Z: ZOMBIE STORIES

Edited by

J.M. Lassen

NIGHT SHADE BOOKS
SAN FRANCISCO

Night Shade Books
http://www.nightshadebooks.com

CONTENTS

FAMILY BUSINESS

JONATHAN MABERRY

I

Benny Imura couldn't hold a job, so he took to killing. It was the family business. He barely liked his family—and by family, that meant his older brother Tom—and he definitely didn't like the idea of "business." Or work. The only part of the deal that sounded like it might be fun was the actual killing.

He'd never done it before. Sure, he'd gone through a hundred simulations in gym class and in the Scouts, but they never let kids do any real killing. Not before they hit fifteen.

"Why not?" he once asked his Scoutmaster, a fat guy named Feeney, who used to be a TV weatherman back in the day.

"Because killing's the sort of thing you should learn from your folks," said Feeney.

"I don't have any folks," Benny countered. "My mom and dad died on First Night."

"Oh, hell," said Feeney, then quickly amended that. "Oh, heck. Sorry, Benny—I didn't know that. Point is, you *got* family of some kind, right?"

"I guess. I got 'I'm Mr. Freaking Perfect Tom Imura' for a brother, and I don't want to learn *anything* from him."

Feeney had stared at him. "Wow. I didn't know you were related to him. Your brother, huh? Well, there's your answer, kid. Nobody better to teach you the art of killing than a professional killer like Tom Imura." Feeney paused and licked his lips nervously. "I guess, being his brother and all, you've seen a lot of killing."

"No," Benny said, with huge annoyance."He never lets me watch!"

"Ask him when you turn thirteen. A lot of kids get to watch when they hit their teens."

Benny had asked, and Tom had said no. Again. It wasn't a discussion. Just, "No."

That was two years ago, and now Benny was six weeks past his fifteenth birthday. He had four more weeks' grace to find a paying job before county ordinance cut his rations by half. Benny hated being in that position, and if one more person gave him the "Fifteen and Free" speech, he was going to scream. He hated that as much as when people saw someone doing hard work and they said crap like, "Damn, he's going at that like he's fifteen and out of food."

Like it was something to be happy about. Something to be proud of. Working your butt off for the rest of your life. Benny didn't see where the fun was in that.

His buddy, Chong, said it was a sign of the growing cultural oppression that was driving humanity toward acceptance of a slave state. Benny had no freaking idea what Chong meant, or if there was even meaning in anything he said. But he nodded in agreement because the look on Chong's face always made it seem like he knew exactly what was what.

At home, before he even finished eating his birthday cake, Tom had said, "If I want to talk about you joining the family business, are you going to chew my head off?"

Benny stared venomous death at Tom and said, very clearly and distinctly, "I. Don't. Want. To. Work. In. The. Family. Business."

"I'll take that as a no, then."

"Don't you think it's a little late now to try and get me all excited about it? I asked you a zillion times to—"

"You asked me to take you out on kills."

"Right! And every time I did you—"

"There's a lot more to what I do, Benny."

"Yeah, there probably is, and maybe I would have thought the rest was something I could deal with, but you never let me see the cool stuff."

"There's nothing 'cool' about killing," Tom said sharply.

"There is when you're talking about killing zoms!" Benny fired back. That stalled the conversation. Tom stalked out of the room and banged around in the kitchen for a while, and Benny threw himself down on the couch.

Tom and Benny never talked about zombies. They had every reason to, but they never did. Benny couldn't understand it. He hated zoms. Everyone hated them, though with Benny it was a white-hot, consuming hatred that went back to his very first memory—a nightmare image that was there every night when he closed his eyes. It was an image that was seared into him, even though it was something he had seen as a tiny child.

Dad and Mom.

Mom screaming, running toward Tom, shoving a squirming Benny—all of eighteen months—into Tom's arms. Screaming and screaming. Telling him to run.

While the *thing* that had been Dad pushed its way through the bedroom door, which Mom had tried to block with a chair and lamps and anything else she could find.

Benny remembered his mom screaming words, but the memory was so old and he had been so young that he didn't remember what any of them were. Maybe there were no words. Maybe it was just her screaming.

Benny remembered the wet heat on his face as Tom's tears fell on him when he climbed out of the bedroom window. They had lived in a ranch-style house. One story. The window emptied out into a yard that was pulsing with red and blue police lights. There were more shouts and screams. The neighbors. The cops. Maybe the army. Benny thought it was the army. And the constant popping sounds of gunfire, near and far away.

But of all of it, Benny remembered a single, last image. As Tom clutched him to his chest, Benny looked over his brother's shoulder at the bedroom window. Mom leaned out of the window screaming at them as Dad's pale hands reached out of the shadows of the room and dragged her back out of sight.

That was Benny's oldest memory. If there had been older memories, then that image had burned them away. Benny remembered the hammering sound that was Tom's panicked heartbeat vibrating against his own chest, and the long wail that was his own inarticulate cry for his mom and his dad.

He hated Tom for running away. He hated that Tom hadn't stayed and helped Mom. He hated what their Dad had become on that First Night all those years ago. And he hated what Dad had turned Mom into.

In his mind they were no longer Mom and Dad. They were the *things* that had killed them. Zoms. And he hated them with an intensity that made the sun feel cold and small.

A few years ago, when he found out that Tom was a zombie hunter, Benny hadn't been proud of his brother. As far as he was concerned, if Tom really had what it took to be a zombie hunter, he'd have had the guts to help Mom. Instead, Tom had run away and left Mom to die. To become one of *them*.

Tom came back into the living room, looked at the remains of Benny's birthday cake on the table, then looked at Benny on the couch.

"The offer still stands," he said. "If you want to do what I do, then I'll take you on as an apprentice. I'll sign the papers so you can still get full rations."

Benny gave him a long, withering stare.

"I'd rather be eaten by zoms than have you as my boss," Benny said.

Tom sighed, turned, and trudged upstairs. After that they didn't talk to each other for days.

II

The following weekend Benny and Lou Chong had picked up the Saturday edition of the *Town Pump* because it had the biggest helpwanted section, and over the next several weeks, they applied for anything that sounded easy.

Benny and Chong clipped out a bunch of want ads and tackled them one at a time, having first categorized them by "most possible money," "coolness," and "I don't know what it is but it sounds okay." They passed on anything that sounded bad right from the get-go.

The first on their list was "Locksmith Apprentice."

That sounded okay, but it turned out to be humping a couple of heavy toolboxes from house to house at the crack of frigging dawn while an old German guy who could barely speak English repaired fence locks and installed dial combinations on both sides of bedroom doors and installed bars and wire grilles.

It was kind of funny watching the old guy explain to his customers how to use the combination locks. Benny and Chong began making bets on how many times per conversation a customer would say "What? Could you repeat that?" or "Beg pardon?"

The work was important, though. Everyone had to lock themselves in their rooms at night and then use a combination to get out. Or a key; some people still locked with keys. That way, if they died in their sleep, they wouldn't be able to get out of the room and attack the rest of the family. There had been whole settlements wiped out because someone's grandfather popped off in the middle of the night and then started chowing down on the kids and grandkids.

Zoms can't work a combination lock. They can't work keys either. The German guy installed double-sided locks, so that the doors could be opened from the other side in a real, non-zombie emergency; or if the town security guys had to come in and do a cleanup on a new zom.

Somehow, Benny and Chong had gotten it into their heads that locksmiths got to see this stuff, but the old guy said that he hadn't seen a single living dead that was in any way connected to his job. Boring.

To make it worse, the German guy paid them a little more than pocket lint and said that it would take three years to learn the actual trade. That meant that Benny wouldn't even pick up a screwdriver for six months and wouldn't do anything but carry stuff for a year. Screw that.

"I thought you didn't want to actually work," said Chong, as they walked away from the German with no intention of returning in the morning.

"I don't. But I don't want to be bored out of my freaking mind either."

Next on their list was "Fence Tester."

That was a little more interesting because there were actual zoms on the other side of the fence. Benny wanted to get close to one. He'd never been closer than a hundred yards from an active zom before. The older kids said that if you looked into a zom's eyes, your reflection would show you how you'd look as one of the living dead. That sounded very cool, but he never got the chance for a close-up look, because there was always a guy with a shotgun dogging him all through the shift.

The shotgun guy got to ride a horse. Benny and Chong had to walk the fence line and stop every six or ten feet, grip the chain links, and shake the fence to make sure there were no breaks or rusted weak spots. That was okay for the first mile, but after that the noise attracted the zoms, and by the middle of the third mile he had to grab, shake, and release pretty damn fast to keep his fingers from getting bitten. He wanted a close-up look, but he didn't want to lose a finger over it. If he got bit, the shotgun guy would blast him on the spot. Depending, a zom bite could turn someone from healthy to living dead in anything from a few hours to a few minutes, and in orientation, they told everyone that there was a zero-tolerance policy on infections.

"If the gun bulls even *think* you got nipped, they'll blow you all to hell and gone," said the trainer, "so be careful!" They quit at lunch.

Next morning they went to the far side of town and applied as "Fence Technicians."

The fence ran for hundreds of miles and encircled the town and the harvested fields, so this meant a lot of walking, mostly carrying yet another grumpy old guy's toolbox. In the first three hours they got chased by a zom who had squeezed through a break in the fence.

"Why don't they just shoot all the zoms who come up to the fence?" Benny asked their supervisor.

"'Cause folks would get upset," said the man, a scruffy-looking guy with bushy eyebrows and a tic at the corner of his mouth. "Some of them zoms are relatives of folks in town, and those folks have rights regarding their kin. Been all sorts of trouble about it, so we keep the fence in good shape, and every once in a while one of the townsfolk will suck up enough intestinal fortitude to grant permission for the fence guards to do what's necessary."

"That's stupid," said Benny.

"That's people," said the supervisor.

That afternoon Benny and Chong were sure they'd walked a million miles, had been peed on by a horse, stalked by a horde of zoms—Benny couldn't see anything at all in their dusty eyes—and yelled at by nearly everyone.

At the end of the day, as they trudged home on aching feet, Chong said, "That was about as much fun as getting beaten up in recess."

He thought about it for a moment. "No… getting beaten up is more fun."

Benny didn't have the energy to argue.

There was only one opening for the next job—"Carpet-Coat Salesman"—which was okay because Chong wanted to stay home and rest his feet. Chong hated walking. So Benny showed up neatly dressed in his best jeans and a clean T-shirt and with his hair as combed as it would ever get without glue.

There wasn't much danger in selling carpet coats, but Benny wasn't slick enough to get the patter down. Benny was surprised that they'd be hard to sell, because everybody had a carpet coat or two. Best thing in the world to have on if some zoms were around and feeling bitey. What he discovered, though, was that everyone who could thread a needle was selling them, so the competition was fierce and sales were few and far between. The door-to-door guys worked on straight commission, too.

The lead salesman, a greasy joker named Chick, would have Benny wear a long-sleeved carpet coat—low knap for summer, shag for winter—and then would use a device on him that was supposed to simulate the full-strength bite of an adult male zom. This metal "biter" couldn't break the skin through the coat—and here Chick rolled into his spiel about human bite strength, throwing around terms like *PSI, avulsion, and post-decay dental-ligament strength*—but it pinched really hard, and the coat was so hot the sweat ran down inside Benny's clothes. When he went home that night, he weighed himself to see how many pounds he'd sweated off. Just one, but Benny didn't have a lot of pounds to spare.

"This one looks good," said Chong over breakfast the next morning. Benny read, "'Pit Thrower.' What's that?"

"I don't know," Chong said, with a mouthful of toast. "I think it has something to do with barbecuing."

It didn't. Pit Throwers worked in teams to drag dead zoms off the back of carts and toss them into the constant blaze at the bottom of Brinkers Quarry. Most of the zoms on the carts were in pieces. The woman who ran orientation kept talking about "parts" and went on and on about the risk of secondary infection; then she pasted on the fakest smile Benny had ever seen and tried to sell the applicants on the physical-fitness benefits that came from constant lifting, turning, and throwing. She even pulled up her sleeve and flexed her biceps. She had pale skin with freckles that looked like liver spots, and the sudden pop of her biceps looked like a swollen tumor.

Chong faked vomiting into his lunch bag.

The other jobs offered by the quarry included "Ash Soaker"— "Because we don't want zom smoke drifting over the town, now do we?" asked the freckly muscle freak. And "Pit Raker," which was exactly what it sounded like.

Benny and Chong didn't make it through orientation. They snuck out during the slide show of smiling Pit Throwers handling gray limbs and heads.

"Spotter" was next, and that proved to be a good choice, but only for one of them. Benny's eyesight was too poor to spot zoms at the right distance. Chong was like an eagle, and they offered him a job as soon as he finished reading numbers off a chart. Benny couldn't even tell they were numbers.

Chong took the job, and Benny walked away alone, throwing dispirited looks back at his friend sitting next to his trainer in a high tower.

Later, Chong told Benny that he loved the job. He sat there all day staring out over the valleys into the Rot and Ruin that stretched from California all the way to the Atlantic. Chong said that he could see twenty miles on a clear day, especially if there were no winds coming his way from the quarry. Just him up there, alone with his thoughts. Benny missed his friend, but privately he thought that the job sounded more boring than words could express.

Benny liked the sound of "Bottler" because he figured it for a factory job filling soda bottles. Benny loved soda, but it was sometimes hard to come by. But as he walked up the road, he met an older teenager—his pal Morgie Mitchell's cousin Bert—who worked at the plant.

When Benny fell into step with Bert, he almost gagged. Bert smelled awful, like something found dead behind the baseboards. Worse. He smelled like a zom.

Bert caught his look and shrugged. "Well, what do you expect me to smell like? I bottle this stuff eight hours a day."

"What stuff?"

"Cadaverine. I work a press to get the oils from the rotting meat." Benny's heart sank. Cadaverine was a nasty-smelling molecule produced by protein hydrolysis during putrefaction of animal tissue. Benny remembered that from science class, but he didn't know that it was made from actual rotting flesh. Hunters and trackers dabbed it on their clothes to keep the zoms from coming after them, because the dead were not attracted to rotting flesh.

Benny asked Bert what *kind* of flesh was used to produce the product, but Bert hemmed and hawed and finally changed the subject. Just as Bert was reaching for the door to the plant, Benny spun around and walked back to town.

There was one job Benny already knew about—"Erosion Artist." He'd seen erosion portraits tacked up all over town, and there were thousands of them on every wall of each of the town's fence outposts.

This job had some promise because Benny was a pretty fair artist. People wanted to know what their relatives might look like if they were zoms, so Erosion Artists took family photos and zombified them. Benny had seen dozens of these portraits in Tom's office. A couple of times he wondered if he should take the picture of his parents to an artist and have them redrawn. He'd never actually done it, though. Thinking about his parents as zoms made him sick and angry.

But Sacchetto, the supervising artist, told him to try a picture of a relative first. He said it provided better insight into what the clients would be feeling. So, as part of his audition, Benny took the picture of his folks out of his wallet and tried it.

Sacchetto frowned and shook his head. "You're making them look too mean and scary."

He tried it again with several photos of strangers the artist had on file.

"Still mean and scary," said Sacchetto, with pursed lips and a disapproving shake of his head.

"They are mean and scary," Benny insisted.

"Not to customers, they're not," said Sacchetto.

Benny almost argued with him about it, saying that if he could accept that his own folks would be flesh-eating zombies—and that there was nothing warm and fuzzy about that—then why couldn't everyone else get it through their heads.

"How old were you when your parents passed?" Sacchetto asked.

"Eighteen months."

"So you never really knew them."

Benny hesitated, and that old image flashed once more in his head. Mom screaming. The pale and inhuman face that should have been Dad's smiling face. And then the darkness as Tom carried him away.

"No," he said bitterly. "But I know what they looked like. I know *about* them. I know that they're zoms. Or maybe they're dead now, but I mean—zoms are zoms. Right?"

After the audition, he hadn't been offered the job.

III

September was ten days away, and Benny still hadn't found a job. He wasn't good enough with a rifle to be a Fence Guard, he wasn't patient enough for farming, and he wasn't strong enough to work as Hitter or Cutter. Not that smashing in zombie heads with a sledgehammer or cutting them up for the quarry wagons was much of a draw for him, even with his strong hatred for the monsters. Yes, it was killing, but it also looked like hard work, and Benny wasn't all that interested in something described in the papers as "demanding physical labor." Was that supposed to attract applicants?

So, after soul-searching for a week, during which Chong lectured him pretty endlessly about detaching himself from preconceived notions and allowing himself to become part of the co-creative process of the universe or something like that, Benny asked Tom to take him on as an apprentice.

At first Tom studied him with narrowed, suspicious eyes.

Then his eyes widened in shock when he realized Benny wasn't playing a joke.

As the reality sank in, Tom looked like he wanted to cry. He tried to hug Benny, but that wasn't going to happen in this life, so Tom and he shook hands on it.

Benny left a smiling Tom and went upstairs to take a nap before dinner. He sat down and stared out the window as if he could see tomorrow, and the tomorrow after that, and the one after that. Just him and Tom.

"This is really going to suck," he said.

IV

That evening they sat on the front steps and watched the sun set over the mountains.

"Why do you do this stuff?" Benny asked.

Tom sipped his coffee and was a long time answering. "Tell me, kiddo, what is it you think I do?"

"Duh! You kill zoms."

"Really? That's all that I do? I just walk up to any zombie I see and *pow!*"

"Uh… *yeah.*"

"Uh… no." Tom shook his head. "How can you live in this house and not know what I do, what my job involves?"

"What's it matter? Everybody I know has a brother, sister, father, mother, haggy old grandmother who's killed zoms. What's the big?" He wanted to say that he thought Tom probably used a high-powered rifle with a scope and killed them from a safe distance; not like Charlie and Hammer, who had the stones to do it *mano a mano.*

"Killing the living dead is a part of what I do, Benny. But do you know why I do it? And for whom?"

"For fun?" Benny suggested, hoping Tom would be at least *that* cool.

"Try again."

"Okay… then for money… and for whoever's gonna pay you."

"Are you pretending to be a dope, or do you really not understand?"

"What, you think I don't know you're a bounty hunter? Everybody knows that. Zak Matthias's uncle Charlie is one, too. I heard him tell stories about going deep into the Ruin to hunt zoms."

Tom paused with his coffee cup halfway to his lips. "Charlie—? You know Charlie Pink-Eye?"

"He gets mad if people call him that."

"Charlie Pink-Eye shouldn't be *around* people."

"Why not?" demanded Benny. "He tells the best stories. He's funny."

"He's a killer."

"So are you."

Tom's smile was gone. "God, I'm an idiot. I have to be the worst brother in the history of the world if I let you think that I'm the same as Charlie Pink-Eye."

"Well, you're not exactly like Charlie."

"Oh, that's something then."

"Charlie's cool."

"'Cool,'" murmured Tom. He sat back and rubbed his eyes. "Good God."

He threw the last of his coffee into the bushes beside the porch and stood up.

"Tell you what, Benny… tomorrow we're going to start early and head out into the Rot and Ruin. We'll go deep, like Charlie does. I want you to see firsthand what he does and what I do, and then you can make your own decisions."

"Decisions about what?"

"About a lot of things, kiddo."

And with that, Tom went in and to bed.

V

They left at dawn and headed down to the southeastern gate. The gatekeeper had Tom sign the usual waiver that absolved the town and the gatekeeping staff of all liability if anything untoward happened once they crossed into the Ruin. A vendor sold Tom a dozen bottles of cadaverine—which they sprinkled on their clothing—and a jar of peppermint goo, which they dabbed on their upper lips to kill their own sense of smell.

They were dressed for a long hike. Tom had instructed Benny to wear good walking shoes, jeans, a durable shirt, and a hat to keep the sun from boiling his brains.

"If it's not already too late," Tom said.

Benny made a rude gesture when Tom wasn't looking.

Despite the heat, Tom wore a lightweight jacket with lots of pockets. He had an old army gun-belt around his narrow waist and a pistol snugged into a worn leather holster. Benny wasn't allowed to have a gun yet, though Tom stowed an extra one in a pack. The last thing Tom strapped on was a sword. Benny watched with interest as Tom slung a long strap diagonally across his body from left shoulder to right hip, with the hilt standing above his shoulder so that he could reach up and over for a fast right-handed draw.

The sword was a *katana*, a Japanese long sword, which Benny had seen Tom practice with every day for as long as he could remember. That sword was the only thing about his brother that Benny thought was cool. Benny's Mom—who was Tom's adopted mother—was Irish, but their father had been Japanese. Tom once told Benny that the Imura family went all the way back to the

Samurai days of ancient Japan. He showed Benny picture books of fierce-looking Japanese men in armor. Samurai warriors.

"Are you a samurai?" Benny had asked when he was nine.

"There are no samurai anymore," Tom said, but even back then Benny thought that Tom had a funny look on his face when he said that. Like maybe there was more to say on the subject but he didn't want to say it right then. When Benny brought the subject up a couple of times since, the answer was always the same.

Even so, Tom was pretty damn good with the sword. He could draw fast as lightning, and Benny had seen him do a trick—when Tom thought no one else was looking—where he threw a handful of grapes into the air, then drew his sword and cut five of them in half before they fell to the grass. The blade was a blur. Later, after Tom had gone off to a store, Benny came down and counted the grapes. Tom had thrown six into the air. He'd only missed one.

That was cool.

Of course, Benny would rather be burned at the stake than tell Tom how cool he thought that was.

"Why are you bringing that?" he asked, as Tom adjusted the lay of the strap.

"It's quiet," Tom said.

Benny understood that. Noise attracted zoms. A sword was quieter than a gun, but it also meant getting closer. Benny didn't think that was a very smart idea. He said as much, and Tom just shrugged.

"Then why bring the gun?" persisted Benny.

"'Cause sometimes quiet doesn't matter." Tom patted his pockets to do a quick inventory to make sure he had everything he needed. "Okay," he said, "let's go. We're burning daylight."

Tom tipped a couple of Fence Runners to bang on drums six hundred yards north, and as soon as that drew away the wandering zoms, Tom and Benny slipped out into the great Rot and Ruin and headed for the treeline.

Chong waved to them from the corner tower.

"We need to move fast for the first half mile," cautioned Tom, and he broke into a jog-trot that was fast enough to get them out of scent range but slow enough for Benny to match.

A few of the zombies staggered after them, but the Fence Guards banged on the drums again, and the zombies, incapable of holding on to more than one reaction at a time, turned back toward the noise. The Imura brothers vanished into the shadows under the trees.

When they finally slowed to a walk, Benny was sweating. It was a hot start to what would be a scorcher of a day. The air was thick with mosquitoes and flies, and the trees were alive with the sound of chattering birds. Far above them the sun was a white hole in the sky.

"How far are we going?" Benny asked.

"Far. But don't worry, there are way stations where we can crash if we don't make it back tonight."

Benny looked at him as if he'd just suggested they set themselves on fire and go swimming in gasoline. "Wait—you're saying we could be out all night?"

"Sure. You know I'm out here for days at a time. You're going to have to do what I do. Besides, except for some wanderers, most of the dead in this area have long since been cleaned out. Every week I have to go farther away."

"Don't they just come to you?"

Tom shook his head. "There are wanderers—what the Fence Guards call 'noms,' short for nomadic zombies—but most don't travel. You'll see."

The forest was old but surprisingly lush in the mid-September heat. Tom found fruit trees, and they ate their fill of sweet pears as they walked. Benny began filling his pockets with them, but Tom shook his head.

"They're heavy and they'll slow you. Besides, I picked a route that'll take us through what used to be farm country. Lots of fruit growing wild."

Benny looked at the lush pears in his hand, sighed, and let them fall.

"How come nobody comes out here to farm this stuff?" he asked.

"People are scared."

"Why? There's got to be forty guys working the fence."

"No, it's not the dead that scare them. People in town don't trust anything out here. They think there's a disease infesting everything. Food, the livestock that have run wild over the last fourteen years—everything."

"Yeah…" Benny said diffidently. He'd heard that talk. "So, it's not true?"

"You ate those pears without a thought."

"You handed them to me."

Tom smiled. "Oh, so you trust me now?"

"You're a dork, but I don't think you want to turn me into a zom."

"Wouldn't have to get on you about cleaning your room, so let's not rule it out."

"You're so funny I almost peed my pants," Benny said without expression.

Tom walked a bit before he said, "There's town and then there's the Rot and Ruin. Most of the time they aren't in the same world, you know?" When it was clear that Benny wasn't following, Tom said, "Think about it and we'll talk later."

He stopped and stared ahead with narrowed eyes. Benny couldn't see anything, but then Tom grabbed his arm and pulled him quickly off the road. He led him in a wide circle through the groves of trees. Benny peered between the hundreds of tree trunks and finally caught a glimpse of three zoms shuffling slowly along the road.

He opened his mouth and almost asked Tom how he knew, but Tom made a shushing gesture and continued on, moving soundlessly through the soft summer grass.

When they were well clear, Tom took them back up to the road.

"I didn't even see them!" Benny gasped, turning to look back.

"Neither did I."

"Then how—?"

"You get a feel for this sort of thing."

Benny held his ground, still looking back. "I don't get it. There were only three of them. Couldn't you have… you know…"

"What?"

"Killed them," said Benny flatly. "Charlie Matthias said he'll go out of his way to chop a zom or two. He doesn't run from anything."

"Is that what he says?" Tom murmured, then continued down the road.

Benny shrugged and followed.

VI

Twice more Tom pulled Benny off the road so they could circle around wandering zombies. After the second time, once they were clear of the creatures' olfactory range, Benny grabbed Tom's arm and demanded, "Whyn't you just pop a cap in them?"

Tom gently pulled his arm free. He shook his head and didn't answer.

"What, are you afraid of them?" Benny yelled.

"Keep your voice down."

"Why? You afraid a zom will come after you? Big, tough zombie killer who's afraid to kill a zombie."

"Benny," said Tom with thin patience, "sometimes you say some truly stupid things."

"Whatever," Benny said, and pushed past him.

"Do you know where you're going?" Tom said, when Benny was a dozen paces along the road.

"This way."

"I'm not," said Tom, and he began climbing the slope of a hill that rose gently from the left-hand side of the road. Benny stood in the middle of the road and seethed for a full minute. He was muttering the worst words he knew the whole time he climbed after Tom up the hill.

There was a smaller road at the top of the hill, and they followed that in silence. By ten o'clock they'd entered a series of steeper hills and valleys that were shaded by massive oak trees with cool green leaves. Tom cautioned Benny to be quiet as they climbed to the top of a ridge that overlooked a small country lane. At the curve of the road was a small cottage with a fenced yard and an elm tree so gnarled and ancient that it looked like the world had grown up around it. Two figures stood in the yard, but they were too small to see. Tom flattened out on the top of the ridge and motioned for Benny to join him.

Tom pulled his field glasses from a belt holster and studied the figures for a long minute.

"What do you think they are?" He handed the binoculars to Benny, who snatched them with more force than was necessary. Benny peered through the lenses in the direction Tom pointed.

"They're zoms," Benny said.

"No kidding, boy genius. But what *are* they?"

"Dead people."

"Ah."

"Ah… what?"

"You just said it. They're dead *people*. They were once living people."

"So what? Everybody dies."

"True," admitted Tom. "How many dead people have you seen?"

"What kind of dead? Living dead like them or dead dead like Aunt Cathy?"

"Either. Both."

"I don't know. The zombies at the fence… and a couple people in town, I guess. Aunt Cathy was the first person I ever knew who died. I was, like, six when she died. I remember the funeral and all." Benny continued to watch the zombies. One was a tall man, the other a young woman or teenage girl. "And… Margie Mitchell's dad died after that scaffolding collapsed. I went to his funeral, too."

"Did you see either of them quieted?"

Quieted was the acceptable term for the necessary act of inserting a metal spike at the base of the skull to sever the brain stem. Since First Night, anyone who died would reanimate as a zombie. Bites made it happen, too, but really any recently deceased person would come back. Every adult in town carried at least one spike, though Benny had never seen one used.

"No," he said. "You wouldn't let me stay in the room when Aunt Cathy died. And I wasn't there when Morgie's dad died. I just went to the funerals."

"What were the funerals like? For you, I mean."

"I dunno. Kind of quick. Kind of sad. And then everyone went to a party at someone's house and ate a lot of food. Morgie's mom got totally shitfaced—"

"Language."

"Morgie's mom got drunk," Benny said, in way that suggested correcting his language was as difficult as having his teeth pulled. "Morgie's uncle sat in the corner singing Irish songs and crying with the guys from the farm."

"That was a year, year and a half ago, right? Spring planting?"

"Yeah. They were building a corn silo, and Mr. Mitchell was using the rope hoist to send some tools up to the crew working on the silo roof. One of the scaffolding pipes broke, and a whole bunch of stuff came crashing down on him."

"It was an accident."

"Well, yeah, sure."

"How'd Morgie take it?"

"How do you think he took it? He was fu—He was screwed up." Benny handed back the glasses. "He's still a little screwed up."

"How's he screwed up?"

"I don't know. He misses his dad. They used to hang out a lot. Mr. Mitchell was pretty cool, I guess."

"Do you miss Aunt Cathy?"

"Sure, but I was little. I don't remember that much. I remember she smiled a lot. She was pretty. I remember she used to sneak me extra ice cream from the store where she worked. Half an extra ration."

Tom nodded. "Do you remember what she looked like?"

"Like Mom," said Benny. "She looked a lot like Mom."

"You were too little to remember Mom."

"I remember her," Benny said, with an edge in his voice. He took out his wallet and showed Tom the image behind the glassine cover. "Maybe I don't remember her really well, but I think about her. All the time. Dad too."

Tom nodded again. "I didn't know you carried this." His smile was small and sad. "I remember Mom. She was more of a mother to me than my mom ever was. I was so happy when Dad married her. I can remember every line on her face. The color of her hair. Her smile. Cathy was a year younger, but they could have been twins."

Benny sat up and wrapped his arms around his knees. His brain felt twisted around. There were so many emotions wired into memories, old and new. He glanced at his brother. "You were older than I am now when—y'know—*it* happened."

"I turned twenty a few days before First Night. I was in the police academy. Dad married your mom when I was sixteen."

"You got to know them. I never did. I wish I…" He left the rest unsaid.

Tom nodded. "Me too, kiddo."

They sat in the shade of their private memories.

"Tell me something, Benny," said Tom. "What would you have done if one of your friends—say, Chong or Margie—had come to Aunt Cathy's funeral and pissed in her coffin?"

Benny was so startled by the question that his answer was unguarded. "I'd have jacked them up. I mean *jacked* them up."

Tom nodded.

Benny stared at him. "What kind of question is that, though?"

"Indulge me. Why would you have freaked out on your friends?"

"Because they dissed Aunt Cathy. Why do you think?"

"But she's dead."

"What the hell does that matter? Pissing in her coffin? I would *so* kick their asses."

"But why? Aunt Cathy was beyond caring."

"It was her funeral! Maybe she was still... I don't know... *there* in some way. Like Pastor Kellogg always says."

"What does he say?"

"That the spirits of those we love are always with us."

"Okay. What if you didn't believe that? What if you believed that Aunt Cathy was only a body in a box? And your friends pissed on her?"

"What do you think?" Benny snapped. "I'd still kick their asses."

"I believe you. But why?"

"Because," Benny began, but then hesitated, unsure of how to express what he was feeling. "Because Aunt Cathy was mine, you know? She was my aunt. My family. They don't have any right to disrespect my family."

"No more than you'd go take a crap on Morgie Mitchell's father's grave. Or dig him up and pour garbage on his bones. You wouldn't do anything like that?"

Benny was appalled. "What's your damage, man? Where do you come up with this crap? Of course I wouldn't do anything sick like that! God, who do you think I am?"

"Shhh… keep your voice down," cautioned Tom. "So, you wouldn't disrespect Morgie's dad… alive or dead?"

"Hell no."

"Language."

Benny said it slower and with more emphasis. "Hell. No."

"Glad to hear it." Tom held out the field glasses. "Take a look at the two dead people down there. Tell me what you see."

"So we're back to business now?" Benny gave him a look. "You're weird, man. Deeply weird."

"Just look."

Benny sighed and grabbed the binoculars out of Tom's hand, put them to his eyes. Stared. Sighed.

"Yep. Two zoms. Same two zoms."

"Be specific."

"Okay. Okay—two zoms. One man, one woman. Standing in the same place as before. Big yawn."

Tom said, "Those dead people…"

"What about them?"

"They used to be somebody's family," said Tom quietly. "The male looks old enough to have been a dad, more likely a grand-dad. He had a family, friends. A name. He was somebody."

Benny lowered the glasses and started to speak.

"No," said Tom. "Keep looking. Look at the woman. She was, what? Eighteen years old when she died? Might have been pretty. Those rags she's wearing might have been a waitress's uniform once. She could have worked at a diner right next to Aunt Cathy. She had people at home who loved her...."

"Don't, man—"

"People who worried when she was late getting home. People who wanted her to grow up happy. People—a mom and a dad. Maybe brothers and sisters. Maybe grandparents. People who believed that girl had a life in front of her. That old man might be her granddad."

"But she's one of them, man. She's dead," Benny said defensively.

"Sure. Almost everyone who ever lived is dead. More than six billion people are dead. And every last one of them had family once. Every last one of them *were* family once. At one time there was someone like you who would have kicked the ass of anyone—stranger or best friend—who harmed or disrespected that girl. Or the old man."

Benny was shaking his head. "No, no, no. It's not the same. These are zoms, man. They kill people. They eat people."

"They used to *be* people."

"But they died!"

"Sure. Like Aunt Cathy and Mr. Mitchell."

"No, Aunt Cathy got cancer. Mr. Mitchell died in an accident." "Sure, but if someone in town hadn't quieted them, they'd have become living dead, too. Don't even pretend you don't know that. Don't pretend you haven't thought about that happening to Aunt Cathy." He nodded down the hill. "These two down there caught a disease."

Benny nodded. He'd learned about it in school, though no one knew for sure what had actually happened. Some sources said it was a virus that was mutated by radiation from a returning space probe. Others said it was a new type of flu that came over from China. Chong believed it was something that got out of a lab somewhere. The only thing everyone agreed on was that it was a disease of some kind.

Tom said, "That guy down there was probably a farmer. The girl was a waitress. I'm pretty sure neither of them was involved in the space program. Or worked in some lab where they researched viruses. What happened to them was an accident. They got sick, Benny, and they died."

Benny said nothing.

"How do you think Mom and Dad died?" No answer.

"Benny...? How do you think...?"

"They died on First Night," Benny said irritably.

"They did. But how?"

Benny said nothing.

"How?"

"You let them die!" Benny said in a savage whisper. Words tumbled out of him in a disjointed sputter. "Dad got sick and... and... then Mom tried to... and you... you just ran away!"

Tom said nothing, but sadness darkened his eyes, and he shook head slowly.

"I remember it," Benny hissed. "I remember you running away."

"You were a baby."

"I remember it."

"You should have told me, Benny."

"Why? So you could make up a lie about why you just ran away and left my mom like that?"

The words *my mom* hung in the air between them. Tom flinched. "You think I just ran away?" he said.

"I don't *think* it, Tom—I remember it."

"Do you remember why I ran?"

"Yeah, 'cause you're a freaking coward, is why!"

"Jesus," Tom whispered. He adjusted the strap that held the sword in place and sighed again. "Benny… this isn't the time or place for this, but someday soon we're going to have a serious talk about the way things were back then, and the way things are now."

"There's nothing you can say that's going to change the truth."

"No. The truth is the truth. What changes is what we know about it and what we're willing to believe."

"Yeah, yeah, whatever."

"If you ever want to know my side of things," said Tom, "I'll tell you. There's a lot you were too young to know then, and maybe you're still too young now."

Silence washed back and forth between them.

"For right now, Benny, I want you to understand that when Mom and Dad died, it was from the same thing that killed those two down there."

Benny said nothing.

Tom plucked a stalk of sweet grass and put it between his teeth. "You didn't *really* know Mom and Dad, but let me ask you this: If someone was to piss on them, or abuse them—even now, even considering what they had to have become during First Night—would it be okay with you?"

"Screw you."

"Tell me."

"No. Okay? No it wouldn't freaking be okay with me? You happy now?"

"Why not, Benny?"

"Because."

"Why not? They're only zoms."

Benny abruptly got up and walked down the hill, away from the farm and away from Tom. He stood looking back along the road they'd traveled as if he could still see the fence line. Tom waited a long time before he got up and joined him.

"I know this is hard, kiddo," he said gently, "but we live in a pretty hard world. We struggle to live. We're always on our guard, and we have to toughen ourselves just to get through each day. And each night."

"I freaking hate you."

"Maybe. I doubt it, but it doesn't matter right now." He gestured toward the path that led back home. "Everybody west of here has lost someone. Maybe someone close, or maybe a distant cousin three times removed. But everybody has lost someone."

Benny said nothing.

"I don't believe that you would disrespect anyone in our town or in the whole west. I also don't believe—I don't want to believe—that you'd disrespect the mothers and fathers, sons and daughters, sisters and brothers who live out here in the great Rot and Ruin."

He put his hands on Benny's shoulders and turned him around. Benny resisted, but Tom Imura was strong. When they were both facing east, Tom said, "Every dead person out there deserves respect. Even in death. Even when we fear them. Even when we have to kill them. They aren't just 'zoms,'

Benny. That's a side effect of a disease or from some kind of radiation or something else that we don't understand. I'm no scientist, Benny. I'm a simple man doing a job."

"Yeah? You're trying to sound all noble, but you *kill* them." Benny had tears in his eyes.

"Yes," Tom said softly, "I do. I've killed hundreds of them. If I'm smart and careful—and lucky—I'll kill hundreds more."

Benny shoved him with both hands. It only pushed Tom back a half step. "I don't understand!"

"No, you don't. I hope you will, though."

"You talk about respect for the dead, and yet you kill them."

"This isn't about the killing. It isn't and never should be about the killing."

"Then what?" Benny sneered. "The money?"

"Are we rich?"

"No."

"Then it's obviously not about the money."

"Then *what?*"

"It's about the *why* of the killing. For the living… for the dead," Tom said. "It's about closure."

Benny shook his head.

"Come with me, kiddo. It's time you understood how the world works. It's time you learned what the family business is all about."

VII

They walked for miles under the hot sun. The peppermint gel ran off with their sweat and had to be reapplied hourly. Benny was quiet for most of the trip, but as his feet got sore and his stomach started to rumble, he turned cranky.

"Are we there yet?"

"No."

"How far is it?"

"A bit."

"I'm hungry."

"We'll stop soon."

"What's for lunch?"

"Beans and jerky."

"I hate jerky."

"You bring anything else?" Tom asked.

"No."

"Jerky it is, then."

The roads Tom picked were narrow and often turned from asphalt to gravel to dirt.

"We haven't seen a zom in a couple of hours," Benny said. "How come?"

"Unless they hear or smell something that draws them, they tend to stick close to home."

"Home?"

"Well… to the places they used to live or work."

"Why?"

Tom took a couple of minutes on that. "There are lots of theories, but that's all we have. Just theories. Some folks say that the dead lack the intelligence to think that there's anywhere other than where they're standing. If nothing attracts them or draws them, they'll just stay right where they are."

"But they need to hunt, don't they?"

"*Need* is a tricky word. Most experts agree that the dead will attack and kill, but it's not been established that they actually hunt. Hunting implies need, and we don't know that the dead need to do anything."

"I don't understand."

They crested a hill and looked down a dirt road to where an old gas station sat beneath a weeping willow.

"Have you ever heard of one of them just wasting away and dying of hunger?"

"No, but—"

"The people in town think that the dead survive by eating the living, right?"

"Well, sure, but—"

"What 'living' do you think they're eating?"

"Huh?"

"Think about it. There're more than three hundred million living dead in America alone. Throw in another thirty-odd million in Canada and a hundred and ten million in Mexico, and you have something like four hundred and fifty million living dead. First Night happened fourteen years ago. So—what are they eating to stay alive?"

Benny thought about it. "Mr. Feeney says they eat each other."

"They don't," said Tom. "Once a body has started to cool, they stop feeding on it. That's why there are so many partially eaten living dead. They won't attack or eat each other even if you locked them in the same house for years on end. People have done it."

"What happens to them?"

"The trapped ones? Nothing."

"Nothing? They don't rot away and die?"

"They're already dead, Benny." A shadow passed over the valley and momentarily darkened Tom's face. "But that's one of the mysteries. They don't rot. Not completely. They decay to a certain point, and then they just stop rotting. No one knows why."

"What do you mean? How can something just stop rotting? That's stupid."

"It's not stupid, kiddo. It's a mystery. It's as much a mystery as why the dead rise in the first place. Why they attack humans. Why they don't attack each other. All mysteries."

"Maybe they eat… like… cows and stuff."

Tom shrugged. "Some do, if they can catch them. A lot of people don't know that, by the way, but it's true. They'll eat anything alive that they can catch. Dogs, cats, birds, even bugs."

"Well, then, that explains—"

"No," Tom said. "Most animals are too fast. Ever try to catch a cat who doesn't want to be caught? Now imagine doing that if you're only able to shuffle along slowly and can't strategize. If a bunch of the dead came upon cows in a pen or fenced field, they might be able to kill them and eat them, but all the penned animals have either long-since escaped or they died off in the first few months. No… the dead don't need to feed at all. They just exist."

They reached the gas station. Tom stopped by the old pump and knocked on the metal casing three times, then twice, and then four more times.

"What are you doing?"

"Saying hello."

"Hello to…?"

There was a low moan, and Benny turned to see a gray-skinned man come shuffling slowly around the corner of the building. He wore ancient coveralls that were stained with dark blotches, but incongruously around his neck was a garland of fresh flowers. Marigolds and honeysuckle. The man's face was in shade for a few steps, but then he crossed into the sunlight and Benny nearly screamed. The man's eyes were missing, and the sockets gaped emptily. The moaning mouth was toothless, the lips and cheeks, sunken in. Worst of all, as the zombie raised its hands toward them, Benny saw that all of its fingers had been clipped off at the primary knuckles.

Benny gagged and stepped back, his muscles tensed to turn and run, but Tom put a hand on his shoulder and gave him a reassuring squeeze.

"Wait," said Tom.

A moment later the door to the gas station opened, and a pair of sleepy-eyed young women came outside followed by a slightly older man with a long brown beard. They were all thin and dressed in tunics that looked like they had been made from old bedsheets. Each wore a thick garland of flowers. The trio looked at Benny and Tom and then at the zombie.

"Leave him be!" cried the youngest woman as she ran across the dirt to the dead man and stood between him and the Imura brothers, her feet planted, her arms spread to shield the zombie.

Tom raised a hand and took his hat off so they could see his face.

"Peace, little sister," he said. "No one's here to do harm."

The bearded man fished eyeglasses from a pocket beneath his tunic and squinted through dirty lenses.

"Tom…?" he said. "Tom Imura?"

"Hey, Brother David." He put his hand on Benny's shoulder. "This is my brother, Benjamin."

"What are you doing here?"

"Passing through," said Tom. "But I wanted to pay my respects. And to teach Benny the ways of *this* world. He's never been outside of the fence before."

Benny caught the way Tom put emphasis on the word *this*.

Brother David walked over, scratching his beard. Up close he was older than he looked—maybe forty, with deep brown eyes and a few missing teeth. His clothing was clean but threadbare. He smelled of flowers, garlic, and mint. The man studied Benny for a long moment, during which Tom did nothing and Benny fidgeted.

"He's not a believer," said Brother David.

"Belief is tough to come by in these times," said Tom. "You believe."

"Seeing is believing."

Benny thought that their exchange had the cadence of a church litany, as if it was something the two of them had said before and would say again.

Brother David bent toward Benny. "Tell me, young brother, do you come here bringing hurt and harm to the Children of God?"

"Um... no?"

"Do you bring hurt and harm to the Children of Lazarus?"

"I don't know who they are, mister, but I'm just here with my brother."

Brother David turned toward the women, who were using gentle pushes to steer the zombie back around the far side of the building. "Old Roger there is one of Lazarus's Children."

"What? You mean he's not a zom—"

Tom made a noise to stop him.

A tolerant smile flickered over Brother David's face. "We don't use that word, little brother."

Benny didn't know how to answer that, so Tom came to his rescue. "The name comes from Lazarus of Bethany, a man who was raised from the dead by Jesus."

"Yeah, I remember hearing about that in church."

The mention of church brightened Brother David's smile. "You believe in God?" he asked hopefully.

"I guess...."

"In these times," said Brother David, "that's better than most." He threw a covert wink at Tom.

Benny looked past him to where the girls had taken the zombie. "I'm like totally confused here. That guy was a... you know. He's dead, right?"

"Living dead," corrected Brother David.

"Right. Why wasn't he trying to... you know." He mimed grabbing and biting.

"He doesn't have teeth," said Tom. "And you saw his hands."

Benny nodded. "Did you guys do that?" he asked Brother David. "No, little brother," Brother David said with a grimace. "No, other people did that to Old Roger."

"Who?" demanded Benny.

"Don't you mean 'Why'?"

"No, *who*. Who'd do something like that?"

Brother David said, "Old Roger is only one of the Children who have been tortured like that. All over this county you can see them. Men and women with their eyes cut out, their teeth pulled, or jaws shot away. Most of them missing fingers or whole hands. And I won't talk about some of the others things I've seen done. Stuff you're too young to know about, little brother."

"I'm fifteen," said Benny.

"You're too young. I can remember when fifteen meant you were still a child." Brother David turned and watched the two young women return without the old zombie.

"He's in the shed," said the blonde.

"But he's agitated," said the redhead.

"He'll quiet down after a spell," said Brother David.

The women stood by the pump and eyed Tom, though Tom seemed to suddenly find something fascinating about the movement of the clouds. Benny's usual inclination would have been to make a joke at Tom's expense, but he didn't feel like it. He turned back to the bearded man.

"Who's doing all this stuff you're talking about? To that old man. To those... others you mentioned. What kind of dirtbags are out here doing that stuff?"

"Bounty hunters," said the redhead.

"Killers," said the blonde.

"Why?"

"If I had an answer to that," said Brother David, "I'd be a saint instead of a way-station monk."

Benny turned to Tom. "I don't get it... *you're* a bounty hunter."

"I guess to some people that's what I am."

"Do you do this kind of stuff?"

"What do you think?"

But Benny was already shaking his head.

Tom said, "What do you even know about bounty hunters?"

"They kill zombies," Benny said, then flinched as he saw the looks of distaste on the faces of Brother David and the two women. "Well, they do! That's what bounty hunters are there for. They come out here into the Rot and Ruin and they hunt the, urn, you know… the living dead."

"Why?" asked Tom.

"For money."

"Who pays them?" asked Brother David.

"People in town. People in other towns," said Benny. "I heard the government pays them sometimes."

"Who'd you hear that from?" asked Tom.

"Charlie Matthias."

Brother David turned a questioning face to Tom, who said, "Charlie Pink-Eye."

The faces of the monk and the two women fell into sickness. Brother David closed his eyes and shook his head slowly from side to side.

"What's wrong?" asked Benny.

"You can stay to dinner," Brother David said stiffly, eyes still closed. "God requires mercy and sharing from all of His Children. But… once you've eaten I'd like you to leave."

Tom put his hand on the monk's shoulder. "We're moving on now."

The redhead stepped toward Tom. "It was a lovely day until you came."

"No," said Brother David sharply, then repeated it more gently. "No, Sarah… Tom's our friend, and we're being rude." He opened his eyes, and Benny thought that the man now looked seventy. "I'm sorry, Tom. Please forgive Sister Sarah, and please forgive me for—"

"No," said Tom. "It's okay. She's right. It was a lovely day, and saying that man's name here was wrong of me. I apologize to you, to her, to Sister Claire, and to Old Roger. This is Benny's first time out here in the Ruin. He met... that man... and had heard a lot of stories. Stories of hunting out here. He's a boy and he doesn't understand. I brought him out here to let him know how things are. How things fall out." He paused. "He's never been to Sunset Hollow. You understand?"

The three Children of God studied him for a while, and then one by one they nodded.

"What's Sunset Hollow?" Benny asked, but Tom didn't answer.

"And I thank you for your offer of a meal," said Tom, "but we've got miles to go, and I think Benny's going to have a lot of questions to ask. Some of them are better asked elsewhere."

Sister Sarah reached up and touched Tom's face. "I'm sorry for my words."

"You've got nothing to be sorry about."

She smiled at him and caressed his cheek; then she turned and placed her hands on either side of Benny's face. "May God protect your heart out here in the world." With that she kissed him on the forehead and walked away. The blonde smiled at the brothers and followed.

Benny turned to Tom. "Did I miss something?"

"Probably," said Tom. "Come on, kiddo, let's roll."

Brother David shifted to stand in Tom's path. "Brother," he said, "I'll ask once and then be done with it."

"Ask away."

"Are you sure about what you're doing?"

"Sure? No. But I'm set on doing it." He fished in his pocket and brought out three vials of cadaverine. "Here, Brother. May it help you in your work."

Brother David nodded his thanks. "God go with you and before you and within you."

They shook hands, and Tom stepped back onto the dirt road. Benny, however, lingered for a moment longer.

"Look, mister," he began slowly, "I don't know what I said or did that was wrong, but I'm sorry, you know? Tom brought me out here, and he's a bit crazy, and I don't know what…" He trailed off. There was no road map in his head to guide him through this conversation.

Brother David offered his hand and gave him the same blessing.

"Yeah," said Benny. "You, too. Okay?"

He hurried to catch up to Tom, who was fifty yards down the road. When he looked back, the monk was standing in the road. He lifted his hand, but whether it was some kind of blessing or a gesture of farewell, Benny didn't know. Either way it creeped him out.

VIII

When they were far down the road, Benny said, "What was that all about? Why'd that guy get so jacked about me mentioning Charlie?"

"Not everyone thinks Charlie's 'cool,' kiddo."

"You jealous?"

Tom laughed. "God! The day I'm jealous of someone like Charlie Pink-Eye is the day I'll cover myself in steak sauce and walk out into a crowd of the dead."

"Hilarious," said Benny sourly. "What's with all that Children of God, Children of Lazarus stuff? What are they doing out here?"

"They're all over the Ruin. I've met travelers who've seen them as far east as Pennsylvania, and all the way down to Mexico City. I first saw them about a year after First Night. A whole bunch of them heading across the country in an old school bus with scripture passages painted all over it. Not sure how they got started or who chose the name. Even Brother David doesn't know. To him it's like they always were."

"Is he nuts?"

"I think the expression used to be 'touched by God.'"

"So… that would be a yes."

"If he's nuts, then at least his heart's in the right place. The Children don't believe in violence of any kind."

"But they're okay with you, even though you kill zoms?"

Tom shook his head. "No, they don't like what I do. But they accept my explanation for why I do it, and Brother David and a few others have seen *how* I do it, and whereas they don't approve, they don't condemn me for it. They think I'm misguided but well-intentioned."

"And Charlie? What do they think of him? Can't be anything good."

"They believe Charlie Pink-Eye to be an evil man. Him and his jackass buddy the Motor City Hammer and a bunch of others. They think most of the bounty hunters are evil, in fact, and I can't fault them for those beliefs."

Benny said nothing. He still thought Charlie Matthias was cool as all hell.

"So… these Children, what do they actually do?"

"Not much. They tend to the dead. If they find a town, they'll go through the houses and look for photos of the people who lived there, and then they try and round up those people if they're still wandering around the town. They put them in their houses, seal the doors, write some prayers on the walls, and then move on. Most of them keep moving. Brother David's been here for a year or so, but I expect he'll move on, too."

"How do they round up zoms? Especially in a town full of them?"

"They wear carpet coats and they know the tricks of moving quietly and using cadaverine to mask their living smells. Sometimes one or another of the Children will come to town to buy some, but more often guys like me bring some out to them."

"Don't they ever get attacked?"

Tom nodded. "All the time, sad to say. I know of at least fifty dead in this part of the country who used to be Children. I've even heard stories that some of the Children give themselves to the dead."

Benny stared at him. *"Why?"*

"Brother David says that some of the Children believe that the dead are the 'meek' who were meant to inherit the earth, and that all things under heaven are there to sustain them. They think that allowing the dead to feed on them is fulfilling God's will."

"That's sick."

Tom shrugged.

"It's stupid," Benny said.

"It is what it is. I think a lot of the Children are people who didn't survive First Night. Oh, sure, their bodies did, but I think some fundamental part of them was broken by what happened. I was there, I can relate."

"You're not crazy."

"I have my moments, kiddo, believe me." Benny gave him a strange look.

That's when they heard the gunshots.

IX

When the first one cracked through the air, Benny dropped to a huddle, but Tom stood straight and looked away to the northeast. When he heard the second shot, he turned his head slightly more to the north.

"Handgun," he said. "Heavy caliber. Three miles."

Benny looked up at him through the arms he'd wrapped over his head. "Bullets can go three miles, can't they?"

"Not usually," said Tom. "Even so, they aren't shooting at us."

Benny straightened cautiously. "You can tell? How?"

"Echoes," he said. "Those bullets didn't travel far. They're shooting at something close and hitting it."

"Um… it's cool that you know that. A little freaky, but cool."

"Yeah, this whole thing is about me showing you how cool I am."

"Oh. Sarcasm," said Benny dryly. "I get it."

"Shut up," said Tom with a grin.

"No, you shut up."

They smiled at each other for the first time all day.

"C'mon," said Tom, "let's go see what they're shooting at." He set off in the direction of the gunshot echoes.

Benny stood watching him for a moment. "Urn… wait… we're going *toward* the shooting?"

Benny shook his head and followed as quickly as he could. Tom picked up the pace, and Benny tried to keep up. They followed a stream down to the lowlands, but Benny noticed that Tom never went closer than a thousand yards to the running water. He asked Tom about this.

Tom asked, "Can you hear the water?"

Benny strained to hear. "No."

"There's your answer. Flowing water is constant noise. It masks other sounds. We'll only go near it to cross it or to fill our canteens; otherwise quiet is better for listening. Always remember that if we can hear something, then it can probably hear us. And if we can't hear something, then it might still be able to hear us and we won't know about it until it's too late."

However, as they followed the gunshot echoes, their path angled toward the stream. Tom stopped for a moment and then shook his head in disapproval. "Not bright," he said, but didn't explain his comment. They ran on.

As they moved, Benny practiced being quiet. It was harder than he thought, and for a while it sounded—to his ears—as if he was making a terrible racket. Twigs broke like firecrackers under his feet; his breath sounded like a wheezing dragon; the legs of his jeans whisked together like a crosscut saw. Tom told him to focus on quieting one thing at a time.

"Don't try to learn too many skills at once. Take a new skill and learn it by using it. Go from there."

By the time they were close to where they'd heard the gunshots, Benny was moving more quietly and found that he enjoyed the challenge. It was like playing ghost tag with Chong and Morgie.

Tom stopped and cocked his head to listen. He put a finger

to his lips and gestured for Benny to remain still. They were in a field of tall grass that led to a dense stand of birch trees. From beyond the trees they could hear the sound of men laughing and shouting and the occasional hollow crack of a pistol shot.

"Stay here," Tom whispered, and then he moved as quickly and quietly as a sudden breeze, vanishing into the tall grass. Benny lost track of him almost at once. More gunshots popped in the dry air.

A full minute passed, and Benny felt a burning constriction in his chest and realized that he was holding his breath. He let it out and gulped in another.

Where was Tom?

Another minute. More laughter and shouts. A few scattered gunshots. A third minute. A fourth.

And then something large and dark rose up in the tall grass a few feet away.

"Tom!" Benny almost screamed the name, but Tom shushed him. His brother stepped close and bent to whisper.

"Benny, listen to me. On the other side of those trees is something you need to see. If you're going to understand how things really are, you need to see."

"What is it?"

"Bounty hunters. Three of them. I've seen these three before, but never this close to town. I want you to come with me. Very quietly. I want you to watch, but don't say or do anything."

"But—"

"This will be ugly. Are you ready?"

"I—"

"Yes or no? We can head southeast and continue on our way. Or we can go home."

Benny shook his head. "No, I'm ready."

Tom smiled and squeezed his arm. "If things get serious, I want you to run and hide. Understand?"

"Yes," Benny said, but the word was like a thorn caught in his throat. Running and hiding. Was that the only strategy Tom knew?

"Promise?"

"I promise."

"Good. Now… follow me. When I move, you move. When I stop, you stop. Step only where I step. Got it? Good."

Tom led the way through the tall grass, moving slowly, shifting his position in time with the fluctuations of the wind. When Benny realized this, it became easier to match his brother step for step. They entered the trees, and Benny could more easily hear the laughter of the three men. They sounded drunk. Then he heard the whinny of a horse.

A horse?

The trees thinned, and Tom hunkered down and pulled Benny down with him. The scene before them was something out of a nightmare. Even as Benny took it in, a part of his mind was whispering to him that he would never forget what he was seeing. He could feel every detail being burned into his brain.

Beyond the trees was a clearing bordered on two sides by switchbacks of the deep stream. The stream vanished around a sheer sandstone cliff that rose thirty feet above the treeline and reappeared on the opposite side of the clearing. Only a narrow dirt path led from the trees in which the Imura brothers crouched to the spit of land framed by stream and cliff. It was a natural clearing that gave the men a clear view of the approaches on all sides. A wagon with two big horses stood in the shade thrown by the birch trees. The back of the wagon was piled high with zombies, who squirmed and writhed in a hopeless attempt to flee or attack. Hopeless, because beside the wagon was a growing pile of severed arms and legs. The zombies in the wagon were limbless cripples.

A dozen other zombies milled around by the sandstone wall, and every time one of them would lumber after one of the men, it was driven back by a vicious kick. It was clear to Benny that two of the men knew some kind of martial art, because they used elaborate jumping and spinning kicks. The more dynamic the kick, the more the others laughed and applauded. When Benny listened, he realized that as one stepped up to confront a zombie, the other two men would name a kick. The men shouted bets at each other and then rated the kicks for points. The two kick-fighters took turns while the third man kept score by drawing numbers in the dirt with a stick.

The zombies had little hope of any effective attack. They were clustered on a narrow and almost water-locked section of the clearing; but far worse than that—each and every one of them was blind. Their eyes were pits of torn flesh and almost colorless blood. Benny looked at the zombies on the cart and saw that they were all blind as well.

He gagged but clamped a hand to his mouth to keep the sound from escaping.

The standing zombies were all battered hulks, barely able to stand, and it was clear that this game had been going on for a while. Benny knew that the zombies were already dead, that they couldn't feel pain or know humiliation, but what he saw seared a mark on his soul.

"That one's 'bout totally messed up," yelled a black man with an eye patch. "Load him up."

The man who apparently didn't know the fancy kicks bent and picked up a sword with a heavy, curved blade. Benny had seen pictures of one in an *Arabian Nights* book. A scimitar.

"Okay," said the swordsman, "what're the numbers?"

"Denny did his in four cuts at three-point-one seconds," said Eyepatch.

"Oh, hell… I got that beat. Time me."

Eyepatch dug a stopwatch out of his pocket. "Ready… steady… *Go!*"

The swordsman rushed toward the closest zombies—a teenage boy who looked like he'd been about Benny's age when he died. The blade swept upward in a glittering line that sheared through the zombie's right arm at the shoulder, and then he checked his swing and chopped down to take the other arm. Instantly he pivoted, swung the sword laterally, and chopped through both legs an inch below the groin. The zombie toppled to the ground, and one leg, against all odds, remained upright.

The three men burst out laughing.

"Time!" yelled Eyepatch, and read the stopwatch. "Holy crap, Stosh. That's two-point-nine-nine seconds!"

"And three cuts," yelled Stash. "I did it in three cuts!"

They howled with laughter, and the third man, called Denny, squatted down, wrapped his burly arms around the limbless zombie's torso, picked it up with a grunt, and carried it over to the wagon. Eyepatch tossed him the limbs—one, two, three, four—and Denny added them to the pile.

The kicking game started up again. Stash drew a pistol and shot one of the remaining zombies in the chest. The bullet did no harm, but the creature turned toward the impact and began lumbering in that direction. Denny yelled, "Jump-spinning back kick!"

Eyepatch leaped into the air, twisted, and drove a savage kick into the zombie's stomach, knocking it backward into the others. They all fell, and the men laughed and handed around a bottle, while the zombies clambered awkwardly to their feet.

Tom leaned close to Benny and whispered, "Time to go."

He moved away, but Benny caught up to him and grabbed his sleeve. "What the hell are you doing? Where are you going?"

"Away from these clowns," said Tom.

"You have to *do* something!"

Tom turned to face him. "What is it you expect me to do?"

"Stop them!" Benny said in an urgent whisper.

"Why?"

"Because they're… because…" Benny sputtered.

"You want me to save the zombies, Benny? Is that it?"

Benny, caught in the fires of his own frustration, glared at him. "They're bounty hunters, Benny," said Tom. "They get a bounty on every zombie they kill. Want to know why they don't just cut the heads off? Because they have to prove that it was they who killed the zombies and didn't just collect heads from someone else's kill. So they bring the torsos back to town and do the killing in front of a bounty judge, who then pays them a half day's rations for every kill. Looks like they have enough there for each of them to get almost five full days' rations. They'll probably swap some of the rations for goods and services with people in town. Especially with women in town. Single moms will do a lot to get enough food for their kids. You following me?"

"I don't believe you!" snarled Benny.

"Keep your voice down," Tom hissed. "And, yes, you do believe me. I can see it in your eyes. I can tell you're thinking about that—and then about what that dirtbag Charlie Pink-Eye told you and the other boys. I'll bet he's told you about all the women he's screwed. How do you think an ugly ape like him *gets* women? Even *he* wouldn't risk rape—not with the death penalty on that—and the only hookers in town are uglier than the zombies. No, Charlie and his buddies buy it with food rations from women who will do *anything* to feed their kids. And as far as I'm concerned, that's not a lot better than rape."

Blotches of fiery red had blossomed on Tom's face as he said this in a fierce whisper. He stopped, took a few breaths, let the fury pass. When he spoke again his face was calmer but his words had as many jagged edges.

"The game these guys are playing? That's ugly, right? It got you so upset that you wanted me to step in and do something. Am I right?"

Benny said nothing. His fists were balled into knuckly knots at his sides.

"Well, as bad as that is... I've seen worse. A whole lot worse. I'm talking pit fights where they put some dumb-ass kid—maybe someone your age—in a hole dug in the ground and then push in a zom. Maybe they give the kid a knife or a sharpened stick or a baseball bat. Sometimes the kid wins, sometimes he doesn't, but the oddsmakers haul in a fortune either way. And where do the kids come from? They *volunteer* for it."

"That's bull...."

"No, it's not. If I wasn't around and you lived with Aunt

Cathy when she was sick with cancer, what would you have done, how much would you have risked to make sure she got enough food and medicine?"

Benny shook his head, but Tom's face was stone.

"Are you going to tell me that you wouldn't take a shot at winning maybe a month's worth of rations—or a whole box of meds—for ninety seconds in a zom pit?"

"That doesn't happen."

"No?"

"I never heard about anything like that."

Tom snorted. "If you did something like that, would you tell anyone? Would you even tell Chong and Morgie?" Benny didn't answer.

Tom pointed. "I can go back there and maybe stop those guys. Maybe even do it without killing them or getting killed myself, but what good would it do? You think they're the only ones doing this sort of thing? This is the great Rot and Ruin, Benny. There's no law out here, not since First Night. Killing zoms is what people do out here."

"That's not killing them! It's sick."

"Yes it is," Tom said softly. "Yes it is, and I can't tell you how relieved and happy I am to hear you say it. To know that you believe it."

There were more shouts and laughter from behind them. And another gunshot.

"I can stop them if you want me to. But it won't stop what's happening out here."

Tears burned in Benny's eyes, and he punched Tom hard in the chest. "But *you* do this stuff! You kill zombies."

Tom grabbed Benny and pulled him close. Benny struggled,

but Tom pulled his brother to his chest and held him. "No," he whispered. "No. Come on, I'll show you what I do."

He released Benny, placed a gentle hand on his brother's back, and guided him back through the trees to the tall grass.

X

They didn't speak for over a mile. Benny kept looking back, but even he didn't know if he was checking to see if they were being followed or if he was regretting that they'd done nothing about what was happening. His jaw ached from clenching it.

They reached the crest of the hill that separated the field of tall grass from an upslope that wound around the base of a huge mountain. There was a road there, a two-lane blacktop that was cracked and choked with weeds. The road spun off toward a chain of mountains that marched into the distance and vanished into heat haze far to the southeast. There were old bones among the weeds, and Benny kept stopping to look at them.

"I don't want to do this anymore," said Benny.

Tom kept walking.

"I don't want to do what you do. Not if it means doing… that sort of stuff."

"I already told you. I don't do that sort of stuff."

"But you're around it. You see it. It's part of your life." Benny kicked a rock and sent it skittering off the road and into the grass. Crows scolded him as they leaped into the air, leaving behind a rabbit carcass on which they'd been feeding.

Tom stopped and looked back. "If we turn back now, you'll only know part of the truth."

"I don't care about the truth."

"Too late for that now. You've seen some of it. If you don't see the rest, it'll leave you—"

"Leave me what? Unbalanced? You can stick that Zen crap up your—"

"Language."

Benny bent and snatched up a shinbone that had been polished white by scavengers and weather. He threw it at Tom, who side-stepped to let it pass.

"Screw you and your truth and all of this stuff!" screamed Benny. "You're just like those guys back there! You come out here all noble and wise and with all that bull, but you're no different. You're a killer. Everyone in town says so!"

Tom stalked over to him and grabbed a fistful of Benny's shirt and lifted him to his toes. "Shut up!" he snarled. "You just shut your damn mouth!"

Benny was shocked to silence.

"You don't know who I am or what I am," Tom growled, giving him a shake. "You don't know what I've done. You don't know the things I've had to do to keep you safe. To keep us safe. You don't know what I—"

He broke off and flung Benny away from him. Benny staggered backward and fell hard on his ass, legs splayed among the weeds and old bones. His eyes bugged with shock, and Tom stood above him, different expressions warring on his face. Anger, shock at his own actions, burning frustration. Even love.

"Benny…"

Benny got to his feet and dusted off his pants. Once more he looked back the way they'd come and then stepped up to Tom, staring up at his big brother with an expression that was equally mixed and conflicted.

"I'm sorry," they both said.

They stared at each other. Benny smiled first.

Tom's smile was slower in coming, though. "You're a total pain in my butt, little brother."

"You're a big dork."

The hot breeze blew past them. Tom said, "If you want to go back, then we'll go back."

Benny shook his head. "No."

"Why not?"

"Do I have to have an answer?"

"Right now? No. Eventually? Probably."

"Yeah," said Benny. "That's okay, I guess. Just tell me one thing. I know you said it already, but I really need to know. Really, Tom." Tom nodded.

"You're not like them. Right? Swear on something." He pulled out his wallet and held up the picture. "Swear on Mom and Dad."

Tom nodded. "Okay, Benny. I swear."

"On Mom and Dad."

"On Mom and Dad." Tom touched the picture and nodded.

"Then let's go."

The afternoon burned on, and they followed the two-lane road around the base of the mountain. Neither spoke for almost an hour, and then Tom said, "This isn't just a walk we're taking, kiddo. I'm out here on a job."

Benny shot him a look. "You're here to kill a zom?"

Tom shrugged. "It's not the way I like to phrase it, but yes, that's the bottom line."

They walked another half mile.

"How does this work? The… job, I mean."

"You saw part of it when you applied to be an Erosion Artist," said Tom. He dug into a jacket pocket and removed an envelope, opened it, and removed a piece of paper, which he unfolded and handed to Benny. There was a small color photograph clipped to one corner that showed a smiling man of about thirty with sandy hair and a sparse beard. The paper it was clipped to was a large portrait of the same man as he might be now if he were a zombie. The name *Harold* was handwritten in one corner.

"*This* is what people do with those pictures?"

"Not always, but a lot of the time. People have the pictures done of wives, husbands, children—anyone they loved, someone they lost. Sometimes they can even remember what a person was wearing on First Night, and that makes it easier for me, because as I said, the dead seldom move far from where they lived or worked. Guys like me find them."

"And kill them?"

Tom answered that with a shrug. They rounded a bend in the road and saw the first few houses of a small town built onto the side of the mountain. Even from a quarter mile away, Benny could see zombies standing in yards or on the sidewalks. One stood in the middle of the road with his face tilted toward the sun.

Nothing moved.

Tom folded the erosion portrait and put it in his pocket, then he took out the vial of cadaverine and sprinkled some on his clothes. He handed it to Benny and then gave him the mint gel after he dabbed some on his upper lip.

"You ready?"

"Not even a little bit," said Benny.

Tom drew his pistol and led the way. Benny shook his head, unsure of how exactly the day had brought him to this moment, and then he followed.

XI

"Won't they attack us?" Benny whispered.

"Not if we're smart and careful. The trick is to move slowly. They respond to quick movements. Smell, too, but we have that covered."

"Can't they hear us?"

"Yes, they can," Tom said. "So once we're in the town, don't talk unless I do, and even then, less is more and quieter is better than loud. I found that speaking slowly helps. A lot of the dead moan, so they're used to slow, quiet sounds."

"This is like the Scouts," Benny said. "Mr. Feeney told us that when we're in nature we should act like we're part of nature."

"For better or worse, Benny, this is part of nature, too."

"That doesn't make me feel good, Tom."

"This is the Rot and Ruin, kiddo. Nobody feels good out here. Now hush and keep your eyes open."

They slowed their pace as they neared the first houses. Tom stopped and spent a few minutes studying the town. The main street ran upward to where they stood, so they had a good view of the whole town. Moving very slowly, Tom removed the envelope from his pocket and unfolded the erosion portrait.

"My client said that it was the sixth house along the main street," Tom murmured. "Red front door and white fence. See it? There, past the old mail truck."

"Uh-huh," Benny said, without moving his lips. He was terrified of the zombies who stood in their yards not more than twenty paces away.

"We're looking for a man named Harold Simmons. There's nobody in the yard, so we may have to go inside."

"Inside?" Benny asked, his voice quavering.

"Come on." Tom began moving slowly, barely lifting his feet. He did not exactly imitate the slow, shuffling gait of the zombies, but his movements were unobtrusive. Benny did his best to mimic everything he did. They passed two houses at which zombies stood in the yard. The first, on their left, had three zombies on the other side of a hip high chain-link fence—two little girls and an older woman. Their clothes were tatters that blew like holiday streamers in the hot breeze. As Tom and Benny passed by them, the old woman turned in their direction. Tom stopped and waited, his pistol ready, but the woman's dead eyes swept past them without lingering. A few paces along, they passed a yard on their right in which a man in a bathrobe stood staring at the corner of the house as if he expected something to happen. He stood among wild weeds, and creeper vines had wrapped themselves around his calves. It looked like he had stood there for years, and with a sinking feeling of horror, Benny realized that he probably had.

Benny wanted to turn and run. His mouth was as dry as paste, and sweat ran down his back and into his underwear.

They moved steadily down the street, always slowly. The sun was heading toward the western part of the sky, and it would be dark in four or five hours. Benny knew that they could never make it home by nightfall. He wondered if Tom would take them back to the gas station, or if he was crazy enough to claim an empty house in this ghost town for the night. If he had to sleep in a zombie's house, even if there was no zombie there, then Benny was sure he'd go completely mad-cow crazy.

"There he is," murmured Tom, and Benny looked at the house with the red door. A man stood looking out of the big bay window. He had sandy hair and a sparse beard, but now the hair and beard were nearly gone and the skin of his face had shriveled to a leather tightness.

Tom stopped outside of the paint-peeling white picket fence. He looked from the erosion portrait to the man in the window and back again.

"Benny?" he said under his breath. "You think that's him?"

"Mm-hm," Benny said with a low squeak.

The zombie in the window seemed to be looking at them. Benny was sure of it. The withered face and the dead pale eyes were pointed directly at the fence, as if he had been waiting there all these years for a visitor to come to his garden gate.

Tom nudged the gate with his toe. It was locked.

Moving very slowly, Tom leaned over and undid the latch. The process took over two minutes. Nervous sweat ran down Benny's face, and he couldn't take his eyes off of the zombie.

Tom pushed on the gate with his knee, and it opened now.

"Very, very slowly," he said. "Red light, green light, all the way to the door."

Benny knew the game, though in truth he had never seen a working stoplight. They entered the yard. The old woman in the first garden suddenly turned toward them. So did the zombie in the bathrobe. "Stop," hissed Tom. He held the pistol close to his chest, his finger lying straight along the trigger guard. "If we have to make a run for it, head into the house. We can lock ourselves in and wait until they calm down."

The old lady and the man in the bathrobe faced them but did not advance.

The tableau held for a minute that seemed an hour long. "I'm scared," said Benny.

"It's okay to be scared," said Tom. "Scared means you're smart. Just don't panic. That'll get you killed."

Benny almost nodded, but he caught himself.

Tom took a slow step. Then a second. It was uneven, his body swaying as if his knees were stiff. The bathrobe zombie turned away and looked at the shadow of a cloud moving up the valley; but the old lady still watched. Her mouth opened and closed as if she was slowly chewing on something.

But then she, too, turned away to watch the moving shadow.

Tom took another step and another, and eventually Benny followed. The process was excruciatingly slow, but to Benny it felt as if they were moving too fast. No matter how slowly they went, he thought that it was all wrong, that the zombies—all of them up and down the street—would suddenly turn toward them and moan with their dry and dusty voices, and then a great mass of the hungry dead would surround them.

Tom reached the door and turned the handle.

The knob turned in his hand, and the lock clicked open. Tom gently pushed it open and stepped into the gloom of the house. Benny cast a quick look at the window to make sure the zombie was still there.

Only he wasn't.

"Tom!" Benny cried. "Look out!"

A dark shape lunged at Tom out of the shadows of the entrance hallway. It clawed for him with wax-white fingers and moaned with an unspeakable hunger. Benny screamed.

Then something happened that Benny could not understand. Tom was there and then he wasn't. His brother's body became a blur of movement, as he pivoted to the outside of the zombie's right arm, ducked low, grabbed the zombie's shins from behind, and drove his shoulder into the former Harold Simmons's back. The zombie instantly fell forward onto his face, knocking clouds of dust from the carpet. Tom leaped onto the zombie's back and used his knees to pin both shoulders to the floor.

"Close the door!" Tom barked, as he pulled a spool of thin silk cord from his jacket pocket. He whipped the cord around the zombie's wrists and shimmied down to be able to bring both of the zombie's hands together and tie them behind the creature's back. He looked up. "The door, Benny—*now!*"

Benny came out of his daze and realized that there was movement in his peripheral vision. He turned to see the old lady, the two little girls and the zombie in his bathrobe lumbering up the garden path. Benny slammed the door and shot the bolt, then leaned against it, panting as if he had been the one to wrestle a zombie to the ground and hog-tie it. With a sinking feeling, he realized that it had probably been his own shouted warning that had attracted the other zombies.

Tom flicked out a spring-blade knife and cut the silk cord. He kept his weight on the struggling zombie while he fashioned a large loop like a noose. The zombie kept trying to turn its head to bite him, but Tom didn't seem to care. The biting teeth were nowhere near him—though Benny was still terrified of those gray, rotted teeth.

With a deft twist of the wrist, Tom looped the noose over the zombie's head, catching it below the chin, and then he jerked the slack so that the closing loop forced the creature's jaws shut with a *clack*. Tom wound silk cord around the zombie's head so that the line passed under the jaw and over the crown. When he had three full turns in place, he tied it tight. He shimmied farther down the zombie's body and pinned its legs and then tied its ankles together.

Then Tom stood up, stuffed the cord into his pocket, and closed his knife. He slapped dust from his clothes as he turned back to Benny.

"Thanks for the warning, kiddo, but I had it."

"Um… holy sh—!"

"Language," Tom interrupted quietly.

Tom went to the window and looked out. "Eight of 'em out there."

"Do-do we… I mean, *shouldn't* we board up the windows?"

Tom laughed. "You've listened to too many campfire tales. If we started hammering nails into boards, the sound would call every living dead person in the whole town. We'd be under siege."

"But we're trapped."

Tom looked at him. "*Trapped* is a relative term," he said. "We can't go out the front. I expect there's a back door. We'll finish our business here and then we'll sneak out nice and quiet and head on our way."

Benny stared at him and then at the struggling zombie, who was on the carpet.

"You—you just…"

"Practice, Benny. I've done this before. C'mon, help me get him up."

They knelt on opposite sides of the zombie, but Benny didn't want to touch it. He'd never touched a corpse of any kind before, and he didn't want to start with one that had tried to bite his brother.

"Benny," Tom said, "he can't hurt you now. He's helpless."

The word *helpless* hit Benny hard. It brought back the image of Old Roger—with no eyes, no teeth, and no fingers—and the two young women who tended to him. And the limbless torsos in the wagon.

"Helpless," he murmured. "God…"

"Come on," Tom said gently.

Together they lifted the zombie. He was light—far lighter than Benny expected—and they half carried, half dragged him into the dining room. Away from the living-room window. Sunlight fell in dusty slants through the moth-eaten curtains. The ruins of a meal had long since decayed to dust on the table. They put him in a chair, and Tom produced the spool of cord and bound him in place. The zombie continued to struggle, but Benny understood. The zombie was actually helpless.

Helpless.

The word hung in the air. Ugly and full of dreadful new meaning. Tom removed the envelope from his pocket. Apart from the folded erosion portrait, there was also a piece of cream-colored stationery on which were several handwritten lines. Tom read through them silently, sighed, and then turned to his brother.

"Restraining the dead is difficult, Benny, but it isn't the hardest part." He held out the letter. "This is."

Benny took the letter.

"My clients—the people who hire me to come out here—they usually want something said. Things they would like to say themselves, but can't. Things they need said so that they can have closure. Do you understand?"

Benny read the letter. His breath caught in his throat and he nodded as the first tears fell down his cheeks.

His brother took the letter back. "I need to read it aloud, Benny. You understand?"

Benny nodded again.

Tom angled the letter into the dusty light and read:

My dear Harold. I love you and miss you. I've missed you so desperately for all these years. I still dream about you every night, and each morning I pray that you've found peace. I forgive you for what you tried to do to me. I forgive you for what you did to the children. I hated you for a long time, but I understand now that it wasn't you. It was this thing that happened. I want you to know that I took care of our children when they turned. They are at peace, and I put flowers on their graves every Sunday. I know you would like that. I have asked Tom Imura to find you. He's a good man, and I know that he will be gentle with you. I love you, Harold. May God grant you His peace. I know that when my time comes, you will be waiting for me, waiting with Bethy and little Stephen, and that we will all be together again in a better world. Please forgive me for not having the courage to help you sooner. I will always love you. Yours forever, Claire.

Benny was weeping when Tom finished. He turned away and covered his face with his hands and sobbed. Tom came and hugged him and kissed his head.

Then Tom stepped away, took a breath, and opened his knife again. Benny didn't think he would be able to watch, but he raised his head and saw Tom as he placed the letter on the table in front of Harold Simmons and smoothed it out. Then he moved behind the zombie and gently pushed its head forward so that he could place the tip of his knife against the hollow at the base of the skull.

"You can look away if you want to, Benny," he said.

Benny did not want to look, but he didn't turn away.

Tom nodded. He took another breath and then thrust the blade into the back of the zombie's neck. The blade slid in with almost no effort in the gap between spine and skull, and the razor-sharp edge sliced completely through the brain stem.

Harold Simmons stopped struggling. His body didn't twitch; there was no death spasm. He just sagged forward against the silken cords and was still. Whatever force had been active in him, whatever pathogen or radiation or whatever had taken the man away and left behind a zombie, was gone.

Tom cut the cords that held Simmons's arms and raised each hand and placed it on the table so that the dead man's palms held the letter in place.

"Be at peace, brother," said Tom Imura.

He wiped and folded his knife and stepped back. He looked at Benny, who was openly sobbing. "This is what I do, Benny."

XII

They left by the back door, and there were no problems. Benny's tears slowed and stopped, but it took a while. They walked in silence, side by side, heading southeast. Miles fell away behind them. They passed another gas station, where Tom greeted another monk. They didn't linger, though. The day was burning away.

"We'll be back in an hour," Tom said to the monk after gifting him with vials of cadaverine and a wrapped package of jerky. "We'll need to stay the night."

"You're always welcome, brother," said the monk.

They walked on for another fifteen minutes, through a grove of trees that were heavy with late season oranges. Tom picked a few, and they peeled and ate them and said almost nothing until they reached the wrought-iron gate of a community that was embowered by a high red-brick wall. A sign over the gate read SUNSET HOLLOW.

Outside of the gate there were trash and old bones and a few burned shells of cars. The outer walls were pocked with bullet scars. To the right of the gate someone had used white paint to write THIS AREA CLEARED. KEEP GATES CLOSED. KEEP OUT. Below that were the initials T. I.

Benny pointed. "You wrote that?" It was the first time he'd spoken a full sentence since leaving the house of Harold Simmons.

"Years ago," Tom said.

The gates were closed, and a thick chain had been threaded through the bars and locked with a heavy padlock. The chain and the lock looked new and gleamed with oil.

"What is this place?" Benny asked.

Tom tucked his hands into his back pockets and looked up at the sign. "This is what they used to call a gated community. The gates were supposed to keep unwanted people out and keep the people inside safe."

"Did it work? I mean… during First Night?"

"No."

"Did all the people die?"

"Most of them. A few got away."

"Why is it locked?"

"For the same reason as always," Tom said. He blew out his cheeks and dug into his right front jeans pocket for a key. He showed it to Benny and then opened the lock, pushed the gates open, restrung the chain, and clicked the lock closed with the keyhole on the inside now.

They walked along the road. The houses were all weather damaged, and the streets were pasted with the dusty remnants of fifteen years of falling leaves. Every garden was overgrown, but there were no zombies in them. Some of the doors had crosses nailed to them, around which hung withered garlands of flowers.

"Your other job's here?" Benny asked.

"Yes," said Tom. His voice was soft and distant.

"Is it like the other one?"

"Sort of."

"That was… hard," said Benny.

"Yes it was."

"Doing this over and over again would drive me crazy. How do you do it?"

Tom turned to him as if that was the question he'd been

waiting for all day. "It keeps me sane," he said. "Do you understand?"

Benny thought about it for a long moment. Birds sang in the trees and the cicadas buzzed continually. "Is it because you knew what the world was before?"

Tom nodded.

"Is it because if you didn't do it... then maybe no one would?"

Tom nodded again.

"It must be lonely."

"It is." Tom glanced at him. "But I always hoped you'd want to join me. To help me do what I do."

"I... don't know if I can."

"That's always going to be your choice. If you can, you can. If you can't, then believe me, I'll understand. It takes a lot out of you to do this. And it takes a lot out of you to know that the bounty hunters are out there doing what they do."

"How come none of them ever came here?"

"They did. Once."

"What happened."

Tom shrugged.

"What happened?" Benny asked again.

"I was here when they came. Pure chance."

"What happened?"

"Maybe it's better that I don't tell you."

Benny looked at him. "You killed them," he said. "Didn't you?"

Tom walked a dozen steps before he said, "Not all of them." A half dozen steps later he added, "I let two of them go."

"Why?"

"To spread the word," Tom said. "To let the other bounty hunters know that this place was off-limits."

"And they listened? The bounty hunters?"

Tom smiled. It wasn't boastful or malicious. It was a thin, cold knife-blade of a smile that was there and gone. "Sometimes you have to go to some pretty extreme lengths to make a point and to make it stick. Otherwise you find yourself having to make the same point over and over again."

Benny stared at him. "How many were there?"

"Ten."

"And you let two go."

"Yes."

"And you killed eight of them?"

"Yes." The late-afternoon sunlight slanting through the trees threw dappled light on the road and painted the sides of all of the houses to their left with purple shadows. A red fox and three kits scampered across the street ahead of them.

Benny opened his mouth to say something to Tom but didn't. Tom stopped in the middle of the street.

"Benny, I don't really want to talk about that day. Not now, not here, and maybe not ever. I did what I thought I had to do, but I'm not proud of it. Telling you the details would feel like bragging, and I think that would make me sick. It's already been a long day."

"I won't ask, Tom," said Benny.

They stood there, taking each other's measure perhaps for the very first time. Taking each other's measure and getting the right values.

Tom pointed, and Benny turned toward the front door of a house with peach trees growing wild in the yard. "This is it."

"There's a zombie in there?"

"Yes," Tom said. "There are two."

"We have to tie them up?"

"No. That's already been done. Years ago. Nearly every house here has a dead person in it. Some have already been released, the rest wait for family members to reach out and want it done."

"I know this sounds gross, but why don't you just go house to house and do it to every one of them? You know... *release* them."

"Because most of the people here have family living in our town. It takes a while, but people usually get to the point where they want someone to go and do this the way I do it. With respect, with words read to their dead family. Closure isn't closure until someone's ready to close the door. Do you understand what I mean?"

Benny nodded.

"Do you have a picture of the... um... people in there? So we know who they are? So we can make sure."

"There are pictures inside. Besides, I know the names of everyone in Sunset Hollow. I come here a lot. I was the one who went house to house and tied the dead up. Some monks helped, but I knew everyone here." Tom walked to the front door. "Are you ready?"

Benny looked at Tom and then at the door.

"You want me to do this, don't you?"

Tom looked sad. "Yes. I guess I do."

"If I do, then I'll be like you. I'll be doing this kind of thing."

"Yes."

"Forever?"

"I don't know, Benny. I hope not. But for a while? Yeah."

"What if I can't?"

"I told you. If you can't, then you can't, and we go to the way station for tonight and head home in the morning."

"Tom, why don't people from town come out to places like this and just take them back? We're so much stronger than the zoms. Why don't we take everything back?"

Tom shook his head. "I don't know. I ask myself that every day. The people on the other side of the fence—for the most part they don't even want to admit to themselves that the rest of the world exists. They feel safe over there."

"That's stupid."

"Yes," Tom said, "it surely is."

He turned the doorknob and opened the door. "Are you coming?"

Benny came as far as the front step. "It's not safe in there, is it?"

"It's not safe anywhere, Benny."

They were both aware in that moment that they were having a different discussion than the words they exchanged.

The brothers went into the house.

Tom led the way down a hall and into a spacious living room that had once been light and airy. Now it was pale and filled with dust. The wallpaper had faded, and there were animal tracks on the floor. There was a cold fireplace and a mantel filled with picture frames. The pictures were of a family. Mother and father. A smiling son in a uniform. A baby in a blue blanket. Brothers and cousins and grandparents. Two sisters who looked like they might have been twins but weren't. Everyone was smiling. Benny stood looking at the pictures for a long time and then reached up and took one down. A wedding picture.

"Where are they?" he asked softly.

"In here," said Tom.

Still holding the picture, Benny followed Tom through a dining room and into a kitchen. The windows were open and the yard was filled with trees. Two straight-backed chairs sat in front of the window, and in the chairs were two withered zombies. Both of them turned their heads toward the sound of footsteps. Their jaws were tied shut with silken cord. The man was dressed in the tatters of an old blue uniform; the woman wore a tailored suit and frilly white blouse. Benny came around front and looked from them to the wedding picture and back again.

"It's hard to tell."

"Not when you get used to it," said Tom. "The shape of the ears, the height of the cheekbones, the angle of the jaw, the distance between the nose and upper lip. Those things won't change even after years."

"I don't know if I can do this," Benny said again.

"That's up to you." Tom took his knife from his pocket and opened it. "I'll do one, and you can do the other. If you're ready. If you can."

Tom went to stand behind the man. He gently pushed the zombie's head forward and placed the tip of the knife in place, doing everything slowly, reminding Benny of how it had to be done.

"Aren't you going to say anything?" said Benny.

"I've already said it," said Tom. "A thousand times. I waited because I knew that you might want to say something."

"I didn't know them," said Benny.

A tear fell from Tom's eye onto the back of the struggling zombie's neck.

He plunged the blade and the struggles stopped. Just like that. Tom hung his head for a moment as a sob broke in his chest. "I'm sorry," he said, and then, "Be at peace."

He sniffed and held the knife out to Benny.

"I can't!" Benny said, backing away. "Jesus fucking Christ, I can't!"

Tom stood there, tears rolling down his cheeks, holding the knife out. He didn't say a word.

"God… please don't make me do this," said Benny. Tom shook his head.

"Please, Tom."

Tom lowered the knife.

The female zombie threw her weight against the cords and uttered a shrill moan that was like a dagger in Benny's mind. He covered his ears and turned away. He dropped into a crouch, face tucked into the corner between the back door and the wall, shaking his head.

Tom stood where he was.

It took Benny a long, long time. He stopped shaking his head and leaned his forehead against the wood. The zombie in the chair kept moaning. Benny turned and dropped onto his knees. He dragged a forearm under his nose and sniffed.

"She'll be like that forever, won't she?" Tom said nothing.

"Yes," said Benny, answering his own question. "Yes." He climbed slowly to his feet.

"Okay," he said, and held out his hand. His hand and arm trembled. Tom's trembled, too, as he handed over the knife.

Benny stood behind the zombie, and it took six or seven tries before he could bring himself to touch her. Eventually he managed it. Tom guided him, touching the spot where the knife had to go. Benny put the tip of the knife in place.

"When you do it," said Tom, "do it quick."

"Can they feel pain?"

"I don't know. But you can. I can. Do it quick."

Benny took a ragged breath and said, "I love you, Mom."

He did it quickly.

And it was over.

He dropped the knife, and Tom gathered him up, and they sank down to their knees together on the kitchen floor, crying so loud that it threatened to break the world. In the chairs, the two dead people sat slumped, their heads tilted toward one another, their withered mouths silent.

The sun was tumbling behind the edge of the mountain by the time they left the house. Together they'd dug graves in the backyard. Tom locked up the house and then relocked the chain on the front gate. Side by side they walked back the way they had come. The knife was in Benny's pocket. He had asked Tom if he could keep it.

"Why?" his brother asked.

Benny's eyes were puffy from crying but they were dry. "I guess I'll need it," he said.

Tom studied him for a long time. His smile was sad but his eyes were filled with love. And with pride.

"Come on," he said. "Let's head back."

Benny Imura looked back at the wrought-iron gates and at the words painted outside. He nodded to himself.

Together they walked through the gathering twilight back to the way station.

:/8:

THE WRONG GRAVE

KELLY LINK

All of this happened because a boy I once knew named Miles Sperry decided to go into the resurrectionist business and dig up the grave of his girlfriend, Bethany Baldwin, who had been dead for not quite a year. Miles planned to do this in order to recover the sheaf of poems he had, in what he'd felt was a beautiful and romantic gesture, put into her casket. Or possibly it had just been a really dumb thing to do. He hadn't made copies. Miles had always been impulsive. I think you should know that right up front.

He'd tucked the poems, handwritten, tear-stained and with cross-outs, under Bethany's hands. Her fingers had felt like candles, fat and waxy and pleasantly cool, until you remembered that they were fingers. And he couldn't help noticing that there was something wrong about her breasts, they seemed larger. If Bethany had known that she was going to die, would she have gone all the way with him? One of his poems was about that, about how now they never would, how it was too late now. Carpe diem before you run out of diem.

Bethany's eyes were closed, someone had done that, too, just like they'd arranged her hands, and even her smile looked composed, in the wrong sense of the word. Miles wasn't sure how you made someone smile after they were dead. Bethany didn't look much like she had when she'd been alive. That had been only a few days ago. Now she seemed smaller, and also, oddly, larger. It was the nearest Miles had ever been to a dead person, and he stood there, looking at Bethany, wishing two things: that he was dead, too, and also that it had seemed appropriate to bring along his notebook and a pen. He felt he should be taking notes. After all, this was the most significant thing that had ever happened to Miles. A great change was occurring within him, moment by singular moment.

Poets were supposed to be in the moment, and also stand outside the moment, looking in. For example, Miles had never noticed before, but Bethany's ears were slightly lopsided. One was smaller and slightly higher up. Not that he would have cared, or written a poem about it, or even mentioned it to her, ever, in case it made her self-conscious, but it was a fact and now that he'd noticed it he thought it might have driven him crazy, not mentioning it: he bent over and kissed Bethany's forehead, breathing in. She smelled like a new car. Miles's mind was full of poetic thoughts. Every cloud had a silver lining, except there was probably a more interesting and meaningful way to say that, and death wasn't really a cloud. He thought about what it was: more like an earthquake, maybe, or falling from a great height and smacking into the ground, really hard, which knocked the wind out of you and made it hard to sleep or wake up or eat or care about things like homework or whether there was anything good on TV. And death was foggy, too, but also prickly, so maybe instead of a cloud, a fog made of little sharp things. Needles. Every death fog has a lot of silver needles. Did that make sense? Did it scan?

Then the thought came to Miles like the tolling of a large and leaden bell that Bethany was dead. This may sound strange, but in my experience it's strange and it's also just how it works. You wake up and you remember that the person you loved is dead. And then you think: Really?

Then you think how strange it is, how you have to remind yourself that the person you loved is dead, and even while you're thinking about that, the thought comes to you again that the person you loved is dead. And it's the same stupid fog, the same needles or mallet to the intestines or whatever worse thing you want to call it, all over again. But you'll see for yourself someday.

Miles stood there, remembering, until Bethany's mother, Mrs. Baldwin, came up beside him. Her eyes were dry, but her hair was a mess. She'd only managed to put eye shadow on one eyelid. She was wearing jeans and one of Bethany's old T-shirts. Not even one of Bethany's favorite T-shirts. Miles felt embarrassed for her, and for Bethany, too.

"What's that?" Mrs. Baldwin said. Her voice sounded rusty and outlandish, as if she were translating from some other language. Something Indo-Germanic, perhaps.

"My poems. Poems I wrote for her," Miles said. He felt very solemn. This was a historic moment. One day Miles's biographers would write about this. "Three haikus, a sestina, and two villanelles. Some longer pieces. No one else will ever read them."

Mrs. Baldwin looked into Miles's face with her terrible, dry eyes. "I see," she said. "She said you were a lousy poet." She put her hand down into the casket, smoothed Bethany's favorite dress, the one with spider webs, and several holes through which you could see Bethany's itchy black tights. She patted Bethany's hands, and said, "Well, good-bye, old girl. Don't forget to send a postcard."

Don't ask me what she meant by this. Sometimes Bethany's mother said strange things. She was a lapsed Buddhist and a substitute math teacher. Once she'd caught Miles cheating on an algebra quiz. Relations between Miles and Mrs. Baldwin had not improved during the time that Bethany and Miles were dating, and Miles couldn't decide whether or not to believe her about Bethany not liking his poetry. Substitute teachers had strange senses of humor when they had them at all.

He almost reached into the casket and took his poetry back. But Mrs. Baldwin would have thought that she'd proved something; that she'd won. Not that this was a situation where anyone was going to win anything. This was a funeral, not a game show. Nobody was going to get to take Bethany home.

Mrs. Baldwin looked at Miles and Miles looked back. Bethany wasn't looking at anyone. The two people that Bethany had loved most in the world could see, through that dull hateful fog, what the other was thinking, just for a minute, and although you weren't there and even if you had been you wouldn't have known what they were thinking anyway, I'll tell you. I wish it had been me, Miles thought. And Mrs. Baldwin thought, I wish it had been you, too.

Miles put his hands into the pockets of his new suit, turned, and left Mrs. Baldwin standing there. He went and sat next to his own mother, who was trying very hard not to cry. She'd liked Bethany. Everyone had liked Bethany. A few rows in front, a girl named April Lamb was picking her nose in some kind of frenzy of grief. When they got to the cemetery, there was another funeral service going on, the burial of the girl who had been in the other car, and the two groups of mourners glared at each other as they parked their cars and tried to figure out which grave site to gather around.

Two florists had misspelled Bethany's name on the ugly wreaths, BERTHANY and also BETHONY, just like tribe members did when they were voting each other out on the television show *Survivor,* which had always been Bethany's favorite thing about *Survivor.* Bethany had been an excellent speller, although the Lutheran minister who was conducting the sermon didn't mention that.

Miles had an uncomfortable feeling: he became aware that he couldn't wait to get home and call Bethany, to tell her all about this, about everything that had happened since she'd died. He sat and waited until the feeling wore off. It was a feeling he was getting used to.

Bethany had liked Miles because he made her laugh. He makes me laugh, too. Miles figured that digging up Bethany's grave, even that would have made her laugh. Bethany had had a great laugh, which went up and up like a clarinetist on an escalator. It wasn't annoying. It had been delightful, if you liked that kind of laugh. It would have made Bethany laugh that Miles Googled grave digging in order to educate himself. He read an Edgar Allan Poe story, he watched several relevant episodes of *Buffy the Vampire Slayer*, and he bought Vicks VapoRub, which you were supposed to apply under your nose. He bought equipment at Target: a special, battery-operated, telescoping shovel, a set of wire cutters, a flashlight, extra batteries for the shovel and flashlight, and even a Velcro headband with a headlamp that came with a special red lens filter, so that you were less likely to be noticed.

Miles printed out a map of the cemetery so that he could find his way to Bethany's grave off Weeping Fish Lane, even—as an acquaintance of mine once remarked—"in the dead of night when naught can be seen, so pitch is the dark." (Not that the dark would be very pitch. Miles had picked a night when the moon would be full.) The map was also just in case, because he'd seen movies where the dead rose from their graves. You wanted to have all the exits marked in a situation like that.

He told his mother that he was spending the night at his friend John's house. He told his friend John not to tell his mother anything.

If Miles had Googled "poetry" as well as "digging up graves," he would have discovered that his situation was not without precedent. The poet and painter Dante Gabriel Rossetti also buried his poetry with his dead lover. Rossetti, too, had regretted this gesture, had eventually decided to dig up his lover to get back his poems. I'm telling you this so that you never make the same mistake.

I can't tell you whether Dante Gabriel Rossetti was a better poet than Miles, although Rossetti had a sister, Christina Rossetti, who was really something. But you're not interested in my views on poetry. I know you better than that, even if you don't know me. You're waiting for me to get to the part about grave digging.

Miles had a couple of friends and he thought about asking someone to come along on the expedition. But no one except for Bethany knew that Miles wrote poetry. And Bethany had been dead for a while. Eleven months, in fact, which was one month longer than Bethany had been Miles's girlfriend. Long enough that Miles was beginning to make his way out of the fog and the needles. Long enough that he could listen to certain songs on the radio again. Long enough that sometimes there was something dreamlike about his memories of Bethany, as if she'd been a movie that he'd seen a long time ago, late at night on television. Long enough that when he tried to reconstruct the poems he'd written her, especially the villanelle, which had been, in his opinion, really quite good, he couldn't. It was as if when he'd put those poems into the casket, he hadn't just given Bethany the only copies of some poems, but had instead given away those shining, perfect lines, given them away so thoroughly that he'd never be able to write them out again. Miles knew that Bethany was dead. There was nothing to do about that. But the poetry was different. You have to salvage what you can, even if you're the one who buried it in the first place.

You might think at certain points in this story that I'm being hard on Miles, that I'm not sympathetic to his situation. This isn't true. I'm as fond of Miles as I am of anyone else. I don't think he's any stupider or any bit less special or remarkable than—for example—you. Anyone might accidentally dig up the wrong grave. It's a mistake anyone could make.

The moon was full and the map was easy to read even without the aid of the flashlight. The cemetery was full of cats. Don't ask me why. Miles was not afraid. He was resolute. The battery-operated telescoping shovel at first refused to untelescope. He'd tested it in his own backyard, but here, in the cemetery, it seemed unbearably loud. It scared off the cats for a while, but it didn't draw any unwelcome attention. The cats came back. Miles set aside the moldering wreaths and bouquets, and then he used his wire cutters to trace a rectangle. He stuck the telescoping shovel under and pried up fat squares of sod above Bethany's grave. He stacked them up like carpet samples and got to work.

By two A.M., Miles had knotted a length of rope at short, regular intervals for footholds, and then looped it around a tree, so he'd be able to climb out of the grave again, once he'd retrieved his poetry. He was waist-deep in the hole he'd made. The night was warm and he was sweating. It was hard work, directing the shovel. Every once in a while it telescoped while he was using it. He'd borrowed his mother's gardening gloves to keep from getting blisters, but still his hands were getting tired. The gloves were too big. His arms ached.

By three thirty, Miles could no longer see out of the grave in any direction except up. A large white cat came and peered down at Miles, grew bored and left again. The moon moved over Miles's head like a spotlight. He began to wield the shovel more carefully. He didn't want to damage Bethany's casket. When the shovel struck something that was not dirt, Miles remembered that he'd left the Vicks VapoRub on his bed at home. He improvised with a cherry ChapStick he found in his pocket. Now he used his garden-gloved hands to dig and to smooth dirt away. The bloody light emanating from his Velcro headband picked out the ingenious telescoping ridges of the discarded shovel, the little rocks and worms and worm-like roots that poked out of the dirt walls of Miles's excavation, the smoother lid of Bethany's casket.

Miles realized he was standing on the lid. Perhaps he should have made the hole a bit wider. It would be difficult to get the lid open while standing on it. He needed to pee: there was that as well. When he came back, he shone his flashlight into the grave. It seemed to him that the lid of the coffin was slightly ajar. Was that possible? Had he damaged the hinges with the telescoping shovel, or kicked the lid askew somehow when he was shimmying up the rope? He essayed a slow, judicious sniff, but all he smelled was dirt and cherry ChapStick. He applied more cherry ChapStick. Then he lowered himself down into the grave.

The lid wobbled when he tested it with his feet. He decided that if he kept hold of the rope, and slid his foot down and under the lid, like so, then perhaps he could cantilever the lid up—

It was very strange. It felt as if something had hold of his foot. He tried to tug it free, but no, his foot was stuck, caught in some kind of vise or grip. He lowered the toe of his other hiking boot down into the black gap between the coffin and its lid, and tentatively poked it forward, but this produced no result. He'd have to let go of the rope and lift the lid with his hands. Balance like so, carefully, carefully, on the thin rim of the casket. Figure out how he was caught.

It was hard work, balancing and lifting at the same time, although the one foot was still firmly wedged in its accidental toehold. Miles became aware of his own breathing, the furtive scuffling noise of his other boot against the coffin lid. Even the red beam of his lamp as it pitched and swung, back and forth, up and down in the narrow space, seemed unutterably noisy. "Shit, shit, shit," Miles whispered. It was either that or else scream. He got his fingers under the lid of the coffin on either side of his feet and bent his wobbly knees so he wouldn't hurt his back, lifting. Something touched the fingers of his right hand.

No, his fingers had touched something. *Don't be ridiculous, Miles.* He yanked the lid up as fast and hard as he could, the way you would rip off a bandage if you suspected there were baby spiders hatching under it. "Shit, shit, shit, shit, shit!"

He yanked and someone else pushed. The lid shot up and fell back against the opposite embankment of dirt. The dead girl who had hold of Miles's boot let go.

This was the first of the many unexpected and unpleasant shocks that Miles was to endure for the sake of poetry. The second was the sickening—no, shocking—shock that he had dug up the wrong grave, the wrong dead girl.

The wrong dead girl was lying there, smiling up at him, and

her eyes were open. She was several years older than Bethany. She was taller and had a significantly more developed rack. She even had a tattoo.

The smile of the wrong dead girl was white and orthodontically perfected. Bethany had had braces that turned kissing into a heroic feat. You had to kiss around braces, slide your tongue up or sideways or under, like navigating through barbed wire: a delicious, tricky trip through No Man's Land. Bethany pursed her mouth forward when she kissed. If Miles forgot and mashed his lips down too hard on hers, she whacked him on the back of his head. This was one of the things about his relationship with Bethany that Miles remembered vividly, looking down at the wrong dead girl.

The wrong dead girl spoke first. "Knock knock," she said.

"What?" Miles said.

"Knock knock," the wrong dead girl said again.

"Who's there?" Miles said.

"Gloria," the wrong dead girl said. "Gloria Palnick. Who are you and what are you doing in my grave?"

"This isn't your grave," Miles said, aware that he was arguing with a dead girl, and the wrong dead girl at that. "This is Bethany's grave. What are you doing in Bethany's grave?"

"Oh no," Gloria Palnick said. "This is my grave and I get to ask the questions."

A notion crept, like little dead cat feet, over Miles. Possibly he had made a dangerous and deeply embarrassing mistake. "Poetry," he managed to say. "There was some poetry that I, ah, that I accidentally left in my girlfriend's casket. And there's a deadline for a poetry contest coming up, and so I really, really needed to get it back."

The dead girl stared at him. There was something about her hair that Miles didn't like.

"Excuse me, but are you for real?" she said. "This sounds like one of those lame excuses. The dog ate my homework. I accidentally buried my poetry with my dead girlfriend."

"Look," Miles said, "I checked the tombstone and everything. This is supposed to be Bethany's grave. Bethany Baldwin. I'm really sorry I bothered you and everything, but this isn't really my fault." The dead girl just stared at him thoughtfully. He wished that she would blink. She wasn't smiling anymore. Her hair, lank and black, where Bethany's had been brownish and frizzy in summer, was writhing a little, like snakes. Miles thought of centipedes. Inky midnight tentacles.

"Maybe I should just go away," Miles said. "Leave you to, ah, rest in peace or whatever."

"I don't think sorry cuts the mustard here," Gloria Palnick said. She barely moved her mouth when she spoke, Miles noticed. And yet her enunciation was fine. "Besides, I'm sick of this place. It's boring. Maybe I'll just come along with."

"What?" Miles said. He felt behind himself, surreptitiously, for the knotted rope.

"I said, maybe I'll come with you," Gloria Palnick said. She sat up. Her hair was really coiling around, really seething now. Miles thought he could hear hissing noises.

"You can't do that!" he said. "I'm sorry, but no. Just no."

"Well then, you stay here and keep me company," Gloria Palnick said. Her hair was really something.

"I can't do that either," Miles said, trying to explain quickly, before the dead girl's hair decided to strangle him. "I'm going to be a poet. It would be a great loss to the world if I never got a chance to publish my poetry."

"I see," Gloria Palnick said, as if she did, in fact, see a great deal. Her hair settled back down on her shoulders and began to act a lot more like hair. "You don't want me to come home with you. You don't want to stay here with me. Then how about this? If you're such a great poet, then write me a poem. Write something about me so that everyone will be sad that I died."

"I could do that," Miles said. Relief bubbled up through his middle like tiny doughnuts in an industrial deep-fat fryer. "Let's do that. You lie down and make yourself comfortable and I'll rebury you. Today I've got a quiz in American History, and I was going to study for it during my free period after lunch, but I could write a poem for you instead."

"Today is Saturday," the dead girl said.

"Oh, hey," Miles said. "Then no problem. I'll go straight home and work on your poem. Should be done by Monday."

"Not so fast," Gloria Palnick said. "You need to know all about my life and about me, if you're going to write a poem about me, right? And how do I know you'll write a poem if I let you bury me again? How will I know if the poem's any good? No dice. I'm coming home with you and I'm sticking around until I get my poem. 'Kay?"

She stood up. She was several inches taller than Miles. "Do you have any ChapStick?" she said. "My lips are really dry."

"Here," Miles said. Then, "You can keep it."

"Oh, afraid of dead girl cooties," Gloria Palnick said. She smacked her lips at him in an upsetting way.

"I'll climb up first," Miles said. He had the idea that if he could just get up the rope, if he could yank the rope up after himself fast enough, he might be able to run away, get to the fence where he'd chained up his bike, before Gloria managed to get out. It wasn't like she knew where he lived. She didn't even know his name.

"Fine," Gloria said. She looked like she knew what Miles was thinking and didn't really care. By the time Miles had bolted up the rope, yanking it up out of the grave, abandoning the telescoping shovel, the wire cutters, the wronged dead girl, and had unlocked his road bike and was racing down the empty 5 A.M. road, the little red dot of light from his headlamp falling into potholes, he'd almost managed to persuade himself that it had all been a grisly hallucination. Except for the fact that the dead girl's cold dead arms were around his waist, suddenly, and her cold dead face was pressed against his back, her damp hair coiling around his head and tapping at his mouth, burrowing down his filthy shirt.

"Don't leave me like that again," she said.

"No," Miles said. "I won't. Sorry."

He couldn't take the dead girl home. He couldn't think of how to explain it to his parents. No, no, no. He didn't want to take her over to John's house either. It was far too complicated. Not just the girl, but he was covered in dirt. John wouldn't be able to keep his big mouth shut.

"Where are we going?" the dead girl said.

"I know a place," Miles said. "Could you please not put your hands under my shirt? They're really cold. And your fingernails are kind of sharp."

"Sorry," the dead girl said.

They rode along in silence until they were passing the 7-Eleven at the corner of Eighth and Walnut, and the dead girl said, "Could we stop for a minute? I'd like some beef jerky. And a Diet Coke."

Miles braked. "Beef jerky?" he said. "Is that what dead people eat?"

"It's the preservatives," the dead girl said, somewhat obscurely.

Miles gave up. He steered the bike into the parking lot. "Let go, please," he said. The dead girl let go. He got off the bike and turned around. He'd been wondering just exactly how she'd managed to sit behind him on the bike, and he saw that she was sitting above the rear tire on a cushion of her horrible, shiny hair. Her legs were stretched out on either side, toes in black combat boots floating just above the asphalt, and yet the bike didn't fall over. It just hung there under her. For the first time in almost a month, Miles found himself thinking about Bethany as if she were still alive: Bethany is never going to believe this. But then, Bethany had never believed in anything like ghosts. She'd hardly believed in the school dress code. She definitely wouldn't have believed in a dead girl who could float around on her hair like it was an anti-gravity device.

"I can also speak fluent Spanish," Gloria Palnick said.

Miles reached into his back pocket for his wallet, and discovered that the pocket was full of dirt. "I can't go in there," he said.

"For one thing, I'm a kid and it's five in the morning. Also I look like I just escaped from a gang of naked mole rats. I'm filthy."

The dead girl just looked at him. He said, coaxingly, "*You* should go in. You're older. I'll give you all the money I've got. You go in and I'll stay out here and work on the poem."

"You'll ride off and leave me here," the dead girl said. She didn't sound angry, just matter of fact. But her hair was beginning to float up. It lifted her up off Miles's bike in a kind of hairy cloud and then plaited itself down her back in a long, business-like rope.

"I won't," Miles promised. "Here. Take this. Buy whatever you want."

Gloria Palnick took the money. "How very generous of you," she said.

"No problem," Miles told her. "I'll wait here." And he did wait. He waited until Gloria Palnick went into the 7-Eleven. Then he counted to thirty, waited one second more, got back on his bike and rode away. By the time he'd made it to the meditation cabin in the woods back behind Bethany's mother's house, where he and Bethany had liked to sit and play Monopoly, Miles felt as if things were under control again, more or less. There is nothing so calming as a meditation cabin where long, boring games of Monopoly have taken place. He'd clean up in the cabin sink, and maybe take a nap. Bethany's mother never went out there. Her ex-husband's meditation clothes, his scratchy prayer mat, all his Buddhas and scrolls and incense holders and posters of Che Guevara were still out here. Miles had snuck into the cabin a few times since Bethany's death, to sit in the dark and listen to the plink-plink of the meditation fountain and think about things. He was sure Bethany's mother wouldn't have minded if she knew, although he hadn't ever asked, just in case. Which had been wise of him.

The key to the cabin was on the beam just above the door, but he didn't need it after all. The door stood open. There was a smell of incense, and of other things: cherry ChapStick and dirt and beef jerky. There was a pair of black combat boots beside the door.

Miles squared his shoulders. I have to admit that he was behaving sensibly here, finally. Finally. Because—and Miles and I are in agreement for once—if the dead girl could follow him somewhere before he even knew exactly where he was going, then there was no point in running away. Anywhere he went she'd already be there. Miles took off his shoes, because you were supposed to take off your shoes when you went into the cabin. It was a gesture of respect. He put them down beside the combat boots and went inside. The waxed pine floor felt silky under his bare feet. He looked down and saw that he was walking on Gloria Palnick's hair.

"Sorry!" Miles said. He meant several things by that. He meant sorry for walking on your hair. Sorry for riding off and leaving you in the 7-Eleven after promising that I wouldn't. Sorry for the grave wrong I've done you. But most of all he meant sorry, dead girl, that I ever dug you up in the first place.

"Don't mention it," the dead girl said. "Want some jerky?"

"Sure," he said. He felt he had no other choice.

He was beginning to feel he would have liked this dead girl under other circumstances, despite her annoying, bullying hair. She had poise. A sense of humor. She seemed to have what his mother called stick-to-itiveness; what the AP English Exam prefers to call tenacity. Miles recognized the quality. He had it in no small degree himself. The dead girl was also extremely pretty, if you ignored the hair. You might think less of Miles that he thought so well of the dead girl, that this was a betrayal of Bethany. Miles felt it was a betrayal. But he thought that Bethany might have liked the dead girl too. She would certainly have liked her tattoo.

"How is the poem coming?" the dead girl said.

"There's not a lot that rhymes with Gloria," Miles said. "Or Palnick."

"Toothpick," said the dead girl. There was a fragment of jerky caught in her teeth. "Euphoria."

"Maybe *you* should write the stupid poem," Miles said. There was an awkward pause, broken only by the almost-noiseless glide of hair retreating across a pine floor. Miles sat down, sweeping the floor with his hand, just in case.

"You were going to tell me something about your life," he said.

"Boring," Gloria Palnick said. "Short. Over."

"That's not much to work with. Unless you want a haiku."

"Tell me about this girl you were trying to dig up," Gloria said. "The one you wrote the poetry for."

"Her name was Bethany," Miles said. "She died in a car crash."

"Was she pretty?" Gloria said.

"Yeah," Miles said.

"You liked her a lot," Gloria said.

"Yeah," Miles said.

"Are you sure you're a poet?" Gloria asked.

Miles was silent. He gnawed his jerky ferociously. It tasted like dirt. Maybe he'd write a poem about it. That would show Gloria Palnick.

He swallowed and said, "Why were you in Bethany's grave?"

"How should I know?" she said. She was sitting across from him, leaning against a concrete Buddha the size of a three-year-old, but much fatter and holier. Her hair hung down over her face, just like a Japanese horror movie. "What do you think, that Bethany and I swapped coffins, just for fun?"

"Is Bethany like you?" Miles said. "Does she have weird hair and follow people around and scare them just for fun?"

"No," the dead girl said through her hair. "Not for fun. But what's wrong with having a little fun? It gets dull. And why should we stop having fun, just because we're dead? It's not all demon cocktails and Scrabble down in the old bardo, you know?"

"You know what's weird?" Miles said. "You sound like her. Bethany. You say the same kind of stuff."

"It was dumb to try to get your poems back," said the dead girl. "You can't just give something to somebody and then take it back again."

"I just miss her," Miles said. He began to cry.

After a while, the dead girl got up and came over to him. She took a big handful of her hair and wiped his face with it. It was soft and absorbent and it made Miles's skin crawl. He stopped crying, which might have been what the dead girl was hoping.

"Go home," she said.

Miles shook his head. "No," he finally managed to say. He was shivering like crazy.

"Why not?" the dead girl said.

"Because I'll go home and you'll be there, waiting for me."

"I won't," the dead girl said. "I promise."

"Really?" Miles said.

"I really promise," said the dead girl. "I'm sorry I teased you, Miles."

"That's okay," Miles said. He got up and then he just stood

there, looking down at her. He seemed to be about to ask her something, and then he changed his mind. She could see this happen, and she could see why, too. He knew he ought to leave now, while she was willing to let him go. He didn't want to fuck up by asking something impossible and obvious and stupid. That was okay by her. She couldn't be sure that he wouldn't say something that would rile up her hair. Not to mention the tattoo. She didn't think he'd noticed when her tattoo had started getting annoyed.

"Good-bye," Miles said at last. It almost looked as if he wanted her to shake his hand, but when she sent out a length of her hair, he turned and ran. It was a little disappointing. And the dead girl couldn't help but notice that he'd left his shoes and his bike behind.

The dead girl walked around the cabin, picking things up and putting them down again. She kicked the Monopoly box, which was a game that she'd always hated. That was one of the okay things about being dead, that nobody ever wanted to play Monopoly.

At last she came to the statue of St. Francis, whose head had been knocked right off during an indoor game of croquet a long time ago. Bethany Baldwin had made St. Francis a lumpy substitute Ganesh head out of modeling clay. You could lift that clay elephant head off, and there was a hollow space where Miles and Bethany had left secret things for each other. The dead girl reached down her shirt and into the cavity where her more interesting and useful organs had once been (she had been an organ donor). She'd put Miles's poetry in there for safekeeping.

She folded up the poetry, wedged it inside St. Francis, and

fixed the Ganesh head back on. Maybe Miles would find it someday. She would have liked to see the look on his face.

We don't often get a chance to see our dead. Still less often do we know them when we see them. Mrs. Baldwin's eyes opened. She looked up and saw the dead girl and smiled. She said, "Bethany."

Bethany sat down on her mother's bed. She took her mother's hand. If Mrs. Baldwin thought Bethany's hand was cold, she didn't say so. She held on tightly. "I was dreaming about you," she told Bethany. "You were in an Andrew Lloyd Webber musical."

"It was just a dream," Bethany said.

Mrs. Baldwin reached up and touched a piece of Bethany's hair with her other hand. "You've changed your hair," she said. "I like it."

They were both silent. Bethany's hair stayed very still. Perhaps it felt flattered.

"Thank you for coming back," Mrs. Baldwin said at last.

"I can't stay," Bethany said.

Mrs. Baldwin held her daughter's hand tighter. "I'll go with you. That's why you've come, isn't it? Because I'm dead too?"

Bethany shook her head. "No. Sorry. You're not dead. It's Miles's fault. He dug me up."

"He did what?" Mrs. Baldwin said. She forgot the small, lowering unhappiness of discovering that she was not dead after all.

"He wanted his poetry back," Bethany said. "The poems he gave me."

"That idiot," Mrs. Baldwin said. It was exactly the sort of

thing she expected of Miles, but only with the advantage of hindsight, because how could you really expect such a thing. "What did you do to him?"

"I played a good joke on him," Bethany said. She'd never really tried to explain her relationship with Miles to her mother. It seemed especially pointless now. She wriggled her fingers, and her mother instantly let go of Bethany's hand.

Being a former Buddhist, Mrs. Baldwin had always understood that when you hold onto your children too tightly, you end up pushing them away instead. Except that after Bethany had died, she wished she'd held on a little tighter. She drank up Bethany with her eyes. She noted the tattoo on Bethany's arm with both disapproval and delight. Disapproval, because one day Bethany might regret getting a tattoo of a cobra that wrapped all the way around her bicep. Delight, because something about the tattoo suggested Bethany was really here. That this wasn't just a dream. Andrew Lloyd Webber musicals were one thing. But she would never have dreamed that her daughter was alive again and tattooed and wearing long, writhing, midnight tails of hair.

"I have to go," Bethany said. She had turned her head a little, towards the window, as if she were listening for something far away.

"Oh," her mother said, trying to sound as if she didn't mind. She didn't want to ask: Will you come back? She was a lapsed Buddhist, but not so very lapsed, after all. She was still working to relinquish all desire, all hope, all self. When a person like Mrs. Baldwin suddenly finds that her life has been dismantled by a great catastrophe, she may then hold on to her belief as if to a life raft, even if the belief is this: that one should hold on to nothing. Mrs. Baldwin had taken her Buddhism very seriously, once, before substitute teaching had knocked it out of her.

Bethany stood up. "I'm sorry I wrecked the car," she said, although this wasn't completely true. If she'd still been alive, she would have been sorry. But she was dead. She didn't know how to be sorry anymore. And the longer she stayed, the more likely it seemed that her hair would do something truly terrible. Her hair was not good Buddhist hair. It did not love the living world or the things in the living world, and it *did not love them* in an utterly unenlightened way. There was nothing of light or enlightenment about Bethany's hair. It knew nothing of hope, but it had desires and ambitions. It's best not to speak of those ambitions. As for the tattoo, it wanted to be left alone. And to be allowed to eat people, just every once in a while.

When Bethany stood up, Mrs. Baldwin said suddenly, "I've been thinking I might give up substitute teaching."

Bethany waited.

"I might go to Japan to teach English," Mrs. Baldwin said. "Sell the house, just pack up and go. Is that okay with you? Do you mind?"

Bethany didn't mind. She bent over and kissed her mother on her forehead. She left a smear of cherry ChapStick. When she had gone, Mrs. Baldwin got up and put on her bathrobe, the one with white cranes and frogs. She went downstairs and made coffee and sat at the kitchen table for a long time, staring at nothing. Her coffee got cold and she never even noticed.

The dead girl left town as the sun was coming up. I won't tell you where she went. Maybe she joined the circus and took part in daring trapeze acts that put her hair to good use, kept it from getting bored and plotting the destruction of all that is good and pure and lovely. Maybe she shaved her head and went on a pilgrimage to some remote lamasery and came back as a superhero with a dark past and some kick-ass martial-arts moves. Maybe she sent her mother postcards from time to time. Maybe she wrote them as part of her circus act, using the tips of her hair, dipping them into an inkwell. These postcards, not to mention her calligraphic scrolls, are highly sought after by collectors nowadays. I have two.

Miles stopped writing poetry for several years. He never went back to get his bike. He stayed away from graveyards and also from girls with long hair. The last I heard, he had a job writing topical haikus for the Weather Channel. One of his best-known haikus is the one about tropical storm Suzy. It goes something like this:

A young girl passes
in a hurry. Hair uncombed.
Full of black devils.

%/{}

THE DAYS OF FLAMING MOTORCYCLES

CATHERYNNE M. VALENTE

To tell you the truth, my father wasn't really that much different after he became a zombie.

My mother just wandered off. I think she always wanted to do that, anyway. Just set off walking down the road and never look back. Just like my father always wanted to stop washing his hair and hunker down in the basement and snarl at everyone he met. He chased me and hollered and hit me before. Once, when I stayed out with some boy whose name I can't even remember, he even bit me. He slapped me and for once I slapped him back, and we did this standing-wrestling thing, trying to hold each other back. Finally, in frustration, he bit me, hard, on the side of my hand. I didn't know what to do—we just stared at each other, breathing heavily, knowing something really absurd or horrible had just happened, and if we laughed it could be absurd and if we didn't we'd never get over it. I laughed. But I knew the look in his eye that meant he was coming for me, that glowering, black look, and now it's the only look he's got.

It's been a year now, and that's about all I can tell you about the apocalypse. There was no flash of gold in the sky, no chasms opened up in the earth, no pale riders with silver scythes. People just started acting the way they'd always wanted to but hadn't because they were more afraid of the police or their boss or losing out on the prime mating opportunities offered by the greater Augusta area. Everyone stopped being afraid. Of anything. And sometimes that means eating each other.

But sometimes it doesn't. They don't always do that, you know. Sometimes they just stand there and watch you, shoulders slumped, blood dripping off their noses, their eyes all unfocused. And then they howl. But not like a wolf. Like something broken and small. Like they're sad.

Now, zombies aren't supposed to get sad. Everyone knows that. I've had a lot of time to think since working down at the Java Shack on Front Street became seriously pointless. I still go to the shop in the morning, though. If you don't have habits, you don't have anything. I turn over the sign, I boot up the register—I even made the muffins for a while, until the flour ran out. Carrot-macadamia on Mondays, mascarpone-mango on Tuesdays, blueberry with a dusting of marzipan on

Wednesdays. So on. So forth. Used to be I'd have a line of senators out the door by 8:00 a.m. I brought the last of the muffins home to my dad. He turned one over and over in his bloody, swollen hands until it came apart, then he made that awful howling-crying sound and licked the crumbs off his fingers. And he starting saying my name over and over, only muddled, because his tongue had gone all puffy and purple in his mouth. Caitlin, Caitlin, Caitlin.

So now I drink the pot of coffee by myself and I write down everything I can think of in a kid's notebook with a flaming motorcycle on the cover. I have a bunch like it. I cleaned out all the stores. In a few months I'll move on to the punky princess covers, and then the Looney Tunes ones. I mark time that way. I don't even think of seasons. These are the days of Flaming Motorcycles. Those were the days of Football Ogres. So on. So forth.

They don't bother me, mostly. And okay, the pot of coffee is just hot water now. No arabica for months. But at least the power's still on. But what I was saying is that I've had a lot of time to think, about them, about me, about the virus—because of course it must have been a virus, right? Which isn't really any better than saying fairies or angels did it. Didn't monks used to argue about how many angels could fit on the head of a pin? I seem to think I remember that, in some book, somewhere. So angels are tiny, like viruses. Invisible, too, or you wouldn't have to argue about it, you'd just count the bastards up. So they said virus, I said it doesn't matter, my dad just bit his own finger off. And he howls like he's so sad he wants to die, but being sad means you have a soul and they don't; they're worse than animals. It's a kindness to put them down. That's what the manuals say. Back when there were new manuals every week. Sometimes I think the only way you can tell if something has a soul is if they can still be sad. Sometimes it's the only way I know I have one.

Sometimes I don't think I do.

I'm not the last person on Earth. Not by a long way. I get radio reports on the regular news from Portland, Boston—just a month ago New York was broadcasting loud and clear, loading zombies into the same hangars they kept protesters in back in '04. They gas them and dump them at sea. Brooklyn is still a problem, but Manhattan is coming around. Channel 3 is still going strong, but it's all emergency directives. I don't watch it. I mean, how many times can you sit through The Warning Signs or What We Know? Plus, I have reason to believe they don't know shit.

I might be the last person in Augusta, though. That wouldn't be hard. Did you ever see Augusta before the angel-virus? It was a burnt-out hole. It is a burnt-out hole. Just about every year, the Kennebec floods downtown, so at any given time there's only about three businesses on the main street, and one of them will have a cheerful We'll Be Back! sign up with the clock hands broken off. There's literally nothing going on in this town. Not now, and not then. Down by the river the buildings are pockmarked and broken, the houses are boarded up, windows shattered, only one or two people wandering dazed down the streets. All gas supplied by the Dead River Company, all your dead interred at Burnt Hill Burying Ground. And that was before. Even our Wal-Mart had to close up because nobody ever shopped there.

And you know, way back in the pilgrim days, or Maine's version of them, which starts in the 1700s sometime, there was a guy named James Purington who freaked out one winter and murdered his whole family with an axe. Eight children and his wife. They hanged him and buried him at the crossroads so he wouldn't come back as a vampire. Which would seem silly, except, well, look around. The point is life in Augusta has been both shitty and deeply warped for quite some time. So we greeted this particular horrific circumstance much as Mainers have greeted economic collapse and the total disregard of the rest of the country for the better part of forever: with no surprise whatsoever. Anyway, I haven't seen anyone else on the pink and healthy side in a long time. A big group took off for Portland on foot a few months ago (the days of Kermit and Company), but I stayed behind. I have to think of my father. I know that sounds bizarre, but there's nothing like a parent who bites you to make you incapable of leaving them. Incapable of not wanting their love. I'll probably turn thirty and still be stuck here, trying to be a good daughter while his blood dries on the kitchen tiles.

Channel 3 says a zombie is a reanimated corpse with no observable sell-by date and seriously poor id-control. But I have come to realize that my situation is not like Manhattan or Boston or even Portland. See, I live with zombies. My dad isn't chained up in the basement. He lives with me like he always lived with me. My neighbors, those of them who didn't wander off, are all among the pustulous and dripping. I watched those movies before it happened and I think we all, for a little while, just reacted like the movies told us to: get a bat and start swinging.

But I've never killed one, and I've never even come close to being bitten. It's not a fucking movie.

And if Channel 3 slaps their bullet points all over everywhere, I guess I should write my own What We Know here. Just in case anyone wonders why zombies can cry.

What Is a Zombie?
by Caitlin Zielinski

Grade…well, if the college were still going I guess I'd be Grade 14.

A zombie is not a reanimated corpse. This was never a Night of the Living Dead scenario. The word zombie isn't even right—a zombie is something a voudoun priest makes, to obey his will. That has nothing to do with the price of coffee in Augusta. My dad didn't die. His skin ruptured and he got boils and he started snorting instead of talking and bleeding out of his eyes and lunging at Mr. Almeida next door with his fingernails out, but he didn't die. If he didn't die, he's not a corpse. QED, Channel 3.

A zombie is not a cannibal. This is kind of complicated: Channel 3 says they're not human, which is why you can't get arrested for killing one. So if they eat us, it wouldn't be cannibalism anyway, just, you know, lunch. Like if I ate a dog. Not what you expect from a nice American girl, but not cannibalism. But also, zombies don't just eat humans. If that were true, I'd have been dinner and they'd have been dead long before now, because, as I said, Augusta is pretty empty of anything resembling bright eyed and bushy tailed. They eat animals, they eat old meat in any freezer they can get open, they eat energy bars if that's what they find. Anything. Once I saw a woman—I didn't know her—on her hands and knees down by the river bank, clawing up the mud and eating it, smearing it on her bleeding breasts, staring up at the sky, her jaw wagging uselessly.

A zombie is not mindless. Channel 3 would have a fit if they heard me say that. It's dogma—zombies are slow and stupid. Well, I saw plenty of people slower and stupider than a zombie in the old days. I worked next to the state capitol, after all. Sometimes I think the only difference is that they're ugly. The world was always full of drooling morons who only wanted me for my body. Anyway, some are fast and some are slow. If the girl was a jogger before, she's probably pretty spry now. If the guy never moved but to change the channel, he's not gonna catch you any time soon. And my father still knows my name. I can't be sure but I think it's only that they can't talk. Their tongues swell up and their throats expand—all of them. One of the early warning signs is slurred speech. They might be as smart as they ever were—see jogging—but they can't communicate except by screaming. I'd scream, too, if I were bleeding from my ears and my skin were melting off.

Zombies will not kill anything that moves. My dad hasn't bitten me. He could have, plenty of times. They're not harmless. I've had to get good at running and I have six locks on every door of the house. Even my bedroom, because my father can't be trusted. He hits me, still. His fist leaves a smear of blood and pus and something darker, purpler, on my face. But he doesn't bite me. At first, he barked and went for my neck at least once a day. But I'm faster. I'm always faster. He doesn't even try anymore. Sometimes he just stands in the living room, drool pooling in the side of his mouth till it falls out, and he looks at me like he remembers that strange night when he bit me before, and he's still ashamed. I laugh, and he almost smiles. He shambles back down the hall and starts peeling off the wallpaper, shoving it into his mouth in long pink strips like skin.

There's something else I know. It's hard to talk about, because I don't understand it. I don't understand it because I'm not a zombie. It's like a secret society, and I'm on the outside. I can watch what they do, but I don't know the code. I couldn't tell Channel 3 about this, even if they came to town with all their cameras and sat me in a plush chair like one of their endless Rockette-line of doctors. What makes you think they have intelligence, Miss Zielinski? And I would tell them about my father saying my name, but not about the river. No one would believe me. After all, it's never happened anywhere else. And I have an idea about that, too. Because people in Manhattan are pretty up on their zombie-killing tactics, and god help a zombie in Texas if he should ever be so unfortunate as to en-counter a human. But here there's nothing left. No one to kill them. They own this town, and they're learning how to live in it, just like anyone does. Maybe Augusta always belonged to them and James Purington and the Dead River Company. All hail the oozing, pestilent kings and queens of the apocalypse.

This is what I know: One night, my father picked up our toaster and left the house. I'm not overly attached to the toaster, but he didn't often leave. I feed him good hamburger, nice and raw, and I don't knock him in his brainpan with a bat. Zombies know a good thing.

The next night he took the hallway mirror. Then the microwave, then the coffeepot, then a sack full of pots and pans. All the zombie movies in the world do not prepare you to see your father, his hair matted with blood, his bathrobe torn and seeping, packing your cooking materiel into a flowered king-size pillowcase. And then one night he took a picture off of the bookshelf. My mother, himself, and me, smiling in one of those terrible posed portraits. I was eight or nine in the picture, wearing a green corduroy jumper and big, long brown pigtails. I was smiling so wide, and so were they. You have to, in those kinds of portraits. The photographer makes you, and if you don't, he practically starts turning cartwheels to get you to smile like an angel just appeared over his left shoulder clutching a handful of pins. My mother, her glasses way too big for her face. My father, in plaid flannel, his big hand holding me protectively.

I followed him. It wasn't difficult; his hearing went about the same time as his tongue. In a way, I guess it's a lot like getting old. Your body starts failing in all sorts of weird ways, and you can't talk right or hear well or see clearly, and you just rage at things because everything is slipping away and you're never going to get any better. If one person goes that way, it's tragic. If everyone does, it's the end of the world.

It gets really dark in Augusta, and the streetlights have all been shot out or burned out. There is no darker night than a Maine night before the first snow, all starless and cold. No friendly pools of orange chemical light to break the long, black street. Just my father, shuffling along with his portrait clutched to his suppurating chest. He turned toward downtown, crossing Front Street after looking both ways out of sheer muscle memory. I crept behind him, down past the riverside shops, past the Java Shack, down to the riverbank and the empty parking lots along the waterfront.

Hundreds of zombies gathered down there by the slowly lapping water. Maybe the whole of dead Augusta, everyone left. My father joined the crowd. I tried not to breathe; I'd never seen so many in one place. They weren't fighting or hunting, either. They moaned, a little. Most of them had brought something—more toasters, dresser drawers, light bulbs, broken kitchen chairs, coat racks, televisions, car doors. All junk, gouged out of houses, out of their old lives. They arranged it, almost lovingly, around a massive tower of garbage, teetering, swaying in the wet night wind. A light bulb fell from the top, shattering with a bright pop. They didn't notice. The tower was sloppy, but even I could see that it was meant to be a tower, more than a tower—bed-slats formed flying buttresses between the main column and a smaller one, still being built. Masses of electric devices, dead and inert, piled up between them, showing their screens and gray, lifeless displays to the water. And below the screens rested dozens of family portraits just like ours, leaning against the dark plasma screens and speakers. A few zombies added to the pile—and some of them lay photos down that clearly belonged to some other family. I thought I saw Mrs. Halloway, my first grade teacher, among them, and she treated her portrait of a Chinese family as tenderly as a child. I don't think they knew who exactly the pictures showed. They just understood the general sense they conveyed, of happiness and family. My father added his picture to the crowd and rocked back and forth, howling, crying, holding his head in his hands.

I wriggled down between a dark streetlamp and a park bench, trying to turn invisible as quickly as possible. But they paid no attention to me. And then the moon crowned the spikes of junk, cresting between the two towers.

The zombies all fell to their knees, their arms outstretched to the white, full moon, horrible black tears streaming down their ruined faces, keening and ululating, throwing their faces down into the river-mud, bits of them falling off in their rapture, their eagerness to abase themselves before their cathedral. I think it was a cathedral, when I think about it now. I think it had to be. They sent up their awful crooning moan, and I clapped my hands over my ears to escape it. Finally, Mrs. Halloway stood up and turned to the rest of them. She dragged her nails across her cheeks and shrieked wordlessly into the night. My father went to her and I thought he was going to bite her, the way he bit me, the way zombies bite anyone when they want to.

Instead, he kissed her.

x/{}

THE BARROW MAID

CHRISTINE MORGAN

The death-cry of Sveinthor Otkelsson ripped through
the din of battle as harsh and sudden as the blade that
had ripped through his mail-coat. Friend and foe, ally
and enemy, all who heard it fell silent. The fighting ceased as
men looked to one another, astonished. Could such a cry truly
have come from the throat of Sveinthor Otkelsson? Sveinthor
Wolf-Helmet? Sveinthor, called the Unkillable?

He had led the first assault against the shield-wall in defense of his uncle Kjartan's fortress, plunging deep into the armies of King Hallgeir the Proud. Arrows had rained all around him but never once touched his flesh. He had beheaded Hallgeir's standard-bearer, then cleaved Hallgeir himself in the shoulder so that the king's torso was hewn nearly to the belt.

A death-cry? Sveinthor Otkelsson, voicing a death-cry?

It could not be believed.

No one moved. No living thing made a sound. Even the cawing of ravens was stilled, and it seemed that the wind itself paused in scudding dark clouds across the sky.

Then, as one, those nearest Sveinthor drew back. He stood alone amidst a mound of bodies, most slain by the thirsty work of his own sword, Wolf's Tooth. And the blood ran thick from his belly, spreading over the earth in a wide red stain.

He was Sveinthor Otkelsson, whose ship *Wulfdrakkar* had gone a'viking to far lands, bringing back plunder of gold and silver, slaves, amber, ivory and jet. He had rescued the beautiful Hildirid from becoming an unwilling bride, unmanning her captor with a knife-stroke.

Even if not for the *wyrd* that had been prophesied by the sorceress, Sigritha, when Sveinthor was no more than a boy, this moment could not have been foreseen. But now Wolf's Tooth had dropped from his grasp, and his hands went to his wound, and the blood was a waterfall between his fingers. His wolf-headed helm, its gilded nasal and eye-pieces red-spattered but still glittering gold, turned this way and that as if seeking out his killer.

A single raven screeched. All who heard it knew it to be an omen of the most fearsome sort. The raven was Odin's own bird, and surely Odin had taken notice of the battle. Perhaps Odin was, even now, dispatching the dreaded Valkyries.

Then, as Sveinthor toppled with his belly split open and the tangle of his guts spilling out of him, there came another cry, furious with rage. It was torn from the throat of Ulfgrim the Squint, long a friend and blood-brother and oathsman of Sveinthor.

In his fury, Ulfgrim charged. Rallied by his actions, the others of Sveinthor's men followed, as did Kjartan's own forces. What came next was not so much battle as butchery. Some of the defenders tried again to form their shield-wall, but too many fled in terror and the rest were soon cut down. The victors moved among the fallen, giving aid to their allies and the final mercy to their enemies, and stripping the dead of their valuables.

Kjartan himself, aged and white-bearded, rode from his fort to the place where Sveinthor had stood. He wept openly and without shame. There had been talk in the mead-halls that Kjartan might make Sveinthor his heir. Now that hope was gone, dashed to pieces like a ship storm-hurled against unforgiving stony shores. Sveinthor was dead. With his last breath, he had closed his blood-soaked fingers around the hilt of Wolf's Tooth and held it now in an unbreakable grip.

They bore him back to Kjartan's hall. The day was won, the enemy scattered and fleeing, but there was precious little joy and celebration. Three others of Sveinthor's men had perished bravely in the battle. In honor, Eyjolf Rust-Beard, and Bork Gunnarsson, and Thrain the Merry were to be placed alongside Sveinthor.

Kjartan had for them a great burial-mound built, a chamber

filled with goods for the afterlife. There were bundles of fire-wood, jugs of mead, furs and blankets, tools, weapons, grain, meat and cheese. Into this tomb was placed Sveinthor's wealth, the plunder of villages and forts and monasteries. Silver cups and platters, gold brooches, piles of hack-silver, beads of amber and jet. Kjartan added many more treasures, so that the mound was as rich as any gold-vault of the dwarfs below the earth.

Sveinthor was laid upon his barrow at the center of the chamber. His helm was polished and shining, the wolf's tail that hung from its crown brushed smooth. He was covered with the pelts of wolves, and his sword, Wolf's Tooth, was set across his breast, its hilt still clutched tightly in his dead hand and its blade still clotted dark with the blood of his enemies.

As these preparations were being done, Ulfgrim the Squint sought out Hildirid, who had been Sveinthor's woman. "Kjartan has promised to provide a slave-girl to accompany Sveinthor into the mound," he told her. "There is no need for you to die with him."

Hildirid, who was tall, slender, and proud-figured, said nothing. She had hair the color of gold seen by torchlight, which fell past her waist in long plaits tucked through the belt of her tunic. Her cloak was seal's skin, pinned at the breast with a brooch of walrus-ivory, and her eyes were sea-blue and steady.

"You can escape this dire fate," Ulfgrim urged her. "Already, Kjartan's wise-woman is preparing the poison. You have but to agree, and the slave-girl will go in your place."

"Does not Unn of the dimpled cheeks go with Eyjolf, her husband?" Hildirid asked. "Is not Ainslinn, Bork's favorite, being readied to follow him? You would have Sveinthor, who loved you like a brother, go to his grave-barrow with a stranger slave-girl?"

"Thrain does," argued Ulfgrim, "for Thrain had no woman of his own and will need one to tend him in the afterlife. You can live, sweet Hildirid. Live and go forth from here, and marry a strong man and have many fine sons and fair daughters."

He touched her hand then, but Hildirid drew away. "I was fated to be his and his alone, forever," she said. "Skarri the Blind prophesied it to us. It is my *wyrd*."

Ulfgrim scoffed. "And we have seen for ourselves how well the *wyrd* prophesied for Sveinthor came to pass. Mad old women and blind old men! Pah!" And he spat on the ground.

"I was fated to be his," Hildirid said again.

"There is no fate but what a man makes his own. Sveinthor went wrapped in the confidence of his *wyrd*, and it did make him bold and daunted his enemies, but in the end, did his *wyrd* prove true? Look there, Hildirid. Sveinthor the Unkill-able ... covered with gold and glory, but as cold and dead as a haunch of beef." He clutched at her hand again. "Come away with me, instead. I may not be as handsome as Sveinthor, but I swear I can love you as much if not better."

This time she did not merely draw away but slapped him so that her palm cracked smartly across his cheek. "I will follow Sveinthor," she said, and her voice was like ice.

Ulfgrim flushed dark, angered and embarrassed. His eyes, already narrow, narrowed further. "It was I who learned of your capture," he said in a snarl. "It was my cunning that formed the plan to rescue you. I would have done it myself, but Sveinthor insisted. By rights, Hildirid, you should have been mine."

She walked away from him then without a word, head high and back straight in her dignity.

Later, when the burial mound was all but finished, Kjartan assembled his people to bid farewell to Sveinthor and his men. There were many verses and poems spoken by skalds, recounting the deeds and honor of their lives, mourning their passing and celebrating their entrance into Valhalla.

Then Kjartan's wise-woman brought forth the cups of poison. Unn of the dimpled cheeks drank first, and kissed Eyjolf's lips before lying down beside him. The woman Kjartan had chosen to accompany Thrain smiled at the great honor she had been given as she raised the cup. Thrain's favorite dog, a great shaggy mongrel called Bryn-Loki, was strangled with a rope and set at his master's feet.

The slave-girl, Ainslinn, wailed and screamed and would not drink. She tried to flee, then tried to fight, and finally had to be strangled as Bryn-Loki had been. A disgrace, but only to be expected from an Irish girl and a Christian.

And then the cup came to Hildirid, who was arrayed like a queen with her long hair loose and shining.

As she took the cup, she saw Ulfgrim with his dark eyes pleading. But she drank deep of the bitter liquid, and as she felt its torpor begin to creep through her limbs, she kissed Sveinthor and sank down next to his barrow, on a blanket of soft wool.

She opened her eyes to the chill, misty dark, and felt a pain all throughout her body so sharp and crushing that it was as if she were being rent asunder by beasts. It was Niflheim, kingdom of the dead, realm of the goddess, Hel. And was it Hel's own hound, Garm, grinding her bones in its fierce mouth? Was it the dragon, Nidhug, leaving off its eternal gnawing at the roots of Yggdrasil the World-Tree?

Then the pain ebbed like a tide, receding from her limbs. Hildirid shivered in the blackness. Her mouth felt dry and parched with a terrible thirst, and her innards were a hollow ache. Slowly, stiffly, she moved. The cold wrapped her like a fog, and she pulled her cloak close around her shoulders.

The air was heavy with a reek of corruption so thick it was like a taste. Yet, beneath it, she could smell other scents. Strong cheese. Heady mead. Her dark-blinded hands sought out carefully over the unseen contours and edges. Soft wool. Hard stone. Rushes and pebbles and loose earth. Stacked logs of wood, the bark coarse beneath her fingers. The lushness of fur. Wolf's fur from the pelts that covered Sveinthor, and that was when she knew where she was. In the barrow. In the burial-mound. Entombed in the black, entombed with the dead.

And was she dead? Was this death? Was this the truth of Niflheim? Alone and sightless and trembling from the chill? Yet she breathed, and when she pressed her hand to her breast she could feel the quick thudding of her heart. With the little knife she kept on her belt, she pricked her thumb and felt warm blood well from it, which she licked away.

Still carefully groping her way, she rose to her knees and found Sveinthor's chest beneath the pelts. She touched the silver Thor's-hammer amulet he wore around his neck, touched his wiry beard, touched his face. His flesh was like a lump of cold tallow, greasy with a residue that smeared off onto her fingertips. His mouth gaped and did not stir with breath.

Hildirid rested her brow on his chest. Then she searched blindly through the goods in the barrow until she had a candle and the means to strike a flame. The flickering light sent shadows dancing over the wealth and the weapons and the bodies.

Unn and the slave-girl were peaceful in death. Ainslinn had died with her eyes bulging in horror, the bruises from the knotted strangling-rope livid on her slim neck. Bryn-Loki, Thrain's dog, lay with tongue protruding and death-rigid legs jutting like sticks. The smells of corruption wafted from them. Hildirid saw skin gone waxen and pallid, flesh sunken and slack. They were dead, dead one and all.

Yet she was alive. Somehow, she was alive. She had drunk of the poison. She had drained the cup to its very dregs. It had coursed through her veins. She remembered sinking, sinking like a rock into the bottomless depths.

Her gaze fell upon the jugs of mead, the loaves, the wheels of cheese. Hunger led her to pull off a chunk of bread, but Hildirid hesitated with it at her lips. Should she? Was there any use in eating, in drinking? Why prolong a life that was doomed to a miserable end? Better if she ignored the urges of her body and lay back down to wait for death. Better still if she took out her knife again and seated it in her breast or sliced it across her wrists, to hurry death along.

Yet the bread was in her hand. It was stale and nearly as hard as stone, but could not have been more appetizing had it just come fresh from the baker's oven. She tore into it with her teeth, and when it soon proved a chore to chew, opened a jug of mead and soaked the bread to soften it in the potent honey-brew.

Sated, she moved the candle so that its light played over the various treasures. Here was a tiny ship, the *Wulfdrakkar* in miniature, with red shields along the sides above the tiny oars, and its growling wolf's head prow. There was a set of *hnefatafl*-men, two armies carved from ivory and soapstone arranged in ranks on their board. A bone flute. A polished-amber figure of a wolf. Chests of silver and gold. Monk's crosses. A heavy silver plate with designs of Christian saints and angels upon it. A fortune, and all of it useless to her now. Likewise were the many weapons useless. What need did she, Hildirid, have for bows and arrows, axes, shields, and spears? What need for swords? She had her knife, the knife of ivory hilt wrapped in gold wire, and it would do as well as any blade for what she might have to do.

How the men had given good-natured jest to Sveinthor when he'd given it to her. "Provide your woman a weapon," they had said, "and you're all but inviting her to use it on you, should you displease her as all men eventually do."

But Sveinthor had never displeased her. They had never quarreled, not once. He had never raised a hand against her. When he had sought counsel, he had listened to hers with as ready an ear as he had that of any of his men. He had been as fervent in love as he'd been in battle. And when his death-cry had rung out, it had been her own ending in that instant.

Yet here she was, alive among the dead. Sveinthor would be in Valhalla, and she would not be there to serve him. Who would bring him the great drinking-horns and joints of roasted meat dripping with good juices? Who would arm and armor him when the final call came and Odin's forces assembled against the giants?

She retreated to his side and sat there huddled in her sealskin cloak. The candle burned low and went out. When hunger and thirst again bestirred her, she rose to take a few bites, a few drinks of mead. Sometimes she would bring out her knife again, and set its point to the swell of her breast, but each time—to her shame—her courage would slip from her. Now and then she lit another candle, but the sight of the treasures did not gladden her spirits, and the sight of the dead as their flesh continued to darken and decay only brought her to despair.

Even in the darkness, though, the dead would make sounds. Tendons creaked as rigor stiffened and relaxed their limbs. Gases gurgled within their bloated bellies. Once, a rancid and rattling corpse-belch produced such a stench that, inured though she was to the odors of the mound, Hildirid was made to vomit up her meager meal.

At last she became aware of new noises. She heard a scratching, like that of rats—faint at first, but gradually growing louder. Next came a harsh grating and scraping, as of metal on stony soil.

And Hildirid understood.

Word of the wealth of Sveinthor's death-hoard must have spread far and wide, the value increasing all the more in the telling, until at last it had won the interest and greed of the lowest kind of dishonorable men—grave-robbers, armed with shovels, come to plunder from the dead, to steal away the gold and silver, the amber and ivory, the cups and platters and other treasures. They would strip the corpses bare of their mail-coats and arm-rings. They would have Wolf's Tooth from Sveinthor's cold grasp even if they had to break off the brittle, rotting husks of his fingers to do so.

In silence and utter darkness, for she by now knew her way as well as she'd ever known her own house, Hildirid took up her knife and went to wait by the entrance. She could hear the digging-sounds louder now, and the voices of the men.

As they dug, and cleared away more of the earth, their words came readily to her ears.

Hildirid was left aghast at all that she heard.

Kjartan's enemies had returned in greater number than before, aided by treachery as some of the king's own men turned against him. The mighty fort had fallen. Hundreds of men had been slain, their weapons and valuables taken and their bodies left unburied.

Now Kjartan's feasting-hall rang and thundered with the revelry of his foes. They gorged on food from his store-houses and drank his mead by the barrel. They butchered his goats and pigs, forced the surviving men to fight like bears or horses for their amusement, and made slaves of the women and children. Worst of all, Kjartan himself had been seized as a prisoner. Night after night, he was made by his captors to appear in one humiliating costume after another. Fool's garb, a monk's robe, the clothes of a woman—these things they dressed him in and led him before the men, who laughed and called and hurled refuse at the white-bearded king. Such mistreatment of the man who had been kindly as a father to Sveinthor filled Hildirid with anger and hate.

Then she heard clearly a voice that she knew.

"If she is dead, old woman, I'll hang you by your heels from a tree-branch and leave your body to be picked by the ravens."

The voice belonged to Ulfgrim the Squint, and it was answered by the cracked and peevish tones of Kjartan's wise-woman, who had prepared the poisons.

"I did as you wished, noble lord," she said. "I mixed in her cup a potion of deep-sleeping, but I told you that you would have to be quick in fetching her out of the tomb before its effects wore off and she woke. I told you that! If she has starved, or died of the cold, it is no fault of mine!"

"Peace, brother," another voice said, and Hildirid knew this one as well. It was Halfgrim the Thief, bastard half-brother to Ulfgrim. "If she is dead, she is dead. There are other women and fairer we can find for you. Wealthy as you are now, you can have your choice of them, and never mind that you are ugly as the rump-end of a troll."

Rough snorts and laughter greeted this, though not enough to keep her from hearing Ulfgrim's next words. "I will have Hildirid," he said. "Or I will have no other."

The deadly determination in his voice made the laughter stop for all but Halfgrim, who chuckled all the more. "Then I hope for your sake the maid lives, or she'll be a bedmate even stiffer and colder than the ones you're used to. Myself, it's Sveinthor's gold that I want."

"And I," said another voice, one that Hildirid did not know, "want only to piss on his rotting bones for what he did to my father."

"As a favor to me, then, Runolf," Halfgrim said, "be patient and save your pissing until I've gotten off his mail-coat. It should fetch a pretty price in silver, for all it has that hole ripped across the guts."

Runolf, she knew, must be Runolf the Younger, whose father's skull Sveinthor had crushed with his shield-boss in the battle. So Ulfgrim had joined with the traitors, and Ulfgrim had seen to it that the poison in her cup had not been poison at all.

"Yes, yes," Ulfgrim said, aggrieved. "And the blame for that hole, we all know, you lay on my head."

"I do, indeed, brother," Halfgrim said. "You were supposed to slash his hamstrings and then skewer him through the neck. What made you stab him in the belly?"

The very breath in Hildirid's lungs had turned to frost, and the blood in her veins to water as icy as that of the far northern seas. "I had no choice," came Ulfgrim's reply. "He realized my intent at the moment before I would have struck, and had I not sunk my blade into his guts, he would have had off my head."

There was more talk as the digging continued, but Hildirid paid it barely any mind. At last the shovels met wood, and were laid aside, and she then heard the splintering crash of axes against the planks. They broke inward. Torchlight poured through the gaps, bright as the brightest sun's rays to her, long accustomed as she was to blackness and feeble candles' flames.

The first man to step through was not Ulfgrim but his half-brother, his gaze fixed greedily on the glitter of gold and the sparkle of silver. Halfgrim never once looked her way until her knife-blade plunged down. He wore no mail, and she embedded the steel to the very hilt in his chest.

Halfgrim screamed like a woman in childbearing and staggered back, then fell sprawled at Ulfgrim's feet. The knife had been yanked from her grip and now Hildirid faced them weaponless, but the sight of her revealed by the torches held the men shocked and motionless with terror. A hag she must have been, a filthy crone with dirt on her clothes and her hair hanging in strings and clumps, her eyes as wild as those of a raving berserk.

Then some fled, casting aside their torches and tools into the crude trench of earth they had made to reach the barrow-mound.

"You see?" said the wise-woman. "She lives, as I told you."

Ulfgrim stared at Hildirid, and spoke her name in a strength-less voice. He stepped over Halfgrim and offered out his hand.

"Traitor," she said to him. "Foul, murdering traitor! You killed Sveinthor!"

"I did it for love of you," Ulfgrim said.

She flung herself at him, although not in the lover's greeting for which he had hoped. Her nails, long and ragged, raked at his face and dug long furrows in his stubble-bearded cheeks. Ulfgrim grappled with her, his strength far more than a match for hers, and soon held her with her arms bent painfully behind her back.

Runolf the Younger pushed his way past them as Hildirid struggled in Ulfgrim's grasp. "You men! There is the treasure, the reward you were promised. I will have satisfaction for my father's death."

"What of Halfgrim?" another asked.

"Leave him," Runolf said. "It is a burial-mound, after all." He turned with torch raised high so that its light was shed over the central barrow.

And there he stopped, for the corpse of Sveinthor was sitting upright.

The wolf's pelts had fallen away to the earthen floor. His torn mail gaped where the fatal blow had been struck, and through it could be seen the bulging maggot-ridden fester of his entrails. His eyes, no longer clear blue but clouded and murky as if rimed with muddy ice, peered around from within the gilded eye-pieces of his helm.

Then Sveinthor rose to his feet.

Some of his guts slipped from him, swinging against his thighs like a grisly apron. His joints groaned and his bones crackled. Bits of his skin had sloughed away, leaving raw muscle glistening. His lips had peeled back from his teeth, giving him a leering death's rictus of a grin. The sword, Wolf's Tooth, he still held in his hand, and he extended it now in challenge and invitation.

"*Draugr!*" the wise-woman cried, and threw herself at his knees, babbling prayers to Thor and Freya and Christ and to other gods of which Hildirid had never heard tell. It was a word most used when a man was lost at sea and denied decent burial, so that his restless corpse was doomed to wander. Sveinthor had not drowned, but he was *draugr* nonetheless.

A fierce joy sang within Hildirid's breast, and she cried her lover's name. "Sveinthor!"

"Kill him!" shouted Ulfgrim, retreating and pulling Hildirid as he went.

Runolf had dropped his torch and snatched out his own sword. As the other men rushed forth, waving their axes and shovels, shrieking their horror at this unnatural foe, Runolf hacked down at Sveinthor's shieldless left arm and severed it at the wrist.

No blood gushed from the stump. There was a trickle of thick blackish ooze, and a fresh whiff of stink. The hand fell to the ground and twitched there, then turned itself over and began finger-clawing toward the oncoming men.

Wolf's Tooth flashed down, and Runolf the Younger spun away with his face sliced open. From cheekbone to chin it hung down in a flap of bleeding meat, exposing his teeth and gums.

But the others were urged on by desperation and terror, and raced wildly at Sveinthor. One of them trod upon the severed left hand, which skittered up his leg as swift as a spider. His charge became a frantic leaping dance as he beat at himself with his shovel, hoping to dislodge the scrambling hand. He was too slow. It vanished beneath the hem of his tunic and crawled to his groin, where it squeezed and mauled and twisted like someone wringing water from a rag. The man squealed.

A hoarse and rumbling howl came from Sveinthor's throat. Though distorted, it was still familiar. It was his battle-cry, his call to arms. At the sound of it, one by one around the burial chamber, his loyal men rose in answer. Eyjolf, with an arrow still jutting from his eye socket. Bork, the knob of his shoulder-bone showing through pulped and mangled flesh where his arm had been cut off. Thrain the Merry sprang up almost eagerly. They seized the weapons with which they had been laid to rest, and took their places at Sveinthor's side.

Their women rose as well. Faithful Unn of the dimpled cheeks—not dimpled now but sagging, and the foam of the poison dried to a crust on her lips. The slave-girl, a little creature and young, but hissing like a cat. Even Ainslinn, head lolling on her puffed and swollen neck, got slowly to her feet.

And the battle was joined in a furious clangor of metal and screams. The close confines of the burial-chamber became a slaughtering-ground. Flesh struck wetly on the floor and blood flew like sea-spray in all directions. The *draugr* women had no swords, not even knives, but they had teeth and fingernails and fists, and a strength that seemed more than the equal of any two mortal men.

Ulfgrim had seen enough and fled, dragging Hildirid with him. In her last glimpse of the scene within the mound, it looked almost to her as though the risen dead were not merely fighting their foes but devouring them… tearing off mouthfuls of meat, lapping hungrily at the blood-spatter, even nuzzling their faces into the guts of the fallen to come up with steaming livers and intestines clenched in their jaws.

The night outside was foggy and damp, turning the distant torches on the walls of Kjartan's mighty fortress to golden smears of elf-light. Though she fought him with every step, Hildirid could not win her way free of Ulfgrim's iron grasp. He pulled her into the broad field, the both of them stumbling over broken spear-shafts and split shields and the scavenger-picked remains of the unburied dead.

"Let me go!" demanded Hildirid, trying to bend back his fingers where they held hard around her wrist.

"They're monsters, you foolish sow!" Ulfgrim shouted. "Did you not see? They'll kill you, or eat you alive!"

"I'd rather that death than life with you!"

But he would not release her, even when she fell full-length and tangled in a pile of corpses. Taking her by a fistful of hair, he made as if to sling her over his shoulder and carry her the rest of the way.

Then a long shaggy shape hurtled out of the swirling fog and slammed into him, ripping his hand loose from Hildirid's hair and leaving long strands caught in it. He was knocked hard to the wet earth, where a shadow-shape loomed over him.

It was Bryn-Loki, Thrain's dog, who had never liked Ulfgrim. Parts of his fur had fallen out in patches, and the rest was slimed green with mold. He smelled dank and horrible. The growl that came from low in his throat was bubbled and strange. His teeth, though, when he skinned his black lips back from his muzzle, looked strong and sharper than ever.

Ulfgrim rolled into a crouch, drawing his sword. It was,

Hildirid suddenly knew, the same one that had struck Svein-thor that treacherous, fatal wound. Now he thrust it into Bryn-Loki's chest as the dog leaped. The blade sheared through ribs and muscle and gristle, loosing a spurt of foul fluid. Bryn-Loki fell shuddering onto his side. Ulfgrim got up, shaking but sneering victoriously, and wiped the reeking blade on the dog's thick fur.

Bryn-Loki raised his head, snarled, and clambered to his feet. He shook, the way a dog will after a hard rain, and more fur dropped in mangy clots from his hide. Stiff-legged, he advanced on Ulfgrim, who turned again and ran for his very life as if all the fiends of Niflheim were close upon his heels.

There were no fiends save Bryn-Loki, but Bryn-Loki was fiend enough. Hildirid, kneeling amid the dead, watched the chase as Ulfgrim made for the safety of the earthen wall around the fort. The churning mist had nearly hidden them when she saw Ulfgrim madly scaling the wall and Bryn-Loki make a final lunging leap. His jaws snapped, tearing a chunk from Ulfgrim's buttock. Then Ulfgrim was up and over and gone from her sight.

The dog trotted back to her. As Bryn-Loki came, the first stirrings of fear gathered in her belly. She wondered if it would hurt, the rending of his teeth. She wondered if it would be quick.

She closed her eyes as his paws thumped to a halt on the damp earth only a few paces distant. It seemed she could smell Ulfgrim's blood on his snout. A cold nose bumped her, snuffling thickly. Then a colder tongue, wet and reeking with decay, lapped at her face.

Hildirid opened her eyes. Bryn-Loki sat hunkered on his haunches before her. His head was cocked, his tail making jerky, lurching wags as if he could not quite remember how to do it properly. When he saw her looking at him, he uttered a hollow whine, and the wagging became so energetic she worried his tail might fall off.

Other figures appeared through the gloom. They were drenched in blood, and gobbets of flesh clung to their garments and hair. She knew them, and as they neared her, she stood to face them with the dog sitting beside her and her hand resting on top of his head.

Eyjolf's leg had been hacked to the bone, so that he staggered along nearly lame, leaning on Unn, who swung a tattered scalp of long grey hair—the wise-woman's hair—from her hand. Bork, already lacking one arm, now carried his own head tucked into the crook of the other, his eyes blazing fiercely. Ainslinn could no longer walk, but pulled herself over the earth by her arms. The little slave-girl who had been buried with Thrain held a man's forearm, and munched happily at it as she might have gnawed a pork rib. Thrain himself wore looping strings of intestine around his neck, and his grin was wider than ever.

And with them came Sveinthor. His mail was shredded and his body scored with countless cuts that seeped and oozed. He still held Wolf's Tooth, a dark red rain falling from the blade. His severed hand rode upon his shoulder like one of Odin's ravens.

Hildirid went to him and embraced him, but then stepped back for she knew that his work was not yet finished. He surveyed the battle-field, strewn as it was with the unburied dead, and once more raised his hoarse voice so that it rang and rolled like thunder.

In the fortress on the hill there was much commotion and alarm. Perhaps when Ulfgrim had come in, they had dismissed his claims as drunken ravings or madness. But now, as one by one the corpses of Kjartan's slaughtered army laboriously raised themselves and armed themselves with what makeshift weapons they could find, the living men flocked to the walls with many torches and stared out in horror.

Sveinthor strode among them. They formed into ranks and lines below the earthen wall and the approach to the fort. At the front was a shield-wall, many of the overlapping shields splintered and broken. With slow but inexorable, relentless purpose, the walking dead began their advance.

A storm of arrows descended upon them, and though many found their mark and lodged in flesh, they could not do much harm. Some of Sveinthor's *draugr* were so bristling with arrow-shafts by the time they reached the base of the wall that they looked like hedgehogs, and still they advanced.

Hildirid stood atop the burial mound, her hair and sealskin cloak streaming around her in the dire wind that had sprung up. Bryn-Loki sat at her side, and her hand still stroked his head and scratched his ears, for he was whining in disappointment at having been left behind from the battle to guard her.

Now from the fort came flaming arrows, but many of the *draugr* had lain so long in the rain and mud that they did little more than smolder. One or two, fatter men in life, burned like tallow, and became shuffling candles in the shapes of men. The smoke from their singed hair and charred, rotting bodies blew back over the wall, filling the fort with an abominable stench.

At last a few of the bravest defenders came out to meet their foes, but they soon fell, and the *draugr* swarmed over the wall and into the fortress. Even from where she stood, Hildirid could hear the cries of pain and anguish and terror, and the ghastly sounds of feeding as Sveinthor's followers feasted on quivering, still-warm flesh.

Later, when quiet had descended and the night was almost done, she took Bryn-Loki and ventured into the fort. Everywhere she looked were *draugr*, plundering the newly-dead and adorning themselves with medallions and arm-rings, or taking trophies of scalps and fingers and jawbones and heads. The living—the women and children and slaves taken from among Kjartan's people—cowered unharmed and ignored.

Then she saw Kjartan himself, freed from his prison and seated upon his great wooden chair draped with bearskins. Ulfgrim's body, bound in ropes, lay before him with a pool of blood around the stump of his neck. His head was held aloft on the point of Wolf's Tooth, raised high by Sveinthor.

Kjartan saw her as well. "He will not stay, Hildirid," the king said. "He must return to the burial-mound, before dawn comes. He has fulfilled his *wyrd*."

No amount of imploring by them could sway Sveinthor. As the sky to the east brightened, the *draugr* left off what they were doing. Almost as one, they left the fort and returned to the field, lying down again where they had died and then arisen. Eyjolf, Bork, Thrain and their women entered the tomb, followed by Bryn-Loki.

Only Sveinthor remained. He had Ulfgrim's head knotted by the hair to his belt, and Wolf's Tooth was finally released from his grip to be sheathed again across his back. With his one good hand, he reached out and caressed the curve of Hildirid's cheek. Then he turned from her and walked toward the mound.

"Farewell, lord," Hildirid said to Kjartan, and kissed him.

"Hildirid!" the king called. "Where do you go? What do you do?"

"As you said, lord, Sveinthor has fulfilled his *wyrd*." She touched the knife at her belt and smiled. "Now I shall fulfill mine."

So saying, she followed Sveinthor into the darkness. When the sun rose, the entrance to the mound was covered over again with planks and stones and earth. Never again was it disturbed by mortal men.

And so ends the saga of Sveinthor the Unkillable, and the beautiful Hildirid, his beloved barrow-maid.

;=+{)

YOU'LL NEVER WALK ALONE

SCOTT NICHOLSON

D addy said them that eat human flesh will suffer under
Hell.

I ain't figured that out yet, how there can be a place
under Hell. Daddy couldn't hardly describe it hisself. It's just
a real bad place, hotter than the regular Hell and probably
lonelier, too, since Hell's about full up and nobody's a stranger.
Been so much sinning the Devil had to build a basement for
the gray people.

It was Saturday when we heard about them. I was watching cartoons and eating a bowl of corn flakes. I like cereal with lots of sugar, so when the flakes are done you can drink down that thick milk at the bottom of the bowl. It come up like a commercial, some square-headed man in a suit sitting at a desk, with that beeping sound like when they tell you a bad storm's coming. Daddy was drinking coffee with his boots off, and he said wasn't a cloud in the sky and the wind was lazy as a cut cat. So he figured it was just another thing about the Aye-rabs and who cared if they blew each other to Kingdom Come, except then they showed some of that TV that looks like them cop shows, the camera wiggly so you can't half see what they're trying to show you.

Daddy kept the cartoons turned down low because he said the music hurt his ears, but this time he took the remote from beside my cereal bowl and punched it three or four times with his thumb. The square-headed man was talking faster than they usually do, like a flatlander, acting like he deserved a pat on the head because he was doing such a good job telling about something bad. Then the TV showed somebody in rags moving toward the camera and Daddy said, Lordy, looked like something walked out of one of them suicide bombs, because its face was gray and looked like the meat had melted off the bone.

But the square-headed man said the picture was live from Winston-Salem, that's about two hours from us here in the mountains. The man said it was happening all over, the hospitals was crowded and the governor done called out the National Guard. Then the television switched and it was the president standing at a bunch of microphones, saying something about a new terror threat but how everybody ought to stay calm because you never show fear in the face of the enemy.

Daddy said them damned ragheads must have finally let the bugs out of the bottle. I don't see how bugs could tear up a man's skin that way, to where it looked like he'd stuck his head in a lawn mower and then washed his face with battery acid and grease rags. I saw a dead raccoon once, in the ditch when I was walking home from school, and maggots was squirming in its eye holes and them shiny green dookie flies was swarming around its tail. I reckon that's what kind of bugs Daddy meant, only worse, because these ones get you while you're still breathing.

I was scared then, but it was the kind where you just sort of feel like the ashes in the pan at the bottom of the woodstove. Where you don't know what to be afraid of. At least when you hear something moving in the dark woods, your hands get sweaty and your heart jumps a mite faster and you know which way to run. But looking at the TV, all I could think of was the time I woke up and Momma wasn't making breakfast, and Momma didn't come home from work, and Momma didn't make supper. A kind of scared that fills you up belly first, and you can't figure it out, and you can't take a stick to it like you can that thing in the dark woods. And then there was the next day when Momma still didn't come home, and that's how I felt about the bugs out of the bottle, because it seems like you can't do nothing to stop it. Then I felt bad because the president would probably say I was showing fear in the face of the enemy, and Daddy voted for the president because it was high time for a change.

I asked Daddy what we was going to do, and he said the Lord would show the way. Said he was loading the shotgun just in case, because the Lord helped those that helped themselves. Said he didn't know whether them things could drive a car or not. If they had to walk all the way from the big city, they probably wouldn't get here for three days. If they come here at all.

Daddy told me to go put up the cows. Said the TV man said they liked living flesh, but you can't trust what the TV says half the time because they want to sell you something. I didn't figure how they could sell anything by scaring people like that. But I was awful glad we lived a mile up a dirt road, in a little notch in the mountains. It was cold for March, maybe too cold for them bugs. But I wasn't too happy about fetching the cows, because they tend to wander in the mornings and not come in 'til dark. Cows like to spend their days all the same. If you do something new, they stomp and stir and start in with the moos, and I was afraid the moos might bring the bugs or them gray people that eat living flesh.

I about told Daddy I was too scared to fetch them by myself, but he might have got mad because of what the president said and all. Besides, he was busy putting on his boots. So I took my hickory stick from by the door and called Shep. He was probably digging for groundhogs up by the creek and couldn't hear me. I walked out to the fields on the north side, where the grass grows slow and we don't put cows except early spring. Some of the trees was starting to get new leaves, but the woods was mostly brown rot and granite stone. That made me feel a little better, because a bug-bit gray person would have a harder time sneaking up on me.

We was down to only four cows because of the long drought and we had to cull some steers last year or else buy hay. Four is easy to round up, because all you got to do is get one of them moving and the rest will follow. Cows in a herd almost always point their heads in the same direction, like they all know they're bound for the same place sooner or later. Most people think cows are dumb but some things they got a lot of sense about. You hardly ever see a cow in a hurry. I figure they don't worry much, and they probably don't know about being scared, except when you take them to the barn in the middle of the day. Then maybe they remember the blood on the walls and the steaming guts and the smell of raw meat and the jingle of the slaughter chains.

By the time I got them penned up, Shep had come in from wherever and gave out a bark like he'd been helping the whole time. I took him into the house with me. I don't ever do that unless it's come a big snow or when icicles hang from his fur. Daddy was dressed and the shotgun was laying on the kitchen table. I gave Shep the last of my cereal milk. Daddy said the TV said the gray people was walking all over, even in the little towns, but said some of the telephone wires was down so nobody could tell much what was going on where.

I asked Daddy if these was like the End Times of the Bible, like what Preacher Danny Lee Aldridge talked about when the sermon was almost over and the time had come to pass the plate. I always got scared about the End Times, even sitting in the church with all the wood and candles and that soft red cloth on the back of the pews. The End Times was the same as Hell to me. But Preacher Aldridge always wrapped up by saying that the way out of Hell was to walk through the House of the Lord, climb them stairs and let the loving light burn ever little shred of sin out of you. All you had to do was ask, but you had to do it alone. Nobody else could do it for you.

So you got to pray to the Lord. I like to pray in church, where there's lots of people and the Lord has to mind everybody at the same time. It's probably wrong, but I get scared when I try to pray all by myself. I used to pray with Momma and Daddy, then just Daddy, and that's okay because I figured Daddy's louder than me and probably has more to talk about. I just get that sharp rock feeling in my belly every time I think about the Lord looking at nobody but me, when I ain't got nothing to hide behind and my stick is out of reach.

But these ain't the End Times, Daddy said, because the gray people don't have horns and the TV didn't say nothing about a dragon coming up out of the sea. But he said since they eat human flesh they're of the Devil, and said their bodies may be walking around but you better believe their souls are roasting under Hell. Especially if they got bit by the Aye-rab bug. I told him the cattle was put up and he said the chickens would be okay. You can't catch a chicken even when your legs is working right, much less when you're wobbling around like somebody beat the tar out of you with an ax handle.

He said to get in the truck. I made Shep jump up in the truck bed, then Daddy come out of the house with a loaf of white bread and some cans of sardines. Had the shotgun, too. He got in the truck and started it, and I asked him where we was headed. He said in troubled times you go get closer to the Lord.

I asked him if maybe he thought Momma would be okay. He said it didn't matter none, since the Devil done got her ages ago. Said she was already a gray person before this bug mess even started. Said to waste no prayers on her.

The dirt road was mushy from winter. The road runs by the

creek for a while, then crosses a little bridge by the Hodges'
place. That's where I always caught the school bus, with Johnny
Hodges and his sister Raylene. Smoke was coming out of their
chimney and I asked Daddy if we ought to stop and tell them
about what the TV said. Daddy said they might be gray people
already. I tried to picture Johnny with his face all slopped
around, or Raylene with bugs eating her soft places. Mister
Hodges didn't go to church and Johnny told me he used to
beat them sometimes when he drank too much. I wondered
if all the people who didn't go to church had turned gray and
started eating human flesh.

We passed a few other houses but didn't see nobody, even
at the preacher's place. The church was right there where the
gravel turned to paved, set up above the road on a little green
hill. The graveyard was tucked away to one side, where barbed
wire strung off a pasture. The church was made of brick, the
windows up high so that people wouldn't look outside during
the preaching. Seeing that white cross jabbed up into the sky
made me feel not so scared.

We parked the truck around back. Daddy had me carry the
food and he carried the shotgun. Said a Bible and a shotgun
was all a man needed. I didn't say nothing about a man needed
food. I found a little pack of sugar in the truck's ashtray and
I hid it in my pocket. We didn't have no Co'-colas.

They keep the church unlocked in case people want to
come in and pray. Daddy said people in the big city lock their
churches. If they don't, people might come in and sleep or steal
the candleholders and hymn books. But this is the mountains,
where people all know each other and get along and you don't
need to lock everything. So we went inside. Daddy made Shep

stay out, said it would be disrespecting to the Lord. We locked the door from the inside. I thought somebody else might want to come get close to the Lord in these troubled times, but Daddy said they could knock if they wanted in.

We went up to the front where the pulpit is and Daddy said we might as well get down and give thanks for deliverance. I didn't feel delivered yet but Daddy was a lot smarter about the Bible, so I went on my knees and kept my eyes closed while Daddy said O Lord, it's looking mighty dark but the clouds will part and Heaven will knock down them gray people and set things right. I joined in on the amen and said

I was hungry.

Daddy opened up the sardines and they stank. I spilled some of the fish juice on the floor. We ate some of the bread. It was gummy and stuck to my teeth. I was tired and tried to lay down in the front pew but it was like sleeping in a rock coffin. I didn't know why people in the big city would want to do such a thing. Daddy started reading from the Bible but the light got bad as the afternoon wore on. The church ain't got electric power.

I asked Daddy how long we was going to stay holed up and he said as long as it took. I wished we had a TV so we could see what was going on. Night finally come, and I was using the bathroom in back when I heard Shep whimpering. I reckon he was lonely out there. Sounded like he was scratching in the dirt out back of the church.

I climbed up on the sink and looked out the little window. Under the moonlight I saw the graveyard, and it looked like somebody had took a shovel to it, tore up the dirt real bad. Something was coming up out of one of the holes, and I reckon that's what Shep was whimpering about.

I went and told Daddy what I seen and he said maybe it was the End Times after all. Shep started barking and I begged Daddy to let me open the door. He said the Lord would take care of Shep, but then I heard him bark again and I was trying to open the door when Daddy knocked me away. Said he'd take a look, stepped outside with the shotgun, and the gun went off and Daddy started cussing goddamn right there on the church steps. Shep started moaning and I ran to the door and Shep was crawling toward the woods on his belly like his back was broke. I thought Daddy had shot him and I started to cry but then I seen somebody coming from the woods. Daddy racked another shell into the chamber and hollered but the person just kept coming. Daddy told me to go in and lock the door but I couldn't. I was too scared to be in that big dark church by myself.

Daddy shot high and the pellets scattered through the tops of the trees and still the person kept coming, walking slow with a limp. Another person came out of the trees, then another. They was all headed in the same direction. Straight toward the church.

One of them bent down and got Shep, and I never heard such a sound from a dog. Daddy was cussing a blue streak and let loose both barrels and one of the people stood still for just a second, and I could see that gray face turned up toward the moon, the eye holes empty. Then his insides tumbled out but he kept on coming for us and Daddy was pushing me back through the door and we got inside and locked it.

Daddy went up front and I could hear him crying. Except for that, the church was quiet. I thought the gray people might try to knock the door down but maybe they got scared away because of it being a church and all. I went up beside Daddy and waited until he was hisself again. He said he was sorry for showing fear in the face of the enemy and said O Lord, give me the strength to do your work. I said Lord, protect Momma wherever she is, and Daddy said it was wrong to ask for selfish things.

Daddy said the End Times was a test for the weak. Said you had to stay strong in the Lord. Said it about fifteen hundred times in a row, over and over, in a whisper, and it made me scared.

I was about asleep when Daddy poked me with the gun. Said come here, Son, over by the window where I can see you good. The moon was coming through the window and I could hear the gray people walking outside. They was going around in circles, all headed in the same direction.

Daddy asked me if I got bit by one of them bugs. I said don't reckon. He said, well, you're looking a little gray, and I told him I didn't feel nary bit gray. He asked me if I was getting hungry and I said a little. He gave me the rest of the bread and said eat it. I took a bite and he said you didn't say thanks to the Lord. Then he thanked the Lord for both of us.

I asked Daddy if Shep had gone to Heaven. He said it depended on whether he was dead before the gray people ate him. Said Shep might have done turned gray hisself and might bite me if he saw me again. I almost asked Daddy to say a prayer for Shep but that sounded like a selfish thing.

I must have finally dozed off because I didn't know where I was when I opened my eyes. Daddy was at the front of the church, in the pulpit where Preacher Aldridge stood of a Sunday. The sun was about up and Daddy had the Bible open and was trying to read in the bad light. Somebody was knocking on the church door.

Daddy said the word was made flesh and dwelt among us. Daddy stopped just like Preacher Aldridge did, like he wanted to catch his breath and make you scared at the same time. Then Daddy got louder and said we beheld His glory, the glory as of the only begotten of the Father, full of grace and truth.

I asked what did that mean and Daddy said the Lord come down among people and nobody saw the signs. Said they treated Him just like any normal person, except then He set off doing miracles and people got scared and nailed Him to the cross. Said it was probably gray people that done it. I asked Daddy if we ought to open the church door and see who was knocking.

Daddy said gray people wasn't fit to set foot in the House of the Lord. I asked what if it's the preacher or the Hodges kids or Opalee Rominger from down the road. Daddy said they're all gray, everybody. Said they was all headed under Hell. Said ever sinner is wicked and blind to their sinning ways. I didn't see how Opalee Rominger could eat living flesh, because she ain't got no teeth.

The knocking stopped and I didn't hear no screams so maybe whoever it was didn't get ate up.

I listened to Daddy read the Bible. The sun come up higher and I wondered about the cows. Did the gray people eat them all? It wasn't like they ain't enough sinners to go around. I didn't for a minute believe that everybody was gray. There had to be others like us. There's a hymn that says you11 never walk alone. I don't reckon the Lord breaks promises like that but I was way too scared to ask. Daddy's eyes were getting bloodshot, like he hadn't slept a wink, and he was whispering to hisself again.

I drank water from the plate that Preacher Aldridge passed around on Sundays. The water tasted like old pennies. Daddy didn't drink nothing. I asked him if he wanted the last can of sardines but he said man can't live by bread alone but by the word of the Lord. I wondered what the Lord's words tasted like. I wondered what people tasted like. I ate the sardines by myself.

That night was quiet, like the gray people had done gone on to wherever they were headed. I woke up in the morning plenty sore and I asked Daddy if we could take a peek out the door. Daddy hadn't moved, only stood up there at the pulpit like he was getting ready to let loose with a sermon. He had the shotgun raised toward Heaven and I don't reckon he heard me. I asked it louder and he said you can't see the gray people because ever sinner is blind. I said I ain't no sinner but he said you're looking mighty gray to me.

I said I ain't gray, and then he made me prove it. Said get on your knees and beg the Lord to forgive you. He pointed the shotgun at me. I didn't know if he would use it or not, but the way his eye twitched I wasn't taking no chances. I got on my knees but I was scared to close my eyes. When you close your eyes and pray it's just you and the Lord. You're blind but the Lord sees everything. I asked Daddy to pray with me.

Daddy set in to asking the Lord to forgive us our sins and trespasses. I wondered if we was trespassing on the church. It belonged to the Lord, and we was here so we wouldn't get ate up. I didn't say nothing to Daddy about it, though. I added an extra loud amen just so Daddy would know for sure that I wasn't gray.

Later I asked Daddy how come ever sinner is gray. He said the Lord decides such things. He said Momma was a sinner and that's why she was gray all along and her soul was already under Hell. I didn't say nothing to that. Sometimes Daddy said I took after my Momma. I wished I'd took after Daddy instead and been able to pray all by myself.

I said it sounded like the gray people was gone. Daddy said you can't trust the Devil's tricks. Said the only way out was through the Lord. I said I was getting hungry again. Daddy said get some sleep and pray.

I woke up lost in the dark and Daddy was screaming his head off. He was sitting where the moon come through the window and he said look at me, look at my skin. He held up his hands and said I'm gray, I'm gray, I'm gray. Said he was unfit to be in the House of the Lord. He put the shotgun barrel up to the side of his neck and then there was a flash of light and a sound like the world split in half and then something wet slapped against the walls.

I crawled over to him and laid beside him 'til all the warm had leaked out. I was scared and I wanted to pray but without Daddy to help me the Lord would look right into me and that was worse than anything. Then I thought if Daddy was in Heaven now, maybe I could say a prayer to him instead and he could pass along my words to the Lord.

The sun come up finally and Daddy didn't look gray at all. He was white. His belly gurgled and the blood around his neck hole turned brown. I went to the door and unlocked it. Since it was Sunday morning, I figured people would be coming to hear the sermon. With more people in the church, I could pray without being so scared.

I stacked up some of the hymn books and stood on them so I could look out the window. They was back. More gray people were walking by, all headed in the same direction. I figured they were going to that place under Hell, just like Daddy said, and it made me happy that Daddy died before he turned gray.

Time passed real slow and the bread was long gone and nobody come to church. I never figured so many people that I used to pray with would end up turning gray. Like church didn't do them no good at all. I thought of all the prayers I said with them and it made me scared, the kind of scared that fills you up belly first. I wondered what the Lord thought about all them sinners, and what kind of words the Lord said back to them when they prayed.

Daddy's fingers had gone stiff and I about had to break them to get the shotgun away. He'd used up the last shell. The door was unlocked but nobody set foot in the church. I was hoping whoever had knocked the other day might come back, but they didn't.

The gray people didn't come in the church. I figured if they was eating live flesh they would get me sooner or later. Except maybe they was afraid about the church and all, or being in plain sight of the Lord. Or maybe they ain't figured out doors yet. I wondered if you go through doors to get under Hell.

Night come again. Daddy was dead cold. I was real hungry and I asked Daddy to tell the Lord about it, but I reckon Daddy would call that a selfish thing and wouldn't pass it on. I kept trying to pray but I was scared. Preacher Aldridge said you got to do it alone, can't nobody do it for you.

Maybe one of them Aye-rab bugs got in while the door was open. Maybe the gray people ain't ate me yet because I ain't live flesh no more. Only the Lord knows. All I know is I can't stay in this church another minute. Daddy's starting to stink and the Lord's looking right at me.

Like I'm already gray.

I don't feel like I am, but Daddy said ever sinner is blind. And the hunger gnawing at me is the kind of hungry that hurts.

Outside the church, the morning is fresh and cold and smells like broken flowers. I hear footsteps in the wet grass. I turn and walk, and I fit right in like they was saving a place for me. I'm one of them, following the ones ahead and leading the ones behind. We're all headed in the same direction. Maybe this entire world is the place under Hell, and we've been here all along.

I ain't scared no more, just hungry. The hungry runs deep. You can't live by bread alone. Sometimes you need meat instead of words.

I don't have to pray no more, out here where it ain't never dark. Where the Lord don't look at you. Where we're all sinners. Where you're born gray, again and again, and the End Times never end.

Where you never walk alone.

Xx{P

THE DEAD KID

DARRELL SCHWEITZER

I

It's been a lot of years, but I think I'm still afraid of Luke Bradley, because of what he showed me.

I knew him in the first grade, and he was a tough guy even then, the sort of kid who would sit on a tack and insist it didn't hurt, and then make *you* sit on the same tack (which definitely *did* hurt) because you were afraid of what he'd do if you didn't. Once he found a bald-faced hornet nest on tree branch, broke it off, and ran yelling down the street, waving the branch around and around until finally the nest fell off and the hornets came out like a *cloud.* Nobody knew what happened after that because the rest of us had run away.

We didn't see Luke in school for a couple days afterwards, so I suppose he got stung rather badly. When he did show up he was his old self and beat up three other boys in one afternoon. Two of them needed stitches.

When I was about eight, the word went around the neighborhood that Luke Bradley had been eaten by a werewolf. "Come on," said Tommy Hitchens, Luke's current sidekick. "I'll show you what's left of him. Up in a tree."

I didn't believe any werewolf would have been a match for Luke Bradley, but I went. When Tommy pointed out the alleged remains of the corpse up in the tree, I could tell even from a distance that I was looking at a t-shirt and a pair of blue-jeans stuffed with newspapers.

I said so and Tommy flattened me with a deft right hook, which broke my nose, and my glasses.

The next day, Luke was in school as usual, though I had a splint on my nose. When he saw me, he called me a "pussy" and kicked me in the balls.

Already he was huge, probably a couple of years older than the rest of the class. Though he never admitted it, everybody knew he'd been held back in every grade at least once, even kindergarten.

But he wasn't stupid. He was *crazy.* That was the fascination of hanging out with him, even if you could get hurt in his company. He did *wild* things that no one else dared even think about. There was the stunt with the hornet nest, or the time he picked up fresh dogshit in both his bare hands and claimed he was going to *eat* it right in front of us before everybody got grossed out and ran because we were afraid he was going to make *us* eat it. Maybe he really did. He was just someone for whom the rules, *all* the rules, simply did not apply. That he was usually in detention, and had been picked up by the police several times only added to his mystique.

And in the summer when I was twelve, Luke Bradley showed me the dead kid.

Things had progressed quite a bit since then. No one quite believed all the stories of Luke's exploits, though he would beat the crap out of you if you questioned them to his face. Had he really stolen a car? Did he really hang onto the outside of a P&W light-rail train and ride all the way into Philadelphia without getting caught?

Nobody knew, but when he said to me and to my ten-year-old brother Albert, "Hey you two scuzzes"—*scuzz* being his favorite word of the moment—"there's a *dead kid* in Cabbage Creek Woods. Wanna see?" it wasn't really a question.

Albert tried to turn away, and said, "David, I don't think we should," but I knew what was good for us.

"Yeah," I said. "Sure we want to see."

Luke was already more than a head taller than either of us and fifty pounds heavier. He was cultivating the "hood" image from some hand-me-down memory of James Dean or Elvis, with his hair up in a greasy swirl and a black leather jacket worn even on hot days when he kept his shirt unbuttoned so he could show off that he already had chest hair.

A cigarette dangled from his lips. He blew smoke in my face. I strained not to cough.

"Well come on, then," he said. "It's really cool."

So we followed him, along with a kid called Animal, and another called Spike—the beginnings of Luke's "gang," with which he said he was going to make himself famous one day. My little brother tagged after us, reluctantly at first, but then as fascinated as I was to be initiated into this innermost, forbidden secret of the older, badder set.

Luke had quite a sense of showmanship. He led us under bushes, crawling through natural tunnels under vines and dead trees where, when we were smaller, we'd had our own secret hideouts, as, I suppose, all children do. Luke and his crowd were getting too big for that sort of thing, but they went crashing through the underbrush like bears. I was small and skinny enough. David was young enough. In fact it was all we could do to keep up.

With a great flourish, Luke raised a vine curtain and we emerged into the now half-abandoned Radnor Golf Course. It was an early Saturday morning. Mist was still rising from the poorly tended greens. I saw one golfer, far away. Otherwise we had the world to ourselves.

We ran across the golf course, then across Lancaster Pike, then up the hill and back into the woods on the other side.

I only thought for a minute, *Hey wait a minute, we're going to see a corpse, a kid like us, only dead…* but, as I said, for Luke Bradley or even with him, all rules were suspended, and I knew better than try to ask what the kid died of, because we'd see soon enough.

In the woods again, by secret and hidden ways, we came to the old "fort," which had probably been occupied by generations of boys by then, though of course right now it "belonged" to the Luke Bradley Gang.

I don't know who built the fort or why. It was a rectangle of raised earth and piled stone, with logs laid across for a roof, and vines growing thickly over the whole thing so that from a distance it just looked like a hillock or knoll. That was part of its secret. You had to know it was there.

And only Luke could let you in.

He raised another curtain of vines, and with a sweep of his hand and a bow said, "Welcome to my house, you assholes."

Spike and Animal laughed while Albert and I got down on our hands and knees and crawled inside.

Immediately I almost gagged on the awful smell, like rotten garbage and worse. Albert started to cough. I thought he was going to throw up. But before I could say or do anything, Luke and his two henchmen had come in after us, and we all crowded around a pit in the middle of the dirt floor which didn't used to be there. Now there was a four-foot drop, a roughly square cavity, and in the middle of that, a cardboard box which was clearly the source of the unbelievable stench.

Luke got out a flashlight, then reached down and opened the box.

"It's a dead kid. I found him in the woods in this box. He's mine."

I couldn't help but look. It was indeed a dead kid, an ema-ciated, pale thing, naked but for what might have been the remains of filthy underpants, lying on its side in a fetal posi-tion, little clawlike hands bunched up under its chin.

"A dead kid," said Luke. "Really cool."

Then Albert really was throwing up and screaming at the same time, and scrambling to get *out* of there, only Animal and then Spike had him by the back of his shirt the way you pick up a kitten by the scruff of its neck, and they passed him back to Luke, who held his head in his hands and forced him down into that pit, saying, "Now look at it you fucking pussy faggot, this because it's really cool."

Albert was sobbing and sniffling when Luke let him go, but he didn't try to run, nor did I, even when Luke got a stick and poked the dead kid with it.

"This is the best part," he said.

We didn't run away then because we *had* to watch just to convince ourselves that we weren't crazy, because of what we were seeing.

Luke poked and the dead kid *moved*, spasming at first, then grabbing at the stick feebly, and finally crawling around inside the box like a slow, clumsy animal, just barely able to turn, scratching at the cardboard with bony fingertips.

"What *is* he?" I had to ask.

"A *zombie*," said Luke.

"Aren't zombies supposed to be black?"

"You mean like a nigger?" That was another of Luke's favorite words this year. He called everybody "nigger" no matter what color they were.

"Well, you know. Voodoo. In Haiti and all that."

As we spoke the dead kid reared up and almost got out of the box. Luke poked him in the forehead with his stick and knocked him down.

"I suppose if we let him *rot* long enough he'll be black enough even for *you*."

The dead kid stared up at us and made a bleating sound. The worst thing of all was that he didn't have any eyes, only huge sockets and an oozy mess inside them.

Albert was sobbing for his mommy by then, and after a while of poking and prodding the dead kid, Luke and his friends got tired of this sport. Luke turned to me and said, "You can go now, but you know if you or your piss-pants brother tell about this, I'll kill you both and put you in there for the dead kid to *eat.*"

II

I can't remember much of what Albert and I did for the rest of that day. We ran through the woods, tripped, fell flat on our faces in a stream. Then later we were walking along the old railroad embankment turning over ties to look for snakes, and all the while Albert was babbling on about the dead kid and how we had to do something. I just let him talk until he got it all out of him, and when we went home for dinner and were very quiet when Mom and our stepdad Steve tried to find out what we had been doing all day.

"Just playing," I said. "In the woods."

"It's good for them to be outdoors," Steve said to Mom. "Too many kids spent all their time in front of the TV watching *unwholesome* junk these days. I'm glad our kids are *normal.*"

But Albert ended up screaming in his sleep for weeks and wetting his bed, and things were anything but normal that summer. He was the one with the obvious problems. He was the one who ended up going to a "specialist," and whatever he said in therapy must not have been believed, because the police didn't go tearing up Cabbage Creek Woods, Luke

Bradley and his neanderthals were not arrested, and I was more or less left alone.

In fact, I had more unsupervised time than usual. And I used it to work out problems of my own, like I hated school and I hated Stepdad Steve for the sanctimonious prig he was. I decided, with the full wisdom of my twelve years and some months, that if I was to survive in this rough, tough, evil world, I was going to have to become tough myself, *bad,* and very likely evil.

I decided that Luke Bradley had the answers.

So I sought him out. It wasn't hard. He had a knack for being in the right place at the right time when you're ready to sell your soul, just like the Devil.

I met him in town, in front of the Wayne Toy Town, where I used to go to buy model kits and stuff. I still liked building models, and doing scientific puzzles, though I would never admit it to Luke Bradley.

So I just froze when I saw him there.

"Well, well," he said. "If it ain't the little pussy scuzz." He blew smoke from the perennial cigarette.

"Hello, Luke," I said. I nodded to his companions, who included Spike, Animal, and a virtually hairless, pale gorilla who went by the unlikely name of Corky. As I spoke, I slipped my latest purchase into my shoulder bag and hoped he didn't notice.

Corky grabbed me by the back of the neck and said, "Whaddaya want me to do with him?"

But before Luke could respond, I said, "Hey, have you still got the dead kid at the fort?"

They all hesitated. They weren't expecting that.

"Well he's *cool,*" I said. "I want to see him again."

"Okay," said Luke.

We didn't have any other way to get there, so we walked, about an hour, to Cabbage Creek Woods. Luke dispensed with ceremony. We just crawled into the fort and gathered around the pit.

The smell, if anything, was worse.

This time, the dead kid was already moving around inside the box. When Luke opened the cardboard flaps, the dead kid stood up, with his horrible, pus-filled eye-sockets staring. He made that bleating, groaning sound again. He clawed at the edge of the box.

"Really cool," I forced myself to say, swallowing hard.

"I can make him do tricks," said Luke. "Watch this."

I watched as he shoved his finger *through* the skin under the dead kid's chin and lifted him up like a hooked fish out of the pit. The dead kid scrambled over the edge of the box, then crouched down on the dirt floor at the edge of the pit, staring into space.

Luke passed his hand slowly in front of the dead kid's face. He snapped his fingers. The dead kid didn't respond. Luke smacked him on the side of the head. The dead kid whimpered a little, and made that bleating sound.

"Everybody outside," Luke said.

So we all crawled out, and then Luke reached back inside with a stick and touched the dead kid, who came out too, clinging to the stick, trying to chew on it, but not quite co-ordinated enough, so that he just snapped his teeth in the air and rubbed the side of his face along the stick.

I could see him clearly now. He really *was* rotten, with bone sticking out at his knees and elbows, only scraggly patches of dark hair left on his head, every rib showing in hideous relief on his bare back, and *holes* through his skin between some of them.

"Look!" said Luke. "Look at him dance!" He swirled the stick around and around, and the dead kid clung to it, staggering around in a circle.

Corky spoke up. "Ya think if'n he gets dizzy he'll puke?"

Luke yanked the stick out of the dead kid's hands, then hit him hard with it across the back with a *thwack!* The dead kid dropped to all fours and just stayed there, his head hanging down.

"Can't puke. Got no guts left!" They all laughed at that. I didn't quite get the joke.

But despite everything, I *tried* to get the joke, despite even the incongruity that I really was, like it or not, a more or less "normal" kid and right now I had a model kit for a plastic Fokker Triplane in my schoolbag. I still wanted to measure up to Luke Bradley, for all I was more afraid of him than I had ever been. I figured you had to be afraid of what you did and who you hung out with if you were going to be really *bad*. You did what Luke did. That was what transgression was all about.

So I unzipped my fly and pissed on the dead kid. He made that bleating sound. The others chuckled nervously. Luke grinned.

"Pretty cool, Davey, my boy. Pretty cool."

Then Luke started to play the role of wise elder brother. He put his arm around my shoulders. He took me a little ways apart from the others and said, "I like you. I think you got something special in there." He rapped on my head with his knuckles, hard, but I didn't flinch away.

Then he led me back to the others and said, "I think we're gonna make David here a member of the gang."

So we all sat down in the clearing with the dead kid in our circle, as if he were one of the gang too. Luke got out an old briefcase from inside the fort and produced some very crumpled nudie magazines and passed them around and we all looked at the pictures. He even made a big, funny show of opening out a foldout for the dead kid to admire.

He smoked and passed cigarettes out to all of us. I'd never had one before and it made me feel sick, but Luke told me to hold the smoke in, then breathe it out slowly.

I was amazed and appalled when, right in front of everyone, he unzipped his pants and started to jerk off. The others did it too, making a point of trying to squirt on the dead kid.

Luke looked at me. "Come on, join in with the other gentle-men." The other "gentlemen" brayed like jackasses.

I couldn't move then. I really wanted to be like them, but I knew I wasn't going to measure up. All I could hope for now was to put up a good front so maybe they'd decide I wasn't a pussy after all and maybe let me go after they beat me up a little bit. I could hope for that much.

But Luke had other ideas. He put his hand on the back of my neck. It could have been a friendly gesture, or if he squeezed, he could have snapped my head off for all I could have done anything about it.

"Now David," he said, "I don't care if you've even *got* a dick, any more than I care if *he* does." He jerked his thumb at the dead kid. "But if you want to join our gang, if you want to be cool, you have to meet certain standards."

He flicked a switchblade open right in front of my face. I thought he was going to cut my nose with it, but with a sudden motion he slashed the dead kid's nose right off. It flew into the air. Corky caught it, then threw it away in mindless disgust.

The dead kid whimpered. His face was a black, oozing mess.

Then Luke took hold of my right hand and slashed the back of it. I let out a yell, and tried to stop the bleeding with my other hand.

"No," Luke said. "Let him lick it. He needs a little blood now and then to keep him healthy."

I screamed then, and sobbed, and whimpered the way Albert had that first time, but Luke held onto me with a grip so strong that *I* was the one who wriggled like a fish on a line, and he held my cut hand out to the dead kid.

I couldn't look, but something soft and wet touched my hand, and I could only think, Oh God, what kind of infection or disease am I going to get from this?

"Okay David," Luke said then. "You're doing just fine, but there is one more test. You have to *spend the whole night* in the fort with the dead kid. We've all done it. Now it's your turn."

They didn't wait for my answer, but, laughing, hauled me back inside the fort. Then Luke had the dead kid hooked under the chin again, and lowered him down into his box in the pit.

The others crawled back outside. Before he left, Luke turned to me, "You have to stay here until tomorrow morning. You know what I'll do to you if you pussy out."

So I spent the rest of the afternoon, and the evening, inside that fort with the dead kid scratching around in his box. It was already dark in the fort. I couldn't tell what time it was. I couldn't think very clearly at all. I wondered if anyone was looking for me. I lay very still. I didn't want to be found, especially not by the dead kid, who, for all I knew, could crawl out of the box and the pit if he really wanted to and maybe rip my throat out and drink my blood.

My hand hurt horribly. It seemed to be swelling. I was sure it was already rotten. The air was thick and foul.

But I stayed where I was, because I was afraid, because I was weak with nausea, but also, incredibly, because somehow, somewhere, deep down inside myself I still wanted to show how *tough* I was, to be like Luke Bradley, to be as amazing and crazy as he was. I knew that I *wasn't* cut out for this, and that's why I wanted it—to be *bad,* so no one would ever beat me up again and if I hated my stepdad or my teachers I could just tell them to go fuck off, as Luke would do.

Hours passed, and still the dead kid circled around and around inside his cardboard box, sliding against the sides. He made that bleating, coughing sound, as if he were trying to talk and didn't have any tongue left. For a time I thought there was almost some sense in it, some pattern. He was *clicking* like a cricket. This went on for hours. Maybe I even slept for a while, and fell into a kind of dream in which I was sinking slowly down into incredibly foul-smelling muck and there were thousands of bald-faced hornets swarming over me, all of them with little Luke Bradley faces saying, "Cool... really cool..." until their voices blended together and became a buzzing, then became wind in the trees, then the roar of a P&W light-rail train rushing off toward Philadelphia; and the dead kid and I were hanging onto the outside of the car, swinging wildly. My arm hit a pole and snapped right off, and black ooze was pouring out of my shoulder, and the hornets swarmed over me, eating me up bit by bit.

Once, I am certain, the dead kid *did* reach up and touch me, very gently, running his dry, sharp fingertip down the side of my cheek, cutting me, then withdrawing with a little bit of blood and tears on his fingertip, to drink.

But, strangest of all, I wasn't afraid of him then. It came to me, then, that we too had more in common than not. We were both afraid and in pain and lost in the dark.

III

Then somehow it was morning. The sunlight blinded me when Luke opened the vine curtain over the door.

"Hey. You were really brave. I'm impressed, Davey."

I let him lead me out of the fort, taking comfort in his chum/big-brother manner. But I was too much in shock to say anything.

"You passed the test. You're one of us," he said. "Welcome to the gang. Now there is one last thing for you to do. Not a test. You've passed all the tests. It's just something we do to celebrate."

His goons had gathered once more in the clearing outside the fort.

One of them was holding a can of gasoline.

I stood there, swaying, about to faint, unable to figure out what the gasoline was for.

Luke brought the dead kid outside.

Corky poured gasoline over the dead kid, who just bleated a little and waved his hands in the air.

Luke handed me a cigarette lighter. He flicked it until there was a flame.

"Go on," he said. "It'll be cool."

But I couldn't. I was too scared, too sick. I just dropped to my knees, then onto all fours and started puking.

So Luke lit the dead kid on fire and the others hooted and clapped as the dead kid went up like a torch, staggering and dancing around the clearing, trailing black, oily smoke. Then he fell down and seemed to shrivel up into a pile of blackened, smoldering sticks.

Luke forced me over to where the dead kid had fallen and made me touch what was left with my swollen hand.

And the dead kid *moved*. He made that bleating sound. He whimpered.

"You see? You can't kill him because he's already dead."

They were all laughing, but I just puked again, and finally Luke hauled me to my feet by both shoulders, turned me around, and shoved me away staggering into the woods.

"Come back when you stop throwing up," he said.

IV

Somehow I found my way home, and when I did, Mom just stared at me in horror and said, "My God, what's that awful smell?" But Stepdad Steve shook me and demanded to know where I had been and what I'd been doing? Did I know the police were looking for me? Did I care? (No, and no.) He took me into the bathroom, washed and bandaged my hand, then held me so I couldn't turn away and said, "Have you been taking drugs?"

That was so stupid I started to laugh, and he *smacked* me across the face, something he rarely did, but this time, I think, he was determined to beat the truth out of me, and Mommy, dearest Mommy didn't raise a finger to stop him as he laid on with his hand, then his belt, and I was shrieking my head off.

All they got out of me was the admission that I had been with Luke Bradley and his friends.

"I *don't* want you to associate with *those* boys any further. They're unwholesome."

He didn't know a tenth of it, and I started to laugh again, like I was drunk or something, and he was about to hit me again when Mom finally made him stop.

She told me to change my clothes and take a bath and then go to my room. I wasn't allowed out except for meals and to go to the bathroom.

That was fine with me. I didn't *want* to come out. I wanted to bury myself in there, to be quiet and dead, like the dead kid in his box.

But when I fell asleep, I was screaming in a dream, and I woke up screaming, in the dark, because it was night again.

Mom looked in briefly, but didn't say anything. The expression on her face was more of disgust than concern, as if she really wanted to say, *Serves him damn right but, Oh God, another crazy kid we'll have to send to the so, so expensive psychiatrist and I'd rather spend the money on a new mink coat or a car or something.*

It was my kid brother Albert who snuck over to my bed and whispered, "It's the dead kid, isn't it?"

"Huh?"

"The dead kid. He talks to me in my dreams. He's told me all about himself. He's lost. His father's a magician, who is still trying to find him. There was a war between magicians, or something, and that's how he got lost."

"Huh? Is this something you read in a comic book?"

"*No!* It's the dead kid. You know what we have to do, David. We have to go save him."

I have to give my brother credit for bringing about my moral redemption as surely as if he'd handed me my sanity back on a silver platter and said, *Go on, don't be a pussy. Take it.*

Because he was right. We had to save the dead kid.

Maybe the dead kid talked to Albert in his dreams, but he didn't tell me anything. Why should he?

Still, I'd gotten the message.

So, that night, very late, Albert and I got dressed and slipped out the window of our room, dropping onto the lawn. *He wasn't afraid,* not a little bit. He led me, by the ritual route, under the arching bushes, through the tunnels of vines to all our secret places, as if we had to be *there* first to gain some special strength for the task at hand.

Under the bushes, in the darkness, we paused to scratch secret signs in the dirt.

Then we scurried across the golf course, across the highway, into Cabbage Creek Woods.

We came to the fort by the light of a full moon now flickering through swaying branches. It was a windy night. The woods were alive with sounds of wood creaking and snapping, of animals calling back and forth, and night-birds cawing. Somewhere, very close at hand, an owl cried out.

Albert got down on all fours in the doorway of the fort, poked his head in, and said, "Hey, dead kid! Are you in there?"

He backed out, and waited. There was a rustling sound, but the dead kid didn't come out. So we both crawled in and saw why. There wasn't much left of him. He was just a bundle of black sticks, his head like a charred pumpkin balanced precariously on top. All he could do was sit up weakly and peer over the side of the box.

So we had to lift him out of the pit, box and all.

"Come on," Albert said to him. "We want to show you some stuff."

We carried the dead kid between us. We took him back across the golf course, under the bushes, to our special places. We showed him the secret signs. Then we took him into town. We showed him the storefronts, Wayne Toy Town where I bought models, where there were always neat displays of miniature battlefields or of monsters in the windows. We showed him where the pet store was and the ice cream store, and where you got comic books.

Albert sat down on the merry-go-round in the playground, holding the dead kid's box securely beside him. I pushed them around slowly. Metal creaked.

We stood in front of our school for a while, and Albert and the dead kid were *holding hands,* but it seemed natural and right.

Then we went away in the bright moonlight, through the empty streets. No one said anything, because whatever the dead kid could say or hear wasn't in words anyway. I couldn't hear it. I think Albert could.

In the end the dead kid scrambled out of his box. Somehow he had regained enough strength to walk. Somehow, he was beginning to heal. In the end, he wanted to show *us* something.

He led us back across the golf course but away from Cabbage Creek Woods. We crossed the football field at Radnor

High School, then went across the street, up in back of Wyeth Labs and across the high bridge over the P&W tracks. I was afraid the dead kid would slip on the metal stairs and fall, but he went more steadily than we did. (Albert and I were both a little afraid of heights.)

He led us across another field, into woods again, then through an opening where a stream flowed beneath the Pennsylvania Railroad embankment. We waded ankle-deep in the chilly water and came, at last, to the old Grant Estate, a huge ruin of a Victorian house which every kid knew was haunted, which our parents told us to stay away from because it was dangerous. (There were so many stories about kids murdered by tramps or falling through floors.) But now it wasn't a ruin at all, no broken windows, no holes in the roof. Every window blazed with light.

From a high window in a tower, a man in black gazed down at us.

The dead kid looked up at him, then began to run.

I hurried after him. Now it was Albert (who had better sense) who hung back. I caught hold of the dead kid's arm, as if to stop him, and I felt possessive for a moment, as if I *owned* him the way Luke Bradley had owned him.

"Hey dead kid," I said. "Where are you going?"

He turned to me, and by some trick of the moonlight he seemed to have a face, pale, round, with dark eyes; and he said to me in that bleating, croaking voice of his, actually forming words for once, "My name is Jonathan."

That was the only thing he ever said to me. He never talked to me in dreams.

He went to the front of the house. The door opened. The

light within seemed to swallow him. He turned back, briefly, and looked at us. I don't think he was just a bundle of sticks anymore.

Then he was gone and all the lights blinked out, and it was dawn. My brother and I stood before a ruined mansion in the morning twilight. Birds were singing raucously.

"We'd better get home," Albert said, "or we'll get in trouble."

"Yeah," I said.

V

That autumn, I began junior high school. Because I hadn't been very successful as a bad boy, and my grades were still a lot higher, I wasn't in any of Luke Bradley's classes. But he caught up with me in the locker room after school, several weeks into the term. All he said was, "I know what you did," and beat me so badly that he broke several of my ribs and one arm, and smashed in the whole side of my face, and cracked the socket around my right eye. He stuffed me into a locker and left me there to die, and I spent the whole night in the darkness, in great pain, amid horrible smells, calling out for the dead kid to come and save me as I'd saved him. I made bleating, clicking sounds.

But he didn't come. The janitor found me in the morning. The smell was merely that I'd crapped in my pants.

I spent several weeks in the hospital, and afterwards Stepdad Steve and Mom decided to move out of the state. They put both me and Albert in a prep school.

It was only after I got out of college that I went back to

Radnor Township in Pennsylvania, where I'd grown up. Everything was changed. There was a Sears headquarters where the golf course used to be. Our old house had vanished beneath an apartment parking lot. Most of Cabbage Creek Woods had been cut down to make room for an Altman's department store, and the Grant Estate was gone too, to make room for an office complex.

I didn't go into the remaining woods to see if the fort was still there.

I imagine it is. I imagine other kids own it now.

Later someone told me that Luke Bradley (who turned out to have really been three years older than me) had been expelled from high school, committed several robberies in the company of his three goons, and then all of them were killed in a shootout with the police.

What Luke Bradley inadvertently showed me was that I could have been with the gang all the way to their violent and pointless end, if Albert and the dead kid, whose name was Jonathan, hadn't saved me.

::\{}

SEVEN BRAINS, TEN MINUTES

MARIE ATKINS

The brain was in front of me, pink-gray and pulsing in the sun.

I could see the edge of the skull, sheared off so neatly by the cranial saw. The bony rim of nature's bowl, with its contents bulging up out of it like an extra-large scoop of ice cream. Or maybe gelatin. Hadn't they even, in the dim and gone days before the world ended, made gelatin molds shaped like brains?

If I pretended that's what this was…

No. It might quiver. It might shimmer. It might have the same gelatinous quality. But I knew better. I knew that the temperature would be all wrong. Warm. Body temperature, it'd be.

Of course it would. And why not? The body was still alive.

The guy the brain belonged to was in shock. He'd be dead—and probably glad of it—within minutes. Sooner, if I did what I was up here to do. What I had to do.

I couldn't.

Not even for Val.

Did she even know? Did she even recognize me? Or had fear taken her beyond all that?

The sun beat down. A rusty haze of dust filled the air. I could hear the flap of canvas and the sounds of the crowd. I could hear the Fat Man's laughter from above and behind me.

That's where Val would be. Up there in the bed of the customized pickup truck. With the Fat Man. Naked. Chained. A blue ribbon wrapped around her waist.

The others in the line to either side of me were straining against the iron bar, teeth bared, foamy drool on what was left of their lips. We had our hands tied behind us and number placards strung on ropes around our necks.

The bell rang.

The bar dropped.

"And theeeeeyyyyyy're off!" the Fat Man bellowed.

�֍⋁‹›

We picked up Patty just outside of Bakersfield.

I didn't want to. I would have roared on past and left her

in a whirl of grit and soot. But when Patty waved, Jess said we should stop.

"We can't take care of everybody," I said. "We've got to look out for ourselves."

"Don't be a jerk, Scotty," Val said. "Stop the car."

"Don't call me 'Scotty.' You know I hate it."

"Scotty, Scotty, Scotty," she sneered.

The end of the world hadn't done a thing to Val's looks or her attitude. It hadn't put a shake in her hands or purple circles under her eyes or anything.

Gorgeous. But a bitch.

"I think we should stop," Rick said as he checked out the thin blonde. He was Val's brother but didn't have any of her good looks. Skinny, pimply, a loser from the word *go*.

Two of a kind, that was me and Rick.

"We *are* a girl short," Jess said, putting his arm around Sharon. She only rocked in her seat and hugged the dog. "Us, you and Val, and poor Rick left over."

"Oh, puh-lease." Val's laugh was a snort. "Me and Scotty? Don't make me sick."

I hated her.

I wanted her so much it burned.

When everything started, with the deadies and all, Rick and I were the first ones to figure out what would happen, how it would all go down. We read comic books and horror novels and watched all those old movies. We knew.

Everyone else went around in denial. First they said it was nothing but rumors, urban legends, hoaxes. Then, when the stories were proved real, they said it would blow over. Then that the government would take care of it. Then that scientists would find a cure. Then…

And by *then*, well, there wasn't much of anyone left who wasn't taking bites out of people.

⚥~<>

The crowd roared. Deadies lunged with jaws gaping and putrescent tongues snaking out. They went face-first into the opened domes of the skulls and commenced a smacking, slurping, munching feast.

I shook so hard my teeth clattered. Someone threw a crumpled-up aluminum can at me. It bounced off the filthy rags I'd draped over my chest.

Couldn't do it.

Wouldn't do it.

They'd kill me, though, if I didn't. If they found out.

It had seemed like such a good idea at the time. .

No, that's a lie. It had seemed a stupid, gross, inhuman idea from the get-go. But the *only* idea. The only way to get out of this hell, let alone the only way to save Val.

I turned my head. The mud and gunk with which I'd coated my face cracked and flaked off in places, but that was okay. It made me look authentic, like I was losing skin in the dry, desert heat. My disguise fooled the livies, and somehow it fooled the deadies, too.

That was the part I'd been most worried about. Rick said that they could sense us, that they homed in on the signals our brains gave off or something. I didn't know if the ones in the contest were decomposed beyond that, or if the Fat Man just had them so well-trained that the only time they'd chow on a livie was when it was part of a competition or a prize.

Either way, my ruse had gotten me in. Fooling the livies had turned out to be the easy part. Whenever a livie died, rather than burn the corpse, the guards moved it over to the corral before it could reanimate. They weren't exactly diligent about checking for vital signs, either. I'd made like I had been hiding a wound all along, played dead, and voila. In among the deadies penned up for the contest.

Maneuvering to be one of the contestants had been a little trickier, but it had worked. Here I was, competing for a tempting prize.

I could see Val in the flabby circle of the Fat Man's arm. He was feeling her up, squashing her against his blubbery side.

Val looked on the verge of tears and that decided me. I had to do it no matter how sick it was. For her. Then she'd finally look at me and *see* me—see and appreciate the real Scott Driscoll.

The deadie beside me was gnawing on the side of a hollowed-out head, trying to peel off a flap of scalp. One of the handlers was there to inspect the empty hole of the cranium. "Done!" the handler shouted, thrusting his fist in the air. More people hustled forward. With movements born of practice and efficiency, the contest wranglers unlatched the empty, popped in the refill, and scrambled out of the way as the deadie dove in for the next course.

The stock of a gun rammed into my back. I barely stifled a cry. *They* didn't feel pain. I had to remember not to react.

"What's the matter with you?" the gun-wielder snarled. "Eat up."

"Done down here!" came another cry.

The crowd was clapping rhythmically. On my right, the

female deadie struggled to get the last tasty morsels from the bottom. The deadie popped up, triumphant, with the medulla oblongata hanging out of its mouth, and jerked its head like a bird, gulping it down.

I was losing. I wasn't even on the board yet.

Liver. I'd eaten liver before. Once, on a hunting trip, I'd even had deer liver raw and dripping from the carcass.

If I'd done that, I could do this. For Val.

The handler jabbed me in the back again, and this time I bent forward, toward the rippled folds of brain tissue.

%~<>

My dad had given me the crappy old family station wagon for graduation. When the deadies started ambling, we stashed guns and other supplies in the wagon. Canned food, camping gear, blankets.

Everybody laughed at us, you bet they did. Even Val had, at first. But she'd stopped in a hurry when her mom came home from the beauty shop one day and tried to open her head with freshly manicured acrylic nails.

No one was laughing now. There weren't enough people left to laugh.

The station wagon had held up like a trooper during our entire crazy escape and flight south. Now, as I pulled over to the side of the road, its engine let out a sort of weary rattle. The tires sent up a huge plume of dust and soot.

The girl came running up to the car. "Thank you, oh, thank you, I thought you were going to drive by and leave me. Thank God you stopped."

She was giving me big, adoring, "my hero" eyes. I thought for a minute she was going to hug me, maybe even give me a big "my hero" kiss to go with that look. If she'd been a babe, enough to make Val jealous, I would have been all for it.

The others had climbed out of the car and were looking around nervously. Jess had the shotgun, and pushed his glasses up, squinting. Sharon clung to the bandanna collar on her dog. The girl introduced herself as Patty.

"You'll be safe with us," Rick told Patty, puffing up his chest.

It was kind of funny to see him trying to act all manly. I mean, he's been my friend since grade school, but I'd never had any delusions about either of us. Smart, okay. Jocks, we were not.

"Let's not stand around all day," Jess called. "I don't see anything moving, but..."

"Yeah, 'but.' Back in the car," I said.

The smell was acrid and meaty and awful. I hadn't been aware of it before, not with the stale stink rising off the deadies and the rancid sweat of the crowd.

I could even smell the fine-ground bone dust and the charred, cauterized skin left by the bone saw. The inner membrane—I hadn't even known there was such a thing, but I'd seen them snip through it with kitchen shears—was peeled to the sides in neat folds.

Drying blood streaked the surface of the exposed brain. It had been wet, glistening, when they first clamped the livie into place before me. The desert sun was baking it.

If I waited too long, it would get tough to chew.

My eyes closed. My mouth opened.

I thought of liver. Of oysters. And, of course, I thought of gelatin. "There's always room for Jell-O!" Wasn't that how the old ads went?

A curved, quaking surface touched my lips. I skinned them back from my teeth, which had never needed fillings or braces. That had to give me an edge on the average deadie, whose teeth were chipped or broken from chewing on bone.

For Val.

I took a big, slippery bite.

✠∽◇

I steered in and out of traffic jams, cars and trucks that had been abandoned, overturned, smashed into scrap. Heaps of rotting food spilled from produce trucks dotted the sides of the highway. The only movement besides ours was that of countless scavenger birds and animals, feasting with impunity.

That, and the windfarms. Talk about creepy. Miles and miles of posts with spinning pinwheel blades, whirring around and around. Generating electricity for a dead world.

The station wagon labored as it chugged up to the pass. I wasn't the only one to heave a sigh of relief when we made it over the top and started downhill.

High desert country. Home to military bases and shuttle landings, Joshua trees and borax mines. In the twilight, the desert valley was a brownish purple smear cut by the ruler-straight line of Highway 14.

We descended toward Mojave, hoping there might be something worth finding in that strip of gas stations and burger joints. Thinking about food, lulled by the hazy scenery, I didn't see the pile-up until Patty squealed a warning.

I stood on the brakes. The only reason none of us were thrown into the dashboard was because we were packed in so tight.

Two semis had jackknifed and five cars had rammed into them, entirely blocking the road. The station wagon shuddered to a halt less than a foot from the bumper of a VW van. "Is everybody okay?" I asked, my voice embarrassingly unsteady.

Various replies of assent reached me. I saw a turnoff to the left and a BB-pocked sign reading *Joshua Flats, 6 miles,* with an arrow.

"Can we get around?" Jess asked from the back. "Shoulder's too soft," I said. "We'd get stuck."

"Well, think of something, brainiac," Val sneered.

※~<>

It squelched between my teeth. The texture was hideous, like soft-boiled eggs with striations of chewy gristle. The taste was bad, too, but the texture…

The man clamped into the wooden frame went stiff, then began to jitter and twitch. A fresh stink of voided bladder and bowels wafted up. I could hear his jaw clenching until bone cracked.

I took another bite. Determination drove me on. Once the initial deed was done, the first step taken, the revolting sin committed, it got easier. Don't ask me why or how. All I knew was that I'd gone this far and continuing wasn't going to make things worse. Instead, quitting would. If I quit and it was all for nothing, that would be really losing.

The noise of the crowd was louder than ever, but I ignored it. I ignored the sporadic cries of "Done!" from the handlers. None of that mattered.

Blood pooled in the bottom of the man's skull. I thrust my face in to reach the rest of his brain and wolfed it down. Something in my own brain, some switch or fuse, had blown with a snap and a sizzle.

"Done!" someone near me cried.

I straightened up, chin smeared with blood and cerebrospinal fluid and other assorted goo. They switched victims with the professional speed of an Indy 500 pit crew, and a fresh one was locked into place. I dove in, tearing out ragged, dripping chunks.

Thoughts shut off. I was an animal, a machine. I bit and swallowed, bit and swallowed, barely bothering to chew. My throat worked. My stomach hitched once, in shock maybe, then settled down.

I had the advantage, and not just because of my teeth. I had tendons that weren't withered and stretched. I had functional salivary glands. I had a whole tongue, an esophagus that wasn't riddled with decay.

Most of all, I had the motivation. I wasn't doing this out of hunger or habit. I was in this to win.

We were able to push the VW van out of the way, but it didn't make quite enough room for the station wagon to get by.

Jess turned to me with a questioning look—maybe he was about to ask which car we should try to move next—and that was when the deadie reached out through the broken windshield of one of the semis and clawed the side of his face clear down to the bone.

He stood stock-still for a second, his questioning look transforming to a gape. Blood poured onto his shoulder and rained onto the blacktop.

The deadie's sticklike arms shot out again, seized Jess, and yanked. He flew backward through the shard-ringed gap and into the truck's cab. He dropped the shotgun. Sharon shrieked.

Deadies swarmed over the wrecked vehicles, and the girls screamed and the dog barked. Jess' despairing howls echoed from inside the truck.

I had time to notice how weird they were, the deadies, how different from the ones we'd seen up north. Those had been green, moldy. If you hit them in the middle, they'd belch out clouds of gas. These deadies were dry, their flesh shrunken, their skin leathery. They looked like mummies. Scarecrows. Beef jerky. The arid heat did that, I realized numbly, and then they were on us.

"The guns!" I yelled at Val. "The other guns are in the back!"

Rick panicked and went tearing off into the desert with two deadies in pursuit. The movies always showed them all shambling and slow, but these suckers were quick. Rick was moving faster than I'd ever seen him move in my life, running like he'd made the track team. Didn't matter. They caught up with him, knocked him down, started eating him alive.

A deadie woman with brittle, peroxide hair leaped on Sharon. Another lunged at me, and I danced back, tripped, and almost went down. If I had, that would have been the end. I kept my footing, though, cracked my crazybone on the sideview mirror of the station wagon, and kicked out. My foot struck the deadie in the hip and drove it back.

"The guns!" I yelled again.

Val looked at me, all big blue eyes and wide, surprised mouth. She dove into the car.

She slammed the doors and locked them.

I couldn't believe it.

"Here!" Patty cried. She shoved a stick into my hands.

A deadie in a California highway patrolman's uniform came at me, still wearing mirrored cop shades. Its mouth opened and closed in vicious snaps. I swung that stick like I was in the World Series—and missed by a mile. The effort spun me around.

I pulled Patty with me, getting our backs to the car. I hammered on the window.

"Open up! Open up, Val!"

The CHP snagged Patty's sleeve. She batted at its hand and yodeled a high-pitched cry. I brought the stick down across the deadie's forearm. Both stick and arm broke in half.

"Val, goddammit!"

Deadies were fighting over the bodies of Sharon and the dog. Others were converging on Patty and me. One snared a handful of Patty's hair. She flailed as if the clutching hand were a wayward bat. Dry fingers snapped off; they stayed tangled in her hair like grotesque barrettes. She didn't have time to pluck them out. Another deadie was heading for her with its jaws gaping wide.

A little kid deadie bit my leg. I yelled and punched down,

the broken-off end of the stick still in my grasp. It pushed through the top of the kid's head. Frantic, I probed at my leg and found the heavy denim of my jeans undamaged.

Behind the dirty window, I could see Val. She wasn't doing anything useful, like maybe getting the other guns and saving our asses.

The deadies pulled Patty away from me. She was reaching out, begging for me to save her. But others had started to rock the car, trying to flip it—trying to get at Val. I shook off Patty's trailing, grasping hands and wielded my broken stick like a truncheon.

A rifle-crack split the air. A deadie pitched over, skull bursting apart to reveal a brain like a deflated football. The others froze, shoulders tucking up defensively. Patty, gasping and sobbing, scrambled to my side.

More guns went off, a chattering fusillade of them. Puffs of grit kicked up from the ground. Deadies went down in ruins of desiccated flesh.

I stared incredulously as a vehicle roared into view. It was like some sort or prop from *The Road Warrior*—an SUV painted mottled brown, desert camouflage, with spikes sticking out all over it. Guys—livies—in camo jackets and helmets stood in its makeshift turret, blasting away at the deadies.

And when they had dealt with the deadies, they leveled their guns on Patty and me.

%~<>

An astonished hush fell as I ate and ate and ate.

The handlers struck my rivals with batons, urged them to

keep up. The deadie on my right succeeded in swallowing down another half a brain, then paused, its mummified face taking on a queer look. A moment later, the leathery skin of its belly parted and its overstuffed stomach flopped out through the slit, tore free, hit the planks of the platform, and popped.

Masticated gray matter and deadie digestive acid sprayed the front row of the crowd. A split-second later, the same thing happened to the deadie at the end of the line.

And still I ate. Blood and brain-pulp covered me to the hair-line, welled in my ears. My own stomach felt hugely bloated, smooth and strained, as if it might burst, too.

"Done!" my handler shouted. "What's the score?"

"That's five," the Fat Man proclaimed from on high, where he had Val pressed against his sweaty folds. "A new record!"

"Sev-en, sev-en!" the crowd chanted. That was my number, the one they'd hung around my neck when I shuffled onto the platform with the others.

"How much time left?" my handler asked. "Still two minutes."

"What do you say, dead boy? Got room for more?"

He didn't wait for an answer. A fresh victim was secured, the exposed brain not so neatly prepped this time. They'd run out of pre-made meals. They were grabbing people out of the crowd, doping them and sawing off the tops of their heads just to keep up with the demand.

Before I could make sense of it, the guys in the armor-plated SUV had grabbed me and stuffed me in back. Two soldiers stood watch on Patty and me while the rest broke the windows and dragged Val out of the station wagon.

We tried to talk to them, livie to livie. We pointed out that we were all on the same side and should stick together and all that good stuff. Nothing helped.

They took us to the town, which had been ringed with walls and barbed wire and booby traps. At first I thought it was to keep the deadies out. But the defenses were there to keep *us* in.

The deadies were held in some sort of old barn. They gravitated to the fence of their corral, though never touched it, not after they'd gotten a couple of zaps from the electrified wires. So they just stood there, a handbreadth from the wires, staring vacantly at the activity beyond.

The town was full of livies, most of them prisoners. Some were from town. Others had been nabbed off the highway, like us. The men and women were kept separate. I hadn't seen Val or Patty since we arrived.

I got the lowdown from a local. Big Joe Callup, also known as "the Fat Man," had been Joshua Flats' chief of police until his compulsive overeating and subsequent weight gain had forced him onto disability. Fat? He was beyond obese. He was circus freak fat. He couldn't even get around on his own, so his men hauled him in the back of his customized pickup. Sort of a post-apocalyptic sedan chair.

When the world ended, Big Joe took the town hostage. He set up his own little kingdom with hand-picked soldiers and weapons from the National Guard armory. Raiding parties brought in supplies, more prisoners, and enough deadies to keep them entertained.

"Entertained how?" I asked, not really wanting to hear. "All sorts of ways," my new acquaintance said. "He has them fight each other. He maims them, races them. Sets them on fire. Bull-riding. Rodeos. Football games. He's the emperor, they're his gladiators, and this is his private Colosseum."

"What about us? How do we figure in?"

"Us?" He smiled bitterly. "We're the prizes."

✖~<>

The final buzzer sounded its harsh bray a millisecond after I gagged down the final hunk of my seventh brain.

Seven for lucky number seven. "The winnah!" Big Joe exclaimed.

The livies cheered like they meant it. Anybody who didn't make a sufficient show of enthusiasm was liable to be put on the auction block for the next event.

I wasn't concerned about the next event. All that mattered was winning, getting Val, and getting out of here.

The guards had dragged Val around the outside of the electrified fence earlier that morning, their way of advertising her to the deadies as the day's first prize. In fact, they led her around twice. A shapely or muscular bod usually inspired a better effort from the contestants, and they knew they had something special with her. The deadie that won her would tear her apart, just like the steroid-popping fitness junkie I'd seen pulled to pieces by the winning team from yesterday's soccer match.

That wouldn't happen to Val. I couldn't let it.

I knew I'd only have one chance to save her and escape, before I was revealed as an imposter.

The deadie competitors struggled listlessly as the bar came back up. They were full or falling apart, but either way trained enough to know what came next. Those that were still mobile would go back to their stable. The ones who'd exploded their overstuffed guts would be taken to the edge of town and burned.

I tried to act just like them. I let my shoulders slump, my head loll, my stare go vacant. Inside, though, my pulse was skyrocketing.

I'd won. The prize—Val—was mine.

She was enough to make any deadie feel lively again, all that rosy, lush, firm flesh jiggling about.

The handlers led me toward the Fat Man's pickup truck. The routine was always the same. They herded me up to claim my reward just like they'd herded the deadie soccer team.

I tried not to let my excitement show. This was it. This was my chance.

Big Joe lolled in the truck bed like a sultan, on a layer of old sofa cushions and futons. The rig had all the comforts of home. A tarp on metal poles kept out the worst of the sun. A cord snaked through the cab's rear window, plugging the mini-fridge into the cigarette lighter. The area around him was littered with crumpled pop cans, candy wrappers, and halfempty bags of salty snacks.

He was a human behemoth in sweat pants that could have housed a family of four, and a ship's sail of a T-shirt with a beer company logo on it. Nearly lost amid the bulges and jowls was a hard, mean face that might have once been handsome.

His arm was still around Val, his greasy hand squeezing whatever he could reach. The up-close sight of him touching her almost made me lose it.

"You won a pretty piece of prime cut, here, boy," he boomed.

It was more for the benefit of the crowd than for me, I hadn't a doubt. His eyes were bright and merry. Demented Santa Claus eyes.

I snatched a glance at the pickup's cab. The engine was idling to keep the battery from running down, lest the Fat Man have to suffer the misery of warm soda. The windows were down. No one was in the cab.

Deadie. Had to act like I was a deadie. I gazed at Val with an expression of slack-jawed greed, even while trying to make meaningful eye contact with her.

She wouldn't look at me.

Deadie. Deadie. I shuffled closer to the truck and let a guttural noise come out of my throat. I belched.

That was a mistake. The heavy churning weight in my stomach sent up a vile bubble, and I was tasting the brain meat all over again. My throat hitched. I suddenly knew I was going to spew a geyser.

Somehow, I held it down.

First, Val.

The Fat Man howled with laughter. "Looks like some boy's still hungry. Want your prize, sonny?"

All around me, I could hear livies crowding close, cheering, egging me on, placing bets as to what body part I'd bite first.

Out of the corner of my eye, I saw a familiar, pallid face framed in limp blond hair.

Patty.

The moment I looked at her, I saw that she recognized me. Her eyes got wide, and her mouth dropped open. She was going to screw up everything.

I caught her eye. If ever a guy had wished for telepathy, it was me and it was right then. I silently urged her to stay cool, begged her not to blow my cover.

Her chin quivered. I saw her throat work as she fought down a gag. But then she gave a slight nod. She understood.

Good girl. Smart girl.

Time to move. It was my only chance, the one I'd been waiting for.

I'd have to be quick to take them by surprise. First the handlers, while they were distracted by Val—shoulder them aside. Slam shut the tailgate with Val still in there. Then run around to the driver's door, jump in, and take off. With Val safe in the truck, and the Fat Man as a hostage, we'd get past the guards and out of town.

Next stop, anyplace but here.

I could do it, I knew I could. They weren't expecting any surprises from a deadie. The walking meat in the pens had been too well trained. They knew better than to move against the handlers, or livies not part of a contest.

"Here you go, honey bunch," Big Joe chortled. He nudged Val toward the tailgate.

She stumbled on chained ankles, fell to her knees. A hurt grunt escaped her. She looked up through a veil of hair and saw me. Really *saw* me. Just like with Patty, her mouth dropped open and my name formed on her lips.

I shook my head, trying to make it look like a nerve-jittering deadie impulse. My hungry-sounding moan was a warning.

"Uh-uh-uh," Val said, chains clanking as she trembled. She knew me. "Suh… skuh…"

No! No, oh, goddammit!

Sudden spiking fear made my stomach's heavy cargo slide

and bubble. Because that was *hope* dawning on Val's face. Hope and joy and all the things I'd always wanted to see in her expression. Just not now!

Val let loose a wavering lunatic's laugh. She started to smile, started to reach out toward me.

She was ruining everything! People were looking at me more closely, seeing the solidity of my flesh—scrawny, maybe, but not dried deadie flesh.

"Shut up," I said, low but urgent, under a rising murmur from the crowd. "Shut up, Val."

Any second, suspicion would turn to certainty, and that would be all she wrote. And all because Val couldn't get with the program.

A line of phantom pain lanced around my skull. It traced the curve where the bone saw would grind and scream. Poetic justice, they'd think. I would feel the ripping of capillaries as they took the top off my head like a layer of sod.

The stupid bitch! We were so close! So close to getting out of this with our lives, and she couldn't play along for two minutes?

A glottal howl burst from me. After everything I'd done, after the horrible thing I'd done, this was the thanks I got!

"Scotty—" Val said, but her weak voice was drowned out by my furious cry. No one else could have heard.

But I did.

She called me "Scotty."

Again.

I lunged for her, shouldering the handlers aside just like in my plan. Even better than my plan, because in my surge of angry strength, I sent them flying. I seized a handful of Val's thick, dark hair and dragged her headfirst out of the pickup.

The Colosseum, my acquaintance had said. Like in the days of ancient Rome. I remembered something else they did in Rome. After a feast.

I turned my head to the side and stuck a finger down my throat. My body heaved. A torrent of hot cerebral slush surged up my gullet and splattered everywhere.

I had to make room.

%~<>

The handlers took me to the barn. I could barely walk, my gut felt so bloated. I had consumed a lot of fresh meat. I would probably be days picking the strings of her hair out of my teeth.

I hadn't been able to get through her skull. My jaw just couldn't apply that sort of bone-cracking pressure. I'd had to go for the neck instead.

And then, once it was clear she wasn't going to talk any more and give me away, I guess I sort of went a little nuts.

They put me in with the deadies again. I was too stuffed and lethargic to worry about whether my disguise and their training would hold up. One or the other must have, because none of them made a move against me.

Or maybe, on some instinctual level, they left me alone because they recognized me as one of their own. I had never actually died, but inside, I was a deadie all the same. I had to be. No genuine livie could have done what I'd done.

A few days later, when I was finally starting to feel physically back to normal—mentally and emotionally, I was as much a deadie as ever— they brought a new one to the barn.

Thin. Limp hair that might have started out blond. Sunken

cheeks and hollow eyes, and skin mottled with stains under the rags of clothes.

Not a bad disguise at all.

But then, I knew Patty was a smart girl.

She stood near me, neither of us speaking, as we stared with the deadies out through the fence at the town and waited for the next event.

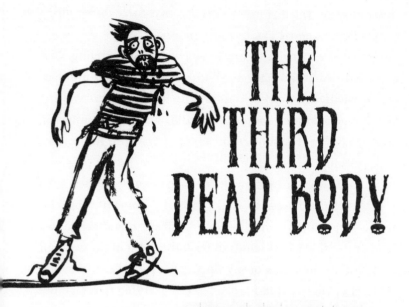

THE THIRD DEAD BODY

NINA KIRIKI HOFFMAN

I didn't even know Richie. I surely didn't want to love him. After he killed me, though, I found him irresistible.

I opened my eyes and dirt fell into them. Having things fall into my eyes was one of my secret terrors, but now I blinked and shook my head and most of the dirt fell away and I felt all right. So I knew something major had happened to me.

With my eyes closed, I shoved dirt away from my face. While I was doing this I realized that the inside of my mouth felt different. I probed with my tongue, my trained and talented tongue, and soon discovered that where smooth teeth had been before there were only broken stumps. What puzzled me about this and about the dirt in my eyes was that these things didn't hurt. They bothered me, but not on a pain level.

I frowned and tried to figure out what I was feeling. Not a lot. Not scared or mad, not hot or cold. This was different too. I usually felt scared, standing on street corners waiting for strangers to pick me up, and cold, working evenings in skimpy clothes that showed off my best features. Right now, I felt nothing.

I sat up, dirt falling away from me, and bumped into branches that gridded my view of the sky. Some of them slid off me. The branches were loose and wilting, not attached to a bush or tree. I used my hands to push them out of the way and noticed that the backs of my fingers were blackened beyond my natural cocoa color. I looked at them, trying to remember what had happened before I fell asleep or whatever—had I dipped my fingers in ink? But no; the skin was scorched. My fingerprints were gone. They would have told police that my name was Tawanda Foote, which was my street name.

My teeth would have led police to call me Mary Jefferson, a name I hadn't used since two years before, when I moved out of my parents' house at fifteen.

In my own mind, I was Sheila, a power name I had given myself no one could have discovered from any evidence about me.

No teeth, no fingerprints; Richie really didn't want anybody to know who I was, not that anybody ever had.

Richie.

With my scorched fingers I tried to take my pulse, though it was hard to find a vein among the rope burns at my wrists.

With my eyes I watched my own naked chest. There were charred spots on my breasts where Richie had touched me with a burning cigarette. No pulse, but maybe that was because the nerves in my fingertips were dead. No breathing. No easy answer to that, so I chose the hard answer:

Dead.

I was dead.

After I pushed aside the branches so I could see trees and sky, I sat in my own grave dirt and thought about this.

My grannie would call this dirt goofer dust; any soil that's been piled on a corpse, whether the body's in a box or just loose like me, turns into goofer dust. Dirt next to dead folk gets a power in it, she used to say.

She used to tell me all kinds of things. She told me about the walking dead; but mostly she said they were just big scary dummies who obeyed orders. When I stayed up too late at night reading library books under my covers with a flashlight, she would say, "Maybe you know somebody who could give those nightwalkers orders. Maybe she can order 'em to come in here and turn off your light."

She had started to train me in recognizing herbs and collecting conjo ingredients, but that was before I told the preacher what really happened when I sat in Grand-père's lap, and Grand-père got in trouble with the church and then with other people in the Parish. I had a lot of cousins, and some of the others started talking up about Grand-père, but I was the first. After the police took Grand-père away, Grannie laid a curse on me: "May you love the thing that hurts you, even after it kills you." She underlined it with virgin blood, the wax of black candles, and the three of spades.

I thought maybe if I left Louisiana I could get the curse off, but nobody I knew could uncross me and the curse followed me to Seattle.

In the midst of what was now goofer dust, I was sitting next to something. I reached out and touched it. It was another dead body. "Wake up," I said to the woman in the shallow grave beside me. But she refused to move.

So: no fingerprints, no teeth. I was dead, next to someone even deader, and off in some woods. I checked in with my body, an act I saved for special times when I could come out of the numb state I spent most of my life in, and found I wasn't hungry or thirsty. All the parts of me that had been hurting just before Richie, my last trick, took a final twist around my neck with the nylon cord he was so fond of, all those parts were quiet, not bothering me at all; but there was a burning desire in my crotch, and a pinprick of fire behind my eyes that whispered to me, "Get up and move. We know where to go."

I looked around. At my back the slope led upward toward a place where sun broke through trees. At my feet it led down into darker woods. To either side, more woods and bushes, plants Grannie had never named for me, foreign as another language.

I moved my legs, bringing them up out of the goofer dust. All of me was naked; dirt caught in my curly hair below. I pulled myself to my feet and something fell out of my money pit, as my pimp Blake liked to call my pussy. I looked down at what had fallen from me. It was a rock flaked and shaped into a blade about the size of a flat hand, and it glistened in the dulled sunlight, wet and dark with what had come from inside me, and maybe with some of his juices too.

The fire in my belly flared up, but it wasn't a feeling like pain; it felt like desire.

I put my hands to my neck and felt the deep grooves the rope had left there. Heat blossomed in my head and in my heart. I wanted to find the hands that had tightened the rope around my neck, wrists, and ankles. I wanted to find the eyes that had watched my skin sizzle under the kiss of the burning cigarette. I wanted to find the mind that had decided to plunge a crude blade into me like that. The compulsion set in along my bones, jetted into my muscles like adrenaline. I straightened, looked around. I had to find Richie. I knew which direction to look: something in my head was teasing me, nudging me—a fire behind my eyes, urging me back to the city.

I fought the urge and lifted more branches off the place where I had lain. If I was going to get to Seattle from here, wherever here was, I needed some clothes. I couldn't imagine anybody stopping to pick me up with me looking the way I did. I knew Richie had worked hard to get rid of all clues to who I was, but I thought maybe my companion in the grave might not be so naked of identity, so I brushed dirt off her, and found she was not alone. There were two bodies in the dirt, with no sign of afterlife in them except maggots, and no trace of clothes. One was darker than me, with fewer marks on her but the same rope burns around her neck. The other one was very light, maybe white. She was really falling apart. They looked like they must smell pretty bad, but I couldn't smell them. I couldn't smell anything. I could see and hear, and my muscles did what I told them, but I didn't feel much except the gathering fire inside me that cried for Richie.

I brushed dirt back over the other women and moved the

branches to cover their resting place again.

Downslope the trees waited, making their own low-level night. Upslope, open sun: a road, probably. I scrambled up toward the light.

The heat in my head and heart and belly burned hotter, and I churned up the hillside and stepped into the sun.

A two-lane highway lay before me, its yellow dotted center stripe bright in the sun. Its edges tailed into the gravel I stood on. Crushed snack bags and Coke and beer cans lay scattered in the bushes beside the road; cellophane glinted. I crossed the road and looked at the wooded hill on its far side, then down in the ditch. No clothes. Not even a plastic bag big enough to make into a bikini bottom.

The heat inside me was like some big fat drunk who will not shut up, yelling for a beer. I started walking, knowing which direction would take me toward town without knowing how I knew.

After a while a car came from behind me. Behind was probably my best side; my microbraids hung down to hide the marks on my neck, and Richie hadn't done any cigarette graffiti on my back that I could remember. A lot of tricks had told me I had a nice ass and good legs; even my pimp had said it, and he never said anything nice unless he thought it was true or it would get him what he wanted. And he had everything he wanted from me.

I could hear the car slowing, but I was afraid to look back. I knew my mouth must look funny because of the missing teeth, and I wasn't sure what the rest of my face looked like. Since I couldn't feel pain, anything could have happened. I bent my head so the sun wasn't shining in my face.

"Miss? Oh, miss?" Either a woman's deep voice came from the car behind me, or a man's high one; it sounded like an older person. The engine idled low as the car pulled up beside me. It was a red Volkswagen Rabbit.

I crossed my arms over my chest, hiding the burn marks and tucking my rope-mark bracelets into the crooks of my elbows.

"Miss?"

"Ya?" I said, trying to make my voice friendly, not sure I had a voice at all.

"Miss, are you in trouble?"

I nodded, my braids slapping my shoulders and veiling my face.

"May I help you, miss?"

I cleared my throat, drew in breath. "Ya-you goin' do down?" I managed to say.

"What?"

"Down," I said, pointing along the road. "Seaddle."

"Oh. Yes. Would you like a ride?"

"Mm-hmm," I said. "Cloze?" I glanced up this time, wondering if the car's driver was man or woman. A man might shed his shirt for me, but a woman, unless she was carrying a suitcase or something, might not have anything to offer.

"Oh, you poor thing, what happened to you?" The car pulled up onto the shoulder ahead of me and the driver got out. It was a big beefy white woman in jeans and a plaid flannel shirt. She came toward me with a no-nonsense stride. She had short dark hair. She was wearing a man's khaki cloth hat with fishing flies stuck in the band, all different feathery colors. "What ha—"

I put one hand over my face, covering my mouth with my palm.

"What happened—" she whispered, stopping while there was still a lot of space between us.

"My boyfriend dreeded me preddy bad," I said behind my hand. My tongue kept trying to touch the backs of teeth no longer there. It frustrated me that my speech was so messy. I thought maybe I could talk more normally if I touched my tongue to the roof of my mouth. "My boyfriend," I said again, then, "treated me pretty bad."

"Poor thing, poor thing," she whispered, then turned back to the car and rummaged in a back seat, came up with a short-waisted Levi's jacket and held it out to me.

I ducked my head and took the jacket. She gasped when I dropped my arms from my chest. I wrapped up in the jacket, which was roomy, but not long enough to cover my crotch. Then again, from the outside, my crotch didn't look so bad. I turned the collar up to cover my neck and the lower part of my face. "Thank you," I said.

Her eyes were wide, her broad face pale under her tan. "You need help," she said. "Hospital? Police?"

"Seattle," I said.

"Medical attention!"

"Won't help me now." I shrugged.

"You could get infections, die from septicemia or something. I have a first aid kit in the car. At least let me—"

"What would help me," I said, "is a mirror."

She sighed, her shoulders lowering. She walked around the car and opened the passenger side door, and I followed her. I looked at the seat. It was so clean, and I was still goofer dusted. "Gonna get it dirty," I said.

"Lord, that's the last thing on my mind right now," she said.

"Get in. Mirror's on the back of the visor."

I slid in and folded down the visor, sighed with relief when I saw my face. Nothing really wrong with it, except my chin was nearer to my nose than it should be, and my lips looked too dark and puffy. My eyes weren't blackened and my nose wasn't broken. I could pass. I gapped the collar just a little and winced at the angry dark rope marks around my neck, then clutched the collar closed.

The woman climbed into the driver's seat. "My name's Marti," she said, holding out a hand. Still keeping the coat closed with my left hand, I extended my right, and she shook it.

"Sheila," I said. It was the first time I'd ever said it out loud. She. La. Two words for woman put together. I smiled, then glanced quickly at the mirror, and saw that a smile was as bad as I'd thought. My mouth was a graveyard of broken teeth, brown with old blood. I hid my mouth with my hand again.

"Christ!" said Marti. "What's your boyfriend's name?"

"Don't worry about it," I said.

"If he did that to you, he could do it to others. My daughter lives in Renton. This has to be reported to the police. Who is he? Where does he live?"

"Near Sea-Tac. The airport."

She took a deep breath, let it out. "You understand, don't you, this is a matter for the authorities?"

I shook my head. The heat in my chest was scorching, urging me on. "I have to go to town now," I said, gripping the door handle.

"Put your seat belt on," she said, slammed her door, and started the car.

Once she got started, she was some ball-of-fire driver. Scared me—even though there wasn't anything I could think of that could hurt me.

"Where were we, anyway?" I asked after I got used to her tire-squealing cornering on curves.

"Well, I was coming down from Kanaskat. I'm on my way in to Renton to see my daughter. She's got a belly-dance recital tonight, and—" She stared at me, then shook her head and focused on the road.

The land was leveling a little. We hit a main road, Highway 169, and she turned north on it.

The burning in my chest raged up into my throat. "No," I said, reaching for her hand on the steering wheel.

"What?"

"No. That way." I pointed back to the other road we had been on. Actually the urge inside me was pulling from some direction between the two roads, but the smaller road aimed closer to where I had to go.

"Maple Valley's this way," she said, not turning, "and we can talk to the police there, and a doctor."

"No," I said.

She looked at me. "You're in no state to make rational decisions," she said.

I closed my hand around her wrist and squeezed. She cried out. She let go of the steering wheel and tried to shake off my grip. I stared at her and held on, remembering my grand-mère's tales of the strength of the dead.

"Stop," I said. I felt strange, totally strange, ordering a woman around the way a pimp would. I knew I was hurting her, too. I knew I could squeeze harder, break the bones in her arm, and I was ready to, but she pulled the car over to the shoulder and stamped on the brake.

"I got to go to Sea-Tac," I said. I released her arm and climbed out of the car. "Thanks for ride. You want the jacket back?" I fingered the denim.

"My Lord," she said, "you keep it, child." She was rubbing her hand over the wrist I had gripped. She heaved a huge sigh. "Get in. I'll take you where you want to go. I can't just leave you here."

"Your daughter's show?" I said.

"I'll phone. We're going someplace with phones, aren't we?"

I wasn't sure exactly where we would end up. I would know when we arrived.... I remembered the inside of Richie's apartment. But that was later. First he had pulled up next to where I was standing by the highway, rolled down the passenger window of his big gold four-door Buick, said he'd like to party and that he knew a good place. Standard lines, except I usually told johns the place, down one of the side streets and in the driveway behind an abandoned house. I had asked him how high he was willing to go. My pimp had been offering me coke off and on but I'd managed not to get hooked, so I was still a little picky about who I went with; but Richie looked clean-cut and just plain clean, and his car was a couple years old but expensive; I thought he might have money.

"I want it all," Richie had said. "I'll give you a hundred bucks."

I climbed into his car.

He took me down off the ridge where the Sea-Tac Strip is to a place like the one where I usually took my tricks, behind one of the abandoned houses near the airport that are due to be razed someday. There's two or three neighborhoods of them handy. I asked him for money and he handed me a hundred, so I got in back with him, but then things went seriously wrong. That was the first time I saw and felt his rope, the first time I heard his voice cursing me, the first time I tasted one of his sweaty socks, not the worst thing I'd ever tasted, but close.

When he had me gagged and tied up and shoved down on the back seat floor, he drove somewhere else. I couldn't tell how long the drive was; it felt like two hours but was probably only fifteen or twenty minutes. I could tell when the car drove into a parking garage because the sounds changed. He put a shopping bag over my head and carried me into an elevator, again something I could tell by feel, and then along a hall to his apartment. That was where I learned more about him than I had ever wanted to know about anybody.

I didn't know his apartment's address, but I knew where Richie was. If he was at the apartment, I would direct Marti there even without a map. The fire inside me reached for Richie like a magnet lusting for a hammer.

Shaping words carefully, I told Marti, "Going to the Strip. Plenty of phones."

"Right," she said.

"On the other road." I pointed behind us.

She sighed. "Get in."

I climbed into the car, and she waited for an RV to pass, then pulled out and turned around.

As soon as we were heading the way I wanted to go, the fire inside me cooled a little. I sat back and relaxed.

"Why are we going to the—to the Strip?" she asked. "What are you going to do when we get there?"

"Don't know," I said. We were driving toward the sun, which was going down. Glare had bothered me before my death, but now it was like dirt in my eyes, a minor annoyance. I blinked and considered this, then shrugged it off.

"Can't you even tell me your boyfriend's name?" she asked.

"Richie."

"Richie what?"

"Don't know."

"Are you going back to him?"

Fire rose in my throat like vomit. I felt like I could breathe it out and it would feel good. It felt good inside my belly already. I was drunk with it. "Oh, yes," I said.

"How can you?" she cried. She shook her head. "I can't take you back to someone who hurt you so much." But she didn't stop driving.

"I have to go back," I said.

"You don't. You can choose something else. There are shelters for battered women. The government should offer you some protection. The police…."

"You don't understand," I said.

"I do," she said. Her voice got quieter. "I know what it's like to live with someone who doesn't respect you. I know how hard it is to get away. But you *are* away, Sheila. You can start over."

"No," I said, "I can't."

"You can. I'll help you. You can live in Kanaskat with me and he'll never find you. Or if you just want a bus ticket some-place—back home, wherever that is—I can do that for you, too."

"You don't understand," I said.

She was quiet for a long stretch of road. Then she said, "Help me understand."

I shook my braids back and opened the collar of the jacket, pulled down the lapels to bare my neck. I stared at her until she looked back.

She screamed and drove across the center lane. Fortunately there was no other traffic. Still screaming, she fought with the steering wheel until she straightened out the car. Then she pulled over to the shoulder and jumped out of the car and ran away.

I shut off the car's engine, then climbed out. "Marti," I yelled. "Okay, I'm walking away now. The car's all yours. I'm leaving. It's safe. Thanks for the jacket. Bye." I buttoned up the jacket, put the collar up, buried my hands in the pockets, and started walking along the road toward Richie.

I had gone about a quarter mile when she caught up with me again. The sun had set and twilight was deepening into night. Six cars had passed going my way, but I didn't hold out my thumb, and though some kid had yelled out a window at me, and somebody else had honked and swerved, nobody stopped.

It had been so easy to hitch before I met Richie. Somehow now I just couldn't do it.

I heard the Rabbit's sputter behind me and kept walking, not turning to look at her. But she slowed and kept pace with me. "Sheila?" she said in a hoarse voice. "Sheila?"

I stopped and looked toward her. I knew she was scared of me. I felt strong and strange, hearing her call me by a name I had given myself, as if I might once have had a chance to make up who I was instead of being shaped by what had happened to me. I couldn't see it being possible now, though, when I was only alive to do what the fire in me wanted.

Marti blinked, turned away, then turned back. "Get in," she said.

"You don't have to take me," I said. "I'll get there sooner or later. Doesn't matter when."

"Get in."

I got back into her car.

For half an hour we drove in silence. She crossed Interstate 5, paused when we hit 99, the Strip. "Which way?"

I pointed right. The fire was so hot in me now I felt like my fingertips might start smoking any second.

She turned the car and we cruised north toward the Sea-Tac Airport, my old stomping grounds. We passed expensive hotels and cheap motels, convenience stores and fancy restaurants. Lighted buildings alternated with dark gaps. The roar of planes taking off and landing, lights rising and descending in the sky ahead of us, turned rapidly into background. We drove past the Goldilocks Motel, where Blake and I had a room we rented by the week, and I didn't feel anything. But as we passed the intersection where the Red Lion sprawls on the corner of 188th Street and the Pacific Highway, fire flared under my skin. "Slowly," I said to Marti. She stared at me and slowed the car. A mile further, past the airport, one of the little roads led down off the ridge to the left. I pointed.

Marti got in the left-turn lane and made the turn, then pulled into a gas station on the corner and parked by the rest rooms. "Now wait," she said. "What are we doing, here?"

"Richie," I whispered. I could feel his presence in the near distance; all my wounds were resonating with his nearness now, all the places he had pressed himself into me with his rope and his cigarette and his sock and his flaked stone knife and his penis, imprinting me as his possession. Surely as a knife slicing into a tree's bark, he had branded me with his heart.

"Yes," said Marti. "Richie. You have any plans for what you're going to do once you find him?"

I held my hands out, open, palms up. The heat was so strong I felt like anything I touched would burst into flame.

"What are you going to do, strangle him? Have you got something to do it with?" She sounded sarcastic.

I was having a hard time listening to her. All my attention was focused down the road. I knew Richie's car was there, and Richie in it. It was the place he had taken me to tie me up. He might be driving this way any second, and I didn't want to wait any longer for our reunion, though I knew there was no place he could hide where I couldn't find him. My love for him was what animated me now.

"Strangle," I said, and shook my head. I climbed out of the car.

"Sheila!" said Marti.

I let the sound of my self-given name fill me with what power it could, and stood still for a moment, fighting the fire inside. Then I walked into the street, stood in the center so a car coming up out of the dark would have to stop. I strode down into darkness, away from the lights and noise of the Strip. My feet felt like match-heads, as if a scrape could strike fire from them.

Presently the asphalt gave way to potholes and gravel; I could tell by the sound of pebbles sliding under my feet. I walked past the first three dark houses to the right and left, looming shapes in a darkness pierced by the flight lights of airplanes, but without stars. I turned left at the fourth house, dark like the others, but with a glow behind it I couldn't see with my eyes but could feel in my bones. Heat pulsed and danced inside me.

I pushed past an overgrown lilac bush at the side of the

house and stepped into the broad drive in back. The car was there, as I had known it would be. Dark and quiet. Its doors were closed.

I heard a brief cry, and then the dome light went on in the car. Richie was sitting up in back, facing away from me.

Richie.

I walked across the crunching gravel, looking at his dark head. He wore a white shirt. He was staring down, focused, his arms moving. As I neared the car, I could see he was sitting on a woman. She still had her clothes on. (Richie hadn't taken my clothes off until he got me in his apartment.) Tape was across her mouth, and her head thrashed from side to side, her upper arms jerking as Richie bound his thin nylon rope around her wrists, her legs kicking. I stood a moment looking in the window. She saw me and her eyes widened. She made a gurgling swallowed sound behind the sock, the tape.

I thought: he doesn't need her. He has me.

I remembered the way my mind had struggled while my body struggled, screaming silently: no, oh no, Blake, where are you? No one will help me, the way no one has ever helped me, and I can't help myself. That hurts, that hurts. Maybe he'll play with me and let me go if I'm very, very good. Oh, God! What do you want? Just tell me, I can do it. You don't have to hurt me! Okay, rip me off, it's not like you're the first, but you don't have to hurt me.

Hurt me.

I love you. I love you so much.

I stared at him through the glass. The woman beneath him had stilled, and she was staring at me. Richie finally noticed, and whirled.

For a moment we stared at each other. Then I smiled, showing him the stumps of my teeth, and his blue eyes widened.

I reached for the door handle, opened it before he could lock it.

"Richie," I said.

"Don't!" he said. He shook his head, hard, as though he were a dog with wet fur. Slowly, he lifted one hand and rubbed his eye. He had a big bread knife in the other hand, had used it to cut the rope, then flicked it across the woman's cheek, leaving a streak of darkness. He looked at me again. His jaw worked.

"Richie."

"Don't! Don't. . . interrupt."

I held out my arms, my fingertips scorched black as if dyed or tattooed, made special, the wrists dark beyond the ends of my sleeves. "Richie," I said tenderly, the fire in me rising up like a firework, a burst of stars. "I'm yours."

"No," he said.

"You made me yours." I looked at him. He had made Tawanda his, and then he had erased her. He had made Mary his, and then erased her. Even though he had erased Tawanda and Mary, these feelings inside me were Tawanda's: *whoever hurts me controls me;* and Mary's: *I spoke up once and I got a curse on me I can't get rid of. If I'm quiet maybe I'll be okay.*

But Sheila? Richie hadn't erased Sheila; he had never even met her.

It was Tawanda who was talking. "You killed me and you made me yours," she said. My fingers went to the jacket, unbuttoned it, dropped it behind me. "What I am I owe to you."

"I—" he said, and coughed. "No," he said.

I heard the purr of car engines in the near distance, not the constant traffic of the Strip, but something closer.

I reached into the car and gripped Richie's arm. I pulled him out, even though he grabbed at the door handle with his free hand. I could feel the bone in his upper arm as my fingers pressed his muscles. "Richie," I whispered, and put my arms around him and laid my head on his shoulder.

For a while he was stiff, tense in my embrace. Then a shudder went through him and he loosened up. His arms came around me. "You're mine?" he said.

"Yours," said Tawanda.

"Does that mean you'll do what I say?" His voice sounded like a little boy's.

"Whatever you say," she said.

"Put your arms down," he said.

I lowered my arms.

"Stand real still." He backed away from me, then stood and studied me. He walked around, looking at me from all sides. "Wait a sec, I gotta get my flashlight." He went around to the trunk and opened it, pulled out a flashlight as long as his forearm, turned it on. He trained the beam on my breasts, my neck. "I did you," he said, nodding. "I did you. You were good. Almost as good as the first one. Show me your hands again."

I held them out and he stared at my blackened fingers. Slowly he smiled, then looked up and met my eyes.

"I was going to visit you," he said. "When I finished with this one. I was coming back to see you."

"I couldn't wait," said Tawanda.

"Don't talk," Richie said gently.

Don't talk! Tawanda and Mary accepted that without a problem, but I, Sheila, was tired of people telling me not to talk. What did I have to lose?

On the other hand, what did I have to say? I didn't even know what I wanted. Tawanda's love for Richie was hard to fight. It was the burning inside me, the sizzling under my skin, all I had left of life.

"Will you scream if I say so?" said Richie in his little boy's voice.

"Yes," said Tawanda; but suddenly lights went on around us, and bullhorn voices came out of the dark.

"Hold it right there, buddy! Put your hands up!"

Blinking in the sudden flood of light, Richie slowly lifted his hand, the knife glinting in the left one, the flashlight in the other.

"Step away from him, miss," said someone else. I looked around too, not blinking; glare didn't bother me. I couldn't see through it, though. I didn't know who was talking. "Miss, move away from him," said another voice from outside the light.

"Come here," Richie whispered, and I went to him. Releasing the flashlight, he dropped his arms around me, held the knife to my neck, and yelled, "Stay back!"

"Sheila!" It was Marti's voice this time, not amplified.

I looked toward her.

"Sheila, get away from him!" Marti yelled. "Do you want him to escape?"

Tawanda did. Mary did. They, after all, had found the place where they belonged. In the circle of his arms, my body glowed, the fire banked but burning steady.

He put the blade closer to my twisted throat. I could almost feel it. I laid my head back on his shoulder, looking at his profile out of the corner of my eye. The light glare brought out the blue in his eye. His mouth was slightly open, the inside of his lower lip glistening. He turned to look down into my face, and a slight smile curved the corner of his mouth. "Okay," he whispered, "we're going to get into the car now." He raised his voice. "Do what I say and don't struggle." Keeping me between him and the lights, he kicked the back door closed and edged us around the car to the driver's side. Moving in tandem, with his arm still around my neck, we slid in behind the wheel, me going first. "Keep close," he said to me. "Slide down a little so I can use my arm to shift with, but keep close."

"Sheila!" screamed Marti. The driver's side window was open. Richie started the car.

"Sheila! There's a live woman in the back of that car!"

Tawanda didn't care, and Mary didn't care, and I wasn't even sure I cared. Richie shifted from park into drive and eased his foot off the brake and onto the gas pedal; I could feel his legs moving against my left shoulder. From the back seat I heard a muffled groan. I looked up at Richie's face. He was smiling.

Just as he gunned the engine, I reached up and grappled the steering-wheel-mounted gear shift into park. Then I broke the shift handle off.

"You said you'd obey me," he said, staring down into my face. He looked betrayed, his eyes wide, his brow furrowed, his mouth soft. The car's engine continued to snarl without effect.

Fire blossomed inside me, hurting me this time because I'd hurt him. Pain came alive. I coughed, choking on my own tongue, my throat swollen and burning, my wrists and ankles burning, my breasts burning, between my legs a column of flame raging up inside me. I tried to apologize, but I no longer had a voice.

"You promised," said Richie in his little boy's voice, looking down at me.

I coughed. I could feel the power leaving me; my arms and legs were stiffening the way a body is supposed to do after death. I lifted my crippling hands as high as I could, palms up, pleading, but by that point only my elbows could bend. It was Tawanda's last gesture.

"Don't make a move," said a voice. "Keep your hands on the wheel."

We looked. A man stood just outside the car, aiming a gun at Richie through the open window.

Richie edged a hand down the wheel toward me.

"Make a move for her and I'll shoot," said the man. Someone else came up beside him, and he moved back, keeping his gun aimed at Richie's head, while the other man leaned in and put handcuffs on Richie.

"That's it," said the first man, and he and the second man heaved huge sighs.

I lay curled on the seat, my arms bent at the elbows, my legs bent at the knees. When they pulled Richie out of the car I slipped off his lap and lay stiff, my neck bent at an angle so my head stuck up sideways. "This woman needs medical attention," someone yelled. I listened to them freeing the woman in the back seat, and thought about the death of Tawanda and Mary.

Tawanda had lifted me out of my grave and carried me for miles. Mary had probably mostly died when Grannie cursed me and drove me out of the house. But Sheila? In a way, I had been pregnant with Sheila for years, and she was born in the grave. She was still looking out of my eyes and listening with my ears even though the rest of me was dead. Even as the pain of death faded, leaving me with clear memories of how Richie had treated me before he took that final twist around my neck, the Sheila in me was awake and feeling things.

"She's in an advanced state of rigor," someone said. I felt a dim pressure around one of my arms. My body slid along the seat toward the door.

"Wait," said someone else. "I got to take pictures."

"What are you talking about?" said another. "Ten minutes ago she was walking and talking."

Lights flashed, but I didn't blink.

"Are you crazy?" said the first person. "Even rapid-onset rigor doesn't come on this fast."

"Ask anybody, Tony. We all saw her."

"Try feeling for a pulse. Are you sure he wasn't just propping her up and moving her around like a puppet? But that wouldn't explain…."

"You done with the pictures yet, Crane?" said one of the cops. Then, to me, in a light voice, "Honey, come on out of there. Don't just lie there and let him photograph you like a corpse. You don't know what he does with the pictures."

"Wait till the civilians are out of here before you start making jokes," said someone else. "Maybe she's just in shock."

"Sheila?" said Marti from the passenger side.

"Marti," I whispered.

Gasps.

"Sheila, you did it. You did it."

Did what? Let him kill me, then kill me again? Suddenly I

was so angry I couldn't rest. Anger was like the fire that had filled me before, only a lower, slower heat. I shuddered and sat up.

Another gasp from one of the men at the driver's side door. "See?" said the one with the shock theory. One of them had a flashlight and shone it on me. I lifted my chin and stared at him, my microbraids brushing my shoulders.

"Kee-rist!"

"Oh, God!"

They fell back a step.

I sucked breath in past the swelling in my throat and said, "I need a ride. And feeling for a pulse? I think you'll be happier if you don't."

Marti gave me back her jacket. I rode in her Rabbit; the cop cars and the van from the medical examiner's office tailed us. Marti had a better idea of where she had found me than I did.

"What's your full name?" she said when we were driving. "Is there anybody I can get in touch with for you?"

"No. I've been dead to them for a couple years already."

"Are you sure? Did you ever call to check with them?"

I waited for a while, then said, "If your daughter was a hooker and dead, would you want to know?"

"Yes," she said immediately. "Real information is much better than not knowing."

I kept silent for another while, then told her my parents' names and phone number. Ultimately, I didn't care if the information upset them or not.

She handed me a little notebook and asked me to write

it down, turning on the dome light so I could see what I was doing. The pain of scorching had left my fingers again. Holding the pen was awkward, but I managed to write out what Marti wanted. When I finished, I slipped the notebook back into her purse and turned off the light.

"It was somewhere along here," she said half an hour later. "You have any feeling for it?"

"No." I didn't have a sense of my grave the way I had had a feeling for Richie. Marti's headlights flashed on three Coke cans lying together by the road, though, and I remembered seeing a cluster like that soon after I had climbed up the slope. "Here," I said.

She pulled over, and so did the three cars following us. Someone gave me a flashlight and I went to the edge of the slope and walked along, looking for my own footprints or anything else familiar. A broken bramble, a crushed fern, a tree with a hooked branch—I remembered them all from the afternoon. "Here," I said, pointing down the mountainside.

"Okay. Don't disturb anything," said the cop named Joe. One of the others started stringing up yellow tape along the road in both directions.

"But—" I was having a feeling now, a feeling that Sheila had lived as long as she wanted. All I needed was my blanket of goofer dust, and I could go back to sleep. When Joe went back to his car to get something, I slipped over the edge and headed home.

I pushed the branches off the other two women and lay down beside their bodies, thinking about my brief life. I had helped somebody and I had hurt somebody, which I figured was as much as I'd done in my first two lives.

I pulled dirt up over me, even over my face, not blinking when it fell into my eyes; but then I thought, Marti's going to see me sooner or later, and she'd probably like it better if my eyes were closed. So I closed my eyes.

THE SKULL-FACED BOY

DAVID BARR KIRTLEY

It was past midnight, and Jack and Dustin were driving along a twisted path through the woods. Jack was at the wheel. He was arguing with Dustin over Ashley.

Jack had always thought she had a pretty face—thin, arching eyebrows, a slightly upturned nose, a delicate chin. She'd dated Dustin in college for six months, until he got possessive and she got restless. Now, Jack thought, maybe she was interested in him.

But Dustin insisted, "She'll give me another chance. Someday."

"Not according to her," Jack said, with a pointed look.

He turned his eyes back to the road, and in the light of the high beams he saw a man stumble into the path of the car. Without thinking, Jack swerved.

The car bounced violently, and then its left front side smashed into a tree. The steering column surged forward, like an ocean wave, and crushed Jack's stomach. Dustin wasn't wearing a seatbelt. He flew face-first through the windshield, rolled across the hood, and tumbled off onto the ground.

Jack awoke, disoriented.

A man was pounding on the side of the car, just beyond the driver's side window, which was cracked and foggy and opaque. Jack pushed at the door, which creaked open just enough for him to make out the man's face. The man stared at Jack, then turned and started to walk off.

Jack shouted, "Call for help."

But the man didn't respond. He wandered toward the woods.

"Hey!" Jack screamed. He brushed aside a blanket of shattered glass and released his seatbelt. He pushed his seat backward, slowly extricating his bleeding stomach from the steering column, then dragged himself out the door and onto the ground, and he crawled after the man, who continued to walk away.

Finally Jack found the strength to stand. He lurched to his feet, grabbed the man by the shirtfront, shoved him back against a tree, and demanded, "What's wrong with you? Get help." Jack glanced about desperately and added, "I have to find my friend."

The man gave a long and wordless moan. Jack stared at him. The man was very pale, with disheveled hair. His face was encrusted with dirt, and his teeth were twisted and rotten. His eyes were... oozing.

Suddenly Dustin's voice burst out, "He's dead."

Jack turned. Dustin stood there, his nose and cheeks torn away. Two giant white eyeballs filled the sockets of his freakishly visible skull. Scraps of flesh hung from his jaw. Jack screamed.

Dustin stumbled over to the wrecked car, to where one of its side-view mirrors hung loosely. He tore off the mirror and stared into it. For a long time, he neither moved nor spoke.

Finally he called out, "That man has come back from the dead. Look at him, Jack. He's dead, and so am I."

Jack shuddered and backed away from the man.

Dustin's eyeballs fixed on Jack's stomach.

Apprehensive, Jack looked down. He lifted his blood-drenched shirt to expose the mangled mess beneath.

"And so are you," Dustin said.

Jack and Dustin set out on foot. They climbed to the top of a high bluff and watched the bodies of dead men stumble through the grassy fields below. Dustin sat with his back turned, so that his ruined face was lost in shadows. He said, "It's everyone. Everyone who died is coming back."

The dead man who had caused the accident was following them. He stumbled from the trees and regarded Jack vacantly.

Jack approached the man and said, "Can you talk?"

The man paused a moment, as if trying to focus, then gave another inarticulate groan. He wandered away.

Jack said to Dustin, "Why is he like that, and we aren't?"

Dustin said, "He dug himself out of the ground. He's been dead a long time—rotted flesh, rotted brains."

"Are there others like us?" Jack said.

"I don't know." Dustin leapt to his feet and called out to the valley below, "Hey! Can you hear me? Can you understand what I'm saying?"

The warm and fetid air carried back only wails. Dustin shrugged.

He and Jack followed the road until they came to a small house with its lights on.

Jack suggested, "We can call for help."

"What help?" Dustin said. "We're past that."

But he followed Jack toward the house, whose front door was open wide. They paused on the porch. They could see into the kitchen, where a woman stood clenching a baseball bat. A dead boy had backed her into a corner, and he shambled across the yellow linoleum toward her. Dry dirt tumbled from his sleeves and fell in a winding trail behind him.

He spoke, in a faint and quavering way: "Mom... help me."

"Stay back," she warned, her voice cracking. "Stay away from me. You're dead. I know you're dead."

Jack started forward, but Dustin held out an arm to stop him.

"Mom," the boy said. "What's wrong? Don't hurt me..."

"Stop it!" the woman shrieked, but her arms shuddered and she collapsed, sobbing. The boy fell upon her. He clawed at her hair, and she thrashed. He tore at her scalp with his teeth.

Jack cringed and turned away. The woman screamed, then gurgled, then was silent. When Jack looked again, he saw that Dustin was regarding the gruesome scene with fascination.

Jack growled, "What's wrong with you? We could've stopped it."

"We're dead now," Dustin said. "We help the dead, not them." He gestured at the woman.

"You're crazy," Jack said.

Dustin ignored him. "I want to see this."

"You—" Jack stopped as the woman rose, her head a cracked and bloody mess. She stepped clumsily forward.

She moaned.

"You'd be like her," Dustin whispered. "Mindless… hungry. If that first one had gotten into the car, chewed up your head, before you rose."

Jack strode into the kitchen, eased around the woman, the boy, and the blood-splattered floor, and stepped toward the phone.

"I'm calling home," Jack said, lifting the receiver. "I have to call my dad. Tell him I'm—"

"What?" Dustin said darkly. "All right?"

Jack hesitated.

Dustin said, "Jack, you're dead. You're lost to him. He'll never take you in."

Jack paused a moment, then began to dial. Dustin turned and stepped out into the night. The phone rang once, and instantly someone answered.

"Jack?" It was his father's voice.

"I'm coming home," Jack said. "I… can't stay on the line." He hung up.

He snatched some keys off the counter and slipped from the house. He spotted Dustin, who had walked out into the fields among the great crowds of the dead and was shouting to them, "Can you understand me? If you can hear me, step forward. If you understand just that much."

Jack circled the house, to where a car was parked. He took the car, and drove north for an hour, along Interstate 95, toward Waterville. He stared at his reflection in the rearview mirror. His face was jaundiced, discolored and sickly, but if he covered his gaping stomach then in dim light he might pass for living.

He pulled up in front of his house and got out of the car. In the front yard lay a dead man whose forehead had a bullet through it. Jack shuddered, and circled around back. The old wood steps creaked as he stepped onto the back porch and knocked. He hung back in the shadows. A curtain was drawn aside, and faces peered out.

From inside the house someone called: "Jack! It's Jack."

The door opened, and Jack's father stood there, clutching a rifle. He stared, then gasped and dropped back, raising the gun.

Jack cowered and said quickly, "Dad. Listen. Please. I'm not like the others." The rifle was now aimed straight at Jack's forehead, and Jack stared into the depths of its barrel. Then the barrel slowly sank, as his father lowered the gun.

Finally his father said, "Come inside, son."

Jack stepped into the house.

His father chained him to the rusty pipe that ran out of the side of the garage and into the ground, and said, "I'm sorry. It's only for the night. It's the only way they'll let you stay here." Nine people were holed up in the house—Jack's father had taken in some vacationers.

Jack whispered sadly, "I understand."

His father went back inside.

The moon was bright, and the garage cast a thick black

shadow over Jack. All across the neighborhood, dogs were barking. The night seemed to go on forever, and Jack never slept. He supposed that he would never sleep again.

Days passed.

Several large groups arrived. Jack stayed out of sight, and most of the visitors departed, headed south. Those who stayed would sometimes let Jack inside, but they kept their distance from him, and always had weapons ready.

During the day the men went out, scavenging for food and ammunition, and at night they told stories of the dead men they'd destroyed. Then they would glance at Jack and fall silent.

He was chained up each night, weeks of that.

One day at dusk, Jack was sitting on a sofa in the living room when gunshots crackled outside. The residents brandished their weapons and took up positions by the windows.

Someone pounded on the front door. A gruff voice outside hollered, "Let us in! For God's sake, let us in. They're coming."

Jack's father, rifle at the ready, leapt forward and threw open the door. Two tall men in hunting gear rushed into the house, each of them carrying several guns. Jack's father slammed the door behind them.

One of the newcomers gasped, "We heard about this house. They said you'd take us in. We've got almost no bullets left."

Jack's father said, "It's my house, and you're—"

Then the newcomer spotted Jack and lurched wildly, falling back against the front wall and violently cocking a shotgun. The man screamed, "They're in the house!," and raised his weapon.

Jack's father leapt in front of the gun and yelled, "Don't shoot! That's my son. He won't hurt you."

The gun's barrel wove in tight circles as the newcomer sought a clear shot.

Jack called out, "Please! It's all right."

The newcomer glanced at his companion, who was now hunched in the corner and moaning, "Oh shit. Oh shit, it's in here with us."

Jack's father said firmly, "You can leave if you want."

There was a long, tense silence. Finally, the newcomer lowered his gun and said, "All right. We'll let it alone." He glared at Jack, and added, "But you stay the hell away from me."

The newcomer was named Sam, and his companion was Todd. Sam was bigger and louder, and leader of the two.

After things had settled down, Todd explained, "We joined up with a militia to hold Portland. But the dead, they…" He stopped and stared at the floor.

Sam said flatly, "It's not good down there. Not good at all."

Jack's father said, "Where did you hear about this house?"

"In Freeport," Todd said. "Some people had stayed here. There was a girl too. She had a note for your son." Todd fished an envelope out of his vest pocket. He glanced uneasily at Jack and said, "I guess that's him."

Sam grumbled, "Maybe that's not such a good idea."

Jack's father scowled and said, "Let him have it."

Todd shrugged and tossed the note out onto the table. Jack scooped up the note and opened it.

It was from Ashley, letting him know that she was all right and that he should join her if he wasn't safe. She gave the address where she was. Jack stuck the note into his pocket.

Sam's voice was shaky: "South of here there's this dead kid

with no face. People call him the skull-faced boy. He's smart, he can talk, like that one there." Sam nodded at Jack.

Jack murmured, "Dustin."

Todd said sharply, "What?"

Jack said, "He hurt his face like that. I saw it."

Sam stared, horrified. "You know him?"

Jack realized that he'd said something wrong.

"Dustin was a friend from school," Jack's father explained. "He was with Jack the night this... all started."

Todd's voice was almost hysterical: "Sam! This is crazy. He's one of them. One of the skull-faced boy's—"

"Shut up!" Sam growled. "Just shut up."

There was a long silence.

Jack's father said, "Come on, son. Let's go outside."

Jack was chained up again. Then he crouched there in the shadow of the garage and listened to the voices that drifted out through the bright cracks in the boarded-up windows.

First came Jack's father's voice: "What's this all about?"

Todd replied anxiously, "We lost Portland because of the skull-faced boy. He's organized the dead down south into some sort of army."

Sam broke in, "He's trained them. They go after people they know—family, friends. The dead act like they have feelings. People hesitate, won't fight, then it's too late."

Jack's father said, "What's that got to do with us?"

"Don't you get it?" It was Todd again. "Jack is part of this. He's friends with the skull-faced boy. He's pretending to be nice, just waiting for his chance to strike."

"He's dangerous," Sam added. "He knows about this house, and now the one in Freeport too. What else does he know?

He's got to be destroyed."

"No," Jack's father said.

Todd pressed him, "He's not your son anymore. Your son is dead and gone. Now it's just a thing, a thing in your son's body. Using your own love against you."

Sam added, "People have a right to protect themselves. If one of these folks here went out one night and shot that thing you keep in the backyard, I wouldn't blame them."

One of the other residents hissed, "Keep your voice down. He might hear."

After that the voices fell to a low, incomprehensible murmur.

Jack waited for hours. Then he watched as the back door swung open. A shadowy figure with a gun crept across the yard toward him.

Was it Sam? Or Todd? Or one of the others? In the darkness, Jack couldn't tell.

It was his father, who stepped from the shadows, then bent to unlock the chains and said, "It's not safe for you here anymore. I'm sorry."

"I'm sorry too," Jack whispered, rising to his feet. He hugged his father, then escaped into the night.

Jack found Dustin's army standing in a great field north of Portland. The thousands of dead milled about in loose formations and watched Jack with their empty eyes. Their groans filled the night.

Jack moved among them and shouted, "Dustin! I'm looking for Dustin. Dustin, can you hear me?"

Finally a voice responded, "Hey! Hey you. What do you want?"

Jack stopped and turned. A balding dead man in olive fatigues was approaching.

Jack said, "I'm looking for the skull-faced boy."

"The Commander, you mean," the man replied. "He'll want to see you too. We can use someone like you."

The man led Jack through the crowds, up to a low hill where a small crowd of dead men conversed in hushed tones. Dustin stood at the peak of the hill, and his back was turned. Standing like that he seemed normal, familiar.

Jack called out, "Dustin."

Dustin glanced backward, so that one white eye showed in his eerie skeletal profile. He wore a ratty army jacket. He said, "You've come back." Then he turned away, so that again all that was visible was the back of his head, and said, "Where have you been?"

"Up north," Jack said.

Dustin asked, "Did you encounter any of the living? Any armed groups?"

"No," Jack lied.

"We'll be headed that way," Dustin continued. "North. Along 95, toward Waterville… Your hometown." He waited for a reaction.

Jack said nothing.

Finally Dustin added, "Anyway, it's time for training." He walked out to the edge of the hill and regarded the hordes below, then shouted, "Don't shoot!"

They moaned back, "Don't… shoot…"

"It's me!" Dustin yelled. "You know me!"

The voices of the dead drifted up toward the sky: "It's me… You know me…"

"Please help me," Dustin shouted.

"Please… help me…" they wailed.

Dustin nodded with satisfaction and turned away from the crowds. "That's our strategy, Jack. My soldiers possess determination, but not much else. A resemblance to loved ones is one of our few assets."

Jack said, "What are you doing? What do you think you're going to accomplish?"

"Peace," Dustin said, then added, "The living want to destroy us. All of us. Our only chance is to convert them, to make them like us."

Jack stared at the lines of moaning dead. They stretched as far as he could see.

Dustin added, "And we're winning, thanks to my plan. I got the idea from that boy, who converted his mother. You remember, that first night, we saw him."

"To hell with your plan," Jack said angrily. "I lost my home because of your plan."

Instantly Dustin turned to face Jack and said, "So you did go home." That menacing skull-face leaned in close. "Are people hiding there?"

Jack turned away.

"At your house?" Dustin pressed. "Is that where they are? My army's fragile, Jack. They're slow and clumsy and stupid. A nest of armed resistance, even a small one, can wreak havoc. I have to know about it."

Jack said, "Leave them alone. Leave my father alone."

"We're headed north, Jack," Dustin said. "The plan is already in motion."

"Don't," Jack insisted, then added, "Just for now. They won't bother you. Push east. Toward Freeport."

"Freeport?" Dustin was dismissive. "What's there?"

Jack reached into his pocket and pulled out the note. He answered in a low voice, "Ashley."

Later that night, Dustin said to Jack, "She'll have to be converted. It's the only way."

Jack said, "Killed, you mean."

"I want her with us," Dustin said. "She's in danger now. Any random dead person might get to her, damage her mind—destroy what makes her special. She'll be safer this way."

Jack wondered: Why did I do it? Why betray Ashley? To protect his father, yes, but… the truth—he wanted to see her again. Would she accept him, if they were the same? If she were dead too?

Jack said, "It won't be easy."

"No," Dustin agreed. "That's why I need you with me. My soldiers follow orders, mostly. I tell them where to march, who to attack, what to say. But I can't stop them from feeding, Jack, which means that most of my new recruits arrive as damaged goods. There's not much officer material around here."

Jack was skeptical. "You want to make me an officer?"

Dustin answered, "I can't use regular troops for this. There's too much risk to Ashley. I have to use officers—men I can trust not to damage her—and I've got few enough of those."

Some of the dumb, moaning ones wandered past, and Jack imagined them ripping at Ashley's soft forehead with their teeth.

"I'll go," Jack said then. "For Ashley. To make sure nothing happens to her."

"For Ashley," Dustin agreed.

Dustin called a meeting of his officers, and held up a photograph that showed him and Ashley standing beside a campfire and embracing. Dustin said, "This is her. Make sure she's not damaged."

The army marched east, thousands of groaning dead shambling along the interstate. Dustin moved among them, shouting orders: "When we reach the town, seek out places you know, people you know. Remember what to say: 'Don't shoot! You know me! Help me!'"

The mumbled replies echoed through the trees: "Don't shoot... you know me... help me..."

Dustin had a dozen officers—dead men armed with rifles and pistols—who stayed close by his side. Dustin himself carried a shotgun, and kept a combat knife tucked in his boot. Jack followed along behind them, and held his rifle limply, and stared down at the damp pine needles that passed beneath his feet. He was full of foreboding.

Dustin lowered his voice and said to his officers, "They've probably never fought dead men like us before—fast, smart, armed. That surprise will be our biggest advantage."

One of the officers grumbled, "They've spent weeks boarding up this house. How are we going to get in?"

Jack called out, "I can get us in."

Dustin turned and studied him, then nodded.

The house was a sprawling Victorian that sat in the middle of a grove of white cedars. Dustin led the squad forward. They all crouched low and scurried across the lawn in a tight column, their weapons held ready. Jack and Dustin hurried up the front steps while the others ducked behind the porch railing or dropped into the long grass.

Jack hammered on the door and shouted, "Let us in! It's Sam! For God's sake, let us in, they're coming!"

After a few moments, he heard the bolt snap out of place. The door opened a crack. Dustin rammed the barrel of his shotgun into the opening and pulled the trigger. Blood exploded through the gap, splattering crimson across the porch, then Dustin kicked open the door.

The officers sprang up, firearms bristling, and charged into the house. Gunfire rang out all around. Jack was swept along into the foyer, which was already littered with bodies. A staircase led up to the second floor.

"Cover the stairs," Dustin ordered Jack. "Make sure no one comes down."

Jack aimed his gun up toward the second floor landing. The other officers poured off into the side rooms, and sounds of violence shook the house.

Suddenly a doorway under the stairs flew open. Jack swung his rifle to cover it, but then a muzzle flashed and a bullet caught him in the chest, and he stumbled back against a small table and knocked over a lamp, which shattered on the floor.

Dustin shouted, "The basement! They're in the basement."

Three of the officers stormed down the basement steps. Beneath Jack's feet the floorboards rattled, and horrible screams filtered up from below. Jack stuck a finger into his chest and rooted out the bullet.

Another officer jogged up to stand at Dustin's side and said, "Sir, we've got your girl. She's in the study. Bleeding."

Dustin nodded. "I want to be with her when she rises. Finish this."

"Yes, sir." The officer walked to the open front door and

called out, "Come here. Come on. Now."

Jack watched, horrified, as crowds of moaning dead men stumbled in through the door and began to gorge on the newly fallen corpses.

Jack grabbed Dustin's arm and said, "What are you doing? We can use these people."

Dustin said, "They'll try to shoot us as soon as they rise. It's better this way."

Jack cast one last grim look at the feeding dead, then followed Dustin through several doorways and into a study.

Ashley lay in an overstuffed chair, flanked by officers. Her pretty face was still. A trickle of blood flowed from a single bullet hole in the center of her chest.

One of the officers said, "She's not breathing. It won't be long."

Dustin ordered, "I want to be alone with her."

The officers herded Jack from the room. He paced down a long, lonely hallway, then out the front door and into the yard, where he sat, leaning back against a tall white cedar and waiting for Ashley to appear.

Finally she did, framed in the light of the doorway. Her figure was slender, her hair long and lustrous. But her beautiful face had been carved away, until there was nothing left but eyeballs and bone.

Dustin came and stood beside her, and their twin skull faces regarded each other.

Later that night, as Jack and Dustin stood together in the yard, Jack said bitterly, "I can't believe you did that. She was beautiful."

To which Dustin replied, "Ashley will always be beautiful. To me. You loved her face. I love her. Who deserves her more?"

"I want to talk to her," Jack said.

"No, you'll stay away." Dustin's voice held a nasty edge. "Or I'll tell her that you led us here. That you betrayed her."

Jack flinched, and Dustin strode away, calling over his shoulder, "I'm the only one who understands her now, understands what she's going through."

For hours Jack wandered aimlessly among the dead, among the masses of rotting flesh. Their awfulness, their stupidity, was overwhelming, and made him want to gag.

Then, through the clusters of corpses, he caught a glimpse of white skull. He walked away.

He wound a path through the dead, and sneaked an occasional backward glance. The skull was there. It gained on him.

Finally, it caught him.

Ashley said, "Jack. It is you." She leaned her horrible skull-face toward him, and her exposed eyeballs studied him. She said, "Dustin didn't tell me you were here. Say something. Do you recognize me, Jack? Do you understand?"

He didn't answer.

Then she was suspicious. "Did you have anything to do with this? Did you help him do this?

Jack turned away and stumbled off into the hordes. In that moment he envied them—their lack of thought, of remorse. He couldn't bear to confront Ashley. Now there was only one thing he could do, that might deceive her, that might make her leave him alone.

"Don't hurt me…" he groaned loudly, desperately. "Please… help me."

THE HUMAN RACE

SCOTT EDELMAN

Paula Gaines felt herself quite ready to die.

Or perhaps it was instead that ever since the phone call that brought her to this distant place to look into her father's dead eyes and have to tell a stranger, "Yes ... that's him," she was no longer ready to live.

As she sat in the bathtub, stroking her forearm with the flat of a knife she had lifted from the hostel's communal dining area, that fine a distinction no longer mattered to her. Whether she was racing toward her death, or racing away from her life, all that mattered now was the speed with which that race could be consummated.

The reflection of her face in the still water, water turned lukewarm so long had she been sitting in it, was unfamiliar to her. Her years on this earth had been full of unfortunate life lessons, and thanks to this added insult from the universe, there seemed little point in going on. Before the call that startled her in the middle of another sleepless night, before her sudden trip to London, she saw herself as a person able to at least keep up a pretense of happiness, even though happiness itself was beyond her. But this day, she no longer had the energy for false smiles, and her expression was far grimmer than she had ever known it.

Grimmer, and almost lifeless already.

As she switched the knife from her right hand to her left, her slight movement gently rippled the water, and as her reflection distorted, she could almost see her sister's face. And when the ripples were at their greatest, even her mother's. She slapped the water angrily, so that the faces went away. She just couldn't bear it. Her mother's face, her sister's face... they were both gone. The explosion that had taken the two of them had been so great that there had been no faces remaining after death, no body parts that the officials at the morgue felt it necessary for her to identify.

While the terrorist attack had left her father's body bloodied but intact, if she was ever going to see the rest of her family again, it would have to be after death.

After *her* death.

She turned the blade so that the edge pressed against her wrist. At the instant that she was about to cut deeply length-wise—as she had learned was necessary for a successful suicide one time when she'd investigated it on the Web—there was a rap at the bathroom door. She startled, and as her hand jerked, the blade sliced shallowly into her flesh. A few drops of blood ran down her arm into the water.

"Who's there?" she asked, with a voice that sounded surprised it had the chance to speak again.

"You're not the only one who needs to use the bath, you know," called out a woman.

"Just a moment," Paula said.

She looked into the water as her red blood dissipated into pink and then was gone, almost as if the thoughts of suicide were a dream. But they weren't, and never would be again. She tried to identify exactly whose voice had called out to her, to remember which of the women with whom she had shared a bustling breakfast it could have possibly been—Lillian, who squeezed her hand briefly after passing the marmalade, Jenni-fer, who found it hard to meet her eyes, or perhaps one of the others—and though she could not put a face to the voice, she remembered them all as friendly, and sympathetic once they realized the purpose of her journey. And so she thought…no, not here. Don't do it here. Paula didn't want to make friends, however new, clean up the mess she'd leave behind. Whatever she was going to do, it had to be done in front of people whom she had never looked in the eye, who would not then be forced to mourn their own failures to save her. The women she'd just met here, even though just passing acquaintances, deserved better. Her mother had raised her that way.

Her mother…

Paula slipped slowly into the water until her head submerged beneath its surface and her knees popped up to cool in the chill air of the room. She held her breath, embracing the silence, and wished that she could just keep holding that breath until all breath was gone, taking with it this room, this city, *everything*. She held the air in her lungs for as long as she could, but then the air exploded from between her lips and she sat up quickly, shivering in a strange room in a strange country.

She dressed quickly and rushed back to her cramped room, which was all that she could afford, and only barely afford at that. She grabbed her backpack, stuffed it with her possessions, told no one she was checking out—almost laughing, but not quite, at the double meaning of that phrase—and fled the hostel.

If she was going to die that day, she was going to do it in front of strangers.

Paula gulped down a mouthful of coffee the moment the waitress brought it over, burning her tongue, which reminded her yet again that life meant pain. At least for her it did. She blew on what liquid remained in the cup, cursing her impatience. She had no idea how others managed to maintain pleasant lives, but hers was one filled with impatience, and blossoming with pain.

She had hoped that the despair which had settled over her, initially back home and now deepening here, would do her a favor for once and demonstrate its own patience, so that she could stave off her suicide long enough to return to die in her home country. But her latest worries made that unlikely. The intricacies of getting her family's remains released, negotiating with a local funeral home for proper caskets, dealing with the airlines to transport the bodies (or what remained of them)… it was all too much for her, and those details buzzed in her head, blotting out both sleep and reason. She found it hard to contemplate the enormity of suddenly being the responsible one in the family. No one could have ever mistaken her for the one in that role before, and now…

Identifying her father's body had been difficult enough. She just didn't have the energy to do all of the other things that remained.

And she didn't have the energy to remain alive either.

She had walked all morning through the streets of a country she had never before thought to visit, stumbled on until her aching feet insisted that she drop into a chair at a corner cafe. She'd sat in the sunshine for hours, unable to summon up the energy to move, shamed by the determination of the passersby rushing on with their lives. Picking at the remains of her plate of squidgy lemon pudding, an odd dessert with an odd name, she wondered why her father had always wanted to visit this odd country.

He had always talked about it, studying maps, poring over guidebooks, and had finally done it, and look what good chasing his dreams had done him. She never understood his dreams anyway. That had always been part of their problem, she figured; she should have been able to understand him better. But then, he never seemed to spend much energy understanding her, either. Still, he *had* reached out to both Paula and her sister Jane, neither of whom had ever married, offering to pay their ways to London to experience it with him. Perhaps she should have taken her father up on it as her sister had. If she'd done so, she would have been on that bus with the three of them, and all of her worrying and despair would now be over.

Instead, she had to sit in an unfamiliar place and contemplate how and when she would…do it. If she'd been home, she would have known exactly what to do. She had been thinking about it long enough, planning for its inevitability. It would have been easy. There was that lake, and the sunset that came with it, and those pills that since Mark had left she had been spending far too many long nights studying, even *before* every living relative of hers had been erased. She cursed her decision to remain home instead of taking her dad up on his invitation. The matter could have been taken out of her hands. She could have died with them, without thought, instead of just sitting there *thinking* about dying.

Now, sitting at the cafe, eating her pastry, drinking her coffee, pondering both her loneliness and the short time she had left in which to be lonely…she had to find another way.

Maybe she could climb up Big Ben, which her father had always talked of visiting. She could climb it and instead of admiring the intricacy of the clockwork and the view, just… jump off, giving herself over to the breeze. She wouldn't have minded that feeling of flight to be real for once, but somehow, it didn't seem right to mingle her father's goal with her own shortcomings. And besides… she knew nothing of Big Ben. She had no idea whether that tourist magnet even contained an accessible window or ledge from which she *could* jump.

Or perhaps she should fill her pockets with rocks, and swim out into the Thames until she could swim no more. A famous writer had done just that. She had even seen a movie about it. She liked the idea of floating off until consciousness faded, but the preparations—finding a river secluded enough so that no one would try to save her, finding a grouping of stones sufficient to her task—it seemed like too much work for her, regardless of how romantic it might sound. She needed a way that was almost effortless. If it could be instantaneous as well, so much the better.

As the traffic blared around her, she took another bite of her pastry and looked at the cars and trucks rushing by, and to the roadway, where she could see painted in large white letters a warning to walkers to look to their right. So many tourists visited London each year that there needed to be constant reminders that the world was not the same all over.

Reading the warning, she realized that she had finally found her answer. She could step blindly into traffic. No one would even have to know that she had done it deliberately. Americans were known for stepping off the curb while looking in the wrong direction. If anyone bothered to research her reasons for coming to London in the first place, they would simply assume that she had been distracted by grief. Unlike the case with the women back at the hostel, no one would have to feel personal responsibility, carrying the weight that it was something she could have been talked out of. There would be no guilt. They would just think it was the unfortunate, accidental passing of another sad American.

In fact, Paula could see one of those quaint double-decker busses approaching right then.

She pushed back from her table and walked away from the cafe. Her waitress stepped toward her from amid the outdoor cluster of tables, calling after her that she had forgotten to pay, which only caused her to walk more quickly. As the bright red bus neared, Paula looked the other way, feigning confusion just in case there was a witness, and began to put her right foot forward to step into the street.

Before she could set it down in the path of the bus, she heard a man scream. She hesitated, hanging there between life and death. When Paula turned, she saw that man pointing, not at her, but past her into the street. The bus went by, her opportunity gone. By then, additional people were pointing, and she followed their outstretched arms to what was revealed after the bus had moved on.

It was a dead man walking.

With his shredded clothes, bloodied body, and gray pallor, another might have thought him merely a man in make-up, costumed for a party or on his way to a movie set, but unfortunately, Paula knew what death looked like. As the creature grew nearer, she could see into its eyes. They were like those of her father; there was no there there.

Unlike her father, however, this corpse *walked*.

It shambled amidst the traffic in her direction, the cars honking for him to move and then swerving when he did not. A few drivers slowed to a crawl so they could look more closely at the impossibility. One man got out of his car and ran over to the thing, placing his hand on its shoulder. Paula could see from the driver's face, no more than ten yards away, that this was only a gesture of concern; perhaps he'd thought the bloodied walker an escapee from a hospital. As a reward for the man's good Samaritanship, the shambler slapped out with a bloodied fist and knocked him dead.

Pedestrians screamed and scattered around her, but Paula

simply stood there. She wondered if she was frozen in shock, but no, she was only waiting, though she wasn't sure for what. She watched as the walking corpse punched a second man to the pavement, then lunged to bring down a third, biting deeply into a woman's neck with crooked teeth.

Then the thing saw her.

With everyone else fleeing, she was the only still target in a sea of flesh. Its lips parted, and she could hear a low, dull growl. She looked away from its bloody lips into its eyes, and thought she now saw an empty hunger there, one that was not unfamiliar to her. She began to ask what force had animated him, what had brought him back to the land of the living, but before she could utter her question, a shot rang out. A police officer had fired on the thing from behind the shelter of a car, hitting the creature in its back. It staggered slightly under the affront, but did not close its dull eyes.

"Wait," she said, holding out one hand toward the officer and the other armed men who joined him. "You can't do this. Not yet."

She took a step forward, the step toward death that she'd been interrupted from taking mere moments before, and further shots rang out. The thing's head exploded, splashing brain matter across her. It crumpled, its knees slamming into the pavement first. Then it sank forward, what remained of its head hitting the roadway at her feet, blood splattering her shoes. Only then did she sag, sitting down hard on the curb. A policeman dashed over, skirting the broken body at their feet.

"Miss?" he asked her. "Are you all right, Miss?"

She didn't know how to even begin to answer. She looked up into the policeman's face and for a moment was unable to tell whether he was alive or dead, or even remember whether she herself was alive or dead. Someone thrust a cup of water into her hands and draped a blanket over her shoulders. Someone else attempted to wipe the blood from her face.

As she sat there limp, hearing the sound of sirens and smelling the scent of death, voices reached her through her fog of shock. The police were saying that this tableaux hadn't just happened on this one street. It was playing itself out all over London. All over the world.

The dead were coming back to life.

And they didn't seem to like us.

She let herself be helped back to her feet, and then she let herself be tugged along, as she had allowed for most of her life, but when she realized that the destination she was being shepherded to was the back of an ambulance, she broke free from those who thought they were helping her. She ran as swiftly as she could, ran away, into the cafe, out a back entrance, and down an alleyway. This was no time to live meekly, to be swept along by the tide.

If the dead were coming back to life, her place wasn't in a hospital, with the living and those who hoped to rejoin the living. It was in the morgue, with the dead.

Her dead.

Paula stared down the barrel of a gun held in the shaking hands of a guard standing in the doorway to the London morgue, and was surprised to realize that all she felt was a calm disinterest.

She felt no alarm. She only thought…how ironic.

Hours before, she would have acted as provocatively as possible in the hopes of setting off the trigger finger of the jittery young man in a uniform at least one size too large for him. She would have made a lunge in his direction, walked with the staggered gait of the living corpses she had seen wandering the streets of London as she'd zigzagged her way to the building in which she'd identified her father's body…anything to provoke that bullet. But now everything had changed, for suddenly she had hope, and so she put her hands out slowly beside her, palms up, and then chose her words carefully.

"I'm not dead," she said, hoping that her calm words would distract from the bits of brain matter that had spotted the front of her blouse when that first corpse had been shot, and from the blood stain that remained on her face, impervious to washing. The guard lowered his gun slightly, but it did not appear to Paula that he had loosened his grip.

"Why did you come here?" he asked. One of his shirt sleeves was missing, and the other was dripping with blood. "This is the last place you should want to be."

"My father's here. Do you remember me? I remember you. You were standing by the elevators when I came in, I think. He died last week and I had to come here yesterday to identify him. What happened to your arm?"

He shook his head, unready to talk about it. He looked like the sort of person who might never be ready to talk about it, holding things in for a lifetime, as she had.

"I'm lucky to be alive," he said. "You should leave."

"I need to be here," she said, taking a careful step forward. "I need to see him. Please."

"No one needs to be here," he said, standing aside and letting her pass through the door to stand beside him in the entrance hall. "And I've been here long enough. They've been coming to life all day. I hope never to see this place again."

Then he was where she had been, outside looking in.

"You're not going to find what you're looking for," he said. "But you're welcome to try. The place is all yours."

He tossed her the keys.

"Just remember—some doors you're not going to want to unlock."

And then he was gone, leaving her alone in a lobby that looked even less welcoming than it had been the day before. The floor was slick with blood and littered with body parts. As she picked her way through the building, that no longer fazed her, because that's what the city had looked like as she'd made her way here. Only luck had let her get this far. She retraced her steps to the room in which she had been asked to identify her father…but it was empty. She feared that she was too late, that her father, animated by the plague that had infected the planet, had already gotten up and staggered away. It could have been his blood on the guard's sleeves. It could have been his body parts on the floor, shredded as the guard had defended himself. But as she looked around the bland room, she realized that no single body ever stayed there for long. This was just a place where people like her came face to face with death. The bodies were shuttled here from somewhere else.

Paula returned to the hallway to find that somewhere else. The floor had become so slippery that she had to steady herself against a wall to stand upright. She'd watched enough television to know what she was looking for, but it wasn't her eyes that first found her goal, that by-now clichéd room with columns and rows of refrigerated cubicles.

It was her ears. She heard her destination before she saw it.

With her hand on the doorknob and the sounds of violence raging inside, she was afraid for the first time that day. The thought that her father was inside, and that she might be stopped from reaching him, stirred up that fear. But she was more afraid of what she would learn about her father than of what would happen to her, and so forced herself into the room.

She had to lean against the door to open it, and only when she had it fully open did she see that her way had been blocked by body parts. A coroner, his internal organs chewed, was split into four pieces. She closed her eyes, took a deep breath, and stepped into the room, which still echoed with noise. Nothing moved to stop her, so she moved slowly to the center of the large room lined with small doors with handles.

She could hear muffled howling, and the dull thuds of bare feet beating against metal doors. People were trapped inside many of the refrigerated cubicles, struggling to get out.

No, not people, she reminded herself. What *used* to be people.

And behind one of those doors was her father.

She moved respectfully through the room, pausing before each column of doors. She noticed that some of the compart-ments emitted no sound, presumably because they contained no body. She walked by someone's mother, someone's father, someone's child, and wondered if others like her were coming to try to collect them. Slots in the doors held cards on which names had been scrawled. She had almost circled the room and returned to where she'd started before she stopped, at last, in front of a door which bore a name she shared.

She placed her hand on the cool metal handle. There was silence within, a silence that sickened her. For it could mean that he was already gone. She rested her head against the door, and was surprised to find herself praying, something she had not done since she was a small child.

She pulled the handle. Once the door opened, she tugged at the tray inside and slid it out from its compartment. It rolled out so effortlessly that she was surprised to see that her father's body was still there, unchanged since the day before.

"Oh, Daddy," she moaned.

He appeared the same as he had been when she had come to identify him. Though they had washed the blood from him as best as they could, the evidence of death was unmistakable. Whatever had brought the other dead back to this new sort of life had not yet touched him. No force had come to animate him again, to wake him so that he could say the things as yet unsaid, so that she could retract the things said that shouldn't have been said.

She dragged a chair over beside his pallet so that she could watch him, and then she sat down to await his transformation.

She jerked awake, startled to realize that she had been asleep. All she remembered was studying her father's face, just as she was doing now. There was no change. Her father still slept.

"He won't be coming back, you know."

She leapt up at the sound of the voice, tumbling her chair on its side. The guard who had earlier abandoned her knelt to pick it up.

"I'm sorry that I frightened you," he said. "But I couldn't leave you alone to face this."

Paula backed away, keeping the righted chair between them. She had not known men to act kindly to her in the past, and she doubted that it was about to start under these circumstances.

"What did you mean when you said that he wasn't coming back?" she asked warily.

"Only that it's too late for him. I've been listening to the news, what news is still broadcasting. All the others, the ones we've seen, the ones we've had to fight…they died today, and yesterday. But your father…he died last week. No one knows why, or what happened, but it's only the newly dead who return."

She sank into the chair and began to cry.

"He wouldn't have been the same anyway, Miss," he said, trying to comfort her. "He wouldn't have recognized you."

The guard didn't understand. That wasn't why she was crying this time, not because her father couldn't join her in life. She was in tears now because it was too late for her to join him in death. She was even worse off than she'd been before. Suicide had been rendered useless. There could be no end to life now. If she were to kill herself, she would just come back for another chapter. And she wanted no further chapters. She wanted her book of life to be closed.

She wanted to die, but the time for death was past. She no longer had a goal. All purpose had been stolen from her.

She dried her tears, but did not get up. She simply sat there, continuing to stare at her father.

"You should go home, Miss. If you can."

"But what about my father? What about him?"

"There is no him anymore."

"I was supposed to bring him home."

"I don't know that there's any home anymore either. From what I hear, the States are just as bad. And at a time like this,

I doubt they would let you return with a dead body. I'm sorry. But it's best to just say goodbye."

The former guard backed away from her, giving her space she did not need, inviting her with his body language to leave with him.

But he didn't get it. She was dead inside. She may have looked alive, but inside, she was just like her father.

She belonged here.

By day, she wandered the wounded city, sure that her wounds were even greater, studying those who still dared to walk the streets in an attempt to get on with their lives in the midst of chaos, and being studied in return. At night, she slept by her father's side, surprised that she even *could* sleep, for the noise in that room, the moaning, the pounding of creatures that could not escape, was unceasing.

As she moved through the city, it was as if she were leading a charmed life, though she was not sure that what she still had was life. She would come upon scenes of great carnage, small battles between the living and the dead, and walk through them unscathed. It was as if the undead took her for one of their own, so dead was she inside. The fugue state in which she existed had seemed to make her invulnerable, though she didn't entirely think of herself as so, because she no longer had the level of consciousness to be self-aware. She existed without conscious choice. She just continued her walking through the city, eating when hungry, returning to sleep when tired.

Around her, some people seemed to be going about their business, but many had abandoned their routines, fleeing the city in search of sanctuary in the countryside. London had become depopulated. It was as if a great city had become a small village in a matter of days. There was no longer a problem getting a seat on the tube, though people now looked at each other with suspicion for new reasons that were just as deadly as the old.

One day after walking, she aimlessly rode the tube for hours, letting it take her where it would. It seemed as useful as anything else she could have been doing. She no longer had anywhere to go. She no longer had anywhere to be. And besides, this is how she felt closest to her family. Riding the public transportation of the city, she felt closer to her father than when she slept next to him at night, propped up in a chair waiting for a metamorphosis she now doubted would ever come. This was the sort of place in which he'd died, after all. This was the sort of place in which her entire family had died, taking her along with them.

She watched others come and go. Most were afraid, eying each other passenger and wondering whether this one or that one was a reanimated corpse. She knew no fear, for she no longer cared. No force, living or dead, had any answers for her.

But at the next station, she felt fear again, as the doors opened to reveal another who was also fearless, though for different reasons.

The man who entered the car wore a hooded sweatshirt, even though the weather had been warm that day, and on his back he carried an olive backpack. Paula tried to read his expression, but there was no expression there to read, and that told her everything she needed to know.

"Don't do it!" she shouted, no longer desiring what came after.

Then came the explosion, brighter than the sun, and then the darkness, as black as death.

Paula heard no screaming as she came to, and she thought at first that the explosion had deafened her by shattering her eardrums. But as she lifted her head, she could see that the reason there was no screaming was because she was the only one on the train left alive. She was on her back, and as she moved her hands about her to rise, her fingers swept against glass that had been blown from the windows.

She sat up in the unmoving train, and through the smoke could see the bodies of the few other occupants of the car that had been brave enough to ride the tube. She had been furthest from the bomber and had only been knocked out, but the half-dozen others had been lifted and thrown against the walls of the train.

She felt an odd sense of cognitive dissonance; it was as if she was visiting the past. This is what her father's last home had looked like, filled with smoke and dust and blood. But somehow she had escaped her family's fate. She leaned against the buckled walls as she moved along the car. She walked gingerly past the dead, the blood streaming from their ears, and threw herself against the door, which would not budge. She looked nervously at the dead, knowing what would happen next.

She had to get out.

Then she saw him, the cause of all this. Or what was left of him. A head, its hair matted with blood, was on the floor, facing away from her. The body that had supported it was nowhere to be seen. She approached the head slowly, circling it and then pushing at it with her toes so she could stare into its face. Yes, it was him. He had thought that he would be in heaven soon, but there was no heaven waiting for him in this new world.

She removed her jacket and kicked the head into the center of the cloth, hands shaking. She tied the corners together so that she could carry her burden along without having to touch it. She had to hurry, for not only would the others soon come back to life, filled with hunger, but she could hear the sounds of rescuers approaching as well, and both living and dead would only be obstacles to her now. She tucked the package under one arm, crawled through a shattered window, and ran down the tracks as quickly as she could in the opposite direction of the voices.

Back at the morgue, Paula unwrapped her parcel and put the head upright on a plate, balanced on its ragged neck. She knew that she might need to move it again, but she never wanted to have to touch it. She placed it on one of the operating tables, turning it carefully away from her, away from her father, so that all she could see was the back of its head. But then she turned it back again, so that she could watch it as she sat by her father. She needed to see the transformation when it came.

The sounds in the room had lessened since the dead first began to wake, but only by degree. The dead feet that had been pounding ceaselessly on the metal doors for hours had splintered, and the throats that roared their anger were wearing away. She imagined that if she could survive here long enough that she would see their bodies break down entirely, just like the systems that kept civilization humming seemed about to do. She wasn't sure that she could get home again even if she wanted to. And she wasn't sure that she wanted to.

She stared at what remained of a man who was willing to die for an ideology. Or, as it turned out, someone who was willing to do something even worse than that, not to die, but to choose a living, mindless death. He and others like him had hoped to bring down the workings of the modern world, but they did no such thing. The zombie plague did what they could not. Yet they still continued, not realizing that their bombs were pointless.

Night fell and morning came again, and there was no change, but then as night fell for the second day, the closed eyes of the terrorist's head snapped open. In that instant, the sounds from within the refrigerated compartments stopped, as if the dead who were locked away sensed a brother outside who might help them. But no help would be forthcoming, for all the manless head could do was rage.

She looked at her father. He had not responded to the resurrection. She guessed she didn't really expect him to. That wasn't what this was about, answers. She dragged her chair forward to sit facing her attacker, who could do nothing but look at her with mindless anger.

"Who *are* you?" she asked. "How can you keep on *doing* something like this, knowing what you had to have known?"

It growled at her, grinding its teeth loudly.

"Killing yourself so that you can go to heaven is barbaric enough. But once you knew that all you'd be getting is *this*, how could you go ahead and do it anyway? The world changed, and you paid it no attention. To choose zombiehood? To make others into zombies? You're dead forever now. I'm not sure that you were ever really alive to begin with."

The head howled, pinning her with unblinking eyes.

"Tell me," she said. "Tell me why you did this."

She stood up, and took a step closer. As she did, the thing's nostrils flared. It snapped its teeth, trying to reach her, but the gap between them was infinite.

"You're not taking a bite out of me. You won't ever be taking a bite out of anyone. Your death is as over as your life. There's nothing left for you. So you might as well tell me."

It rocked back and forth on its severed neck, but could gain no momentum.

"Tell me!" she shouted, and swatted at the head, which flew from the table and bounced several times on the floor, leaving several red splotches. The creatures behind the doors roared. She grabbed the head by its hair and lifted it up to eye level.

"I'll never know, will I?" she said. "Never."

Its answers remained the same as before. It was all senseless. She didn't know whether she could live with that. There seemed little reason to change her earlier plans. She lifted her other hand near to the thing's mouth. It snapped and snarled so ferociously that a tooth flew from between its lips and bounced off her chest. She could do it. She could do it quickly. One bite, and it would be over. She could no longer have death, but she could have something like it, and in a senseless universe, that would have to do.

But behind the head was her father, lying there quietly, speaking to her more eloquently than any member of the living dead ever could. She stepped closer to her father, holding the head out before her like a beacon.

"This is my father," she said, not really caring whether the creature even listened. "He didn't want much out of life. He just wanted to ride a double-decker bus someday, to see the Tower of London, to have a real beer in a real pub. He only wanted to see his daughters grow up to be happy…"

She grew silent. As she held the head by its hair, it rocked below her hand like a pendulum. She didn't know what else to say, but she said it anyway.

"I'm sorry, Dad. Maybe…maybe I can make it up to you."

She hadn't been able to make her father happy while he was alive. But now that he was dead…now that he was dead, maybe she had a chance.

She placed the head in one of the empty cabinets, where it once more began its howling.

"Welcome to your new home," she said. "I have to try to get back to mine."

Then she shut the door on the past and left the room of death forever.

%/(z)

DEEPWATER MIRACLE

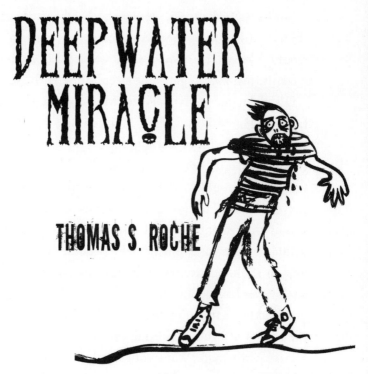

THOMAS S. ROCHE

The laughers come howling; they tend to make noise. It's a creepy sound, sure, and it can paralyze you with fear. But at least you know they're coming.

Pirates aren't like that.

Pirates creep up on you all nice and quiet; they're on you before you know it.

But then, when you're asleep and becalmed, anything can be on you before you realize it. I found that out in the worst possible way. In fact, I'd say there are probably not many worse ways I could have found it out.

That's why I should have never let Harry go downstairs to sleep in the V-berth. Even though we were totally becalmed, I should have made him sit up, to make sure I didn't doze.

But he was exhausted, we were both exhausted, with everything that had happened. And the petroleum stink made us woozy. I knew "Harrison," as he was fond of calling himself recently, just *had* to get some sleep. Apparently, so did I.

His real name is Harry Potter McAvoy and yes, he's named for *that* Harry Potter. He's fourteen and he's my brother, and he's a little bit of a strange egg. He's skinny and he's fast enough when it comes to running but if I was ever in a fight with him I would forfeit just so I didn't have to completely pulverize him. He's got these goofy little round wire-framed glasses that make him look like even more a dork than he would be otherwise. When he doesn't have his nose in a book, he's on the internet, researching things that no sane person would ever have a need to know. He's smart as all get out but not exactly what you might call a "normal" kid. Wanna know the capital of Primorsky Krai, on the Pacific coast of Russia? Harry's your man. Want your brother to get introduced to a girl you're interested in and not completely creep her out? There are better brothers out there, on that count.

About two years ago, Harry started calling himself Harrison, But I can't get my head around that. He'll always be Harry to me. If you think "Harry" is a perfectly fine name, then you're not my brother; he's a straight-A student and I am not kidding you reads Dickens because he thinks it's awesome, so at some point he decided that Harry Potter McAvoy was not a dignified enough name for a future college professor or neurosurgeon or whatever he's going to become. So he renamed himself Harrison, which pleased my Mom no end. "Just like Harrison Ford!" That did not please Harry, especially because I am named Luke after—yes, it's true—Luke Skywalker. The only thing I can say is that at least my Mom did not succumb to the urge to make my middle name Skywalker, because apparently that's just a little bit weirder than calling your second son "Harry Potter." My middle name is Francis, after her uncle—who was essentially her grandfather after her parents died.

Harry picked "Harrison" because it sounded more dignified. He thought this even though to my knowledge that dude in the books isn't named Harrison at all, but Harry from the get-go. I wouldn't know; I haven't read them. In the scheme of things, that's just one more of the many disappointments I handed Mom & Dad that I'll have to answer for if I ever face St. Peter...if *any* of us do. If we're not already in Hell. Well, for what it's worth, they both learned to laugh about it at the end. Ha ha, there, that's a little joke. See? At least I've still got my sense of humor.

It was our sixteenth day at sea and, as far as Harry and I could tell, the sixteenth day after the end of the world. It was the sixteenth day after the Panama Laugh hit the papers and as far as Harry and I could tell, the sixteenth day since the last paper was published.

It was our sixteenth day at sea, and as far as Harry and I could tell for a while there, it would be our very last day on this Earth.

%~⟨⟩

When the Panama Laugh hit, we were in Costa Rica. Mom's grandparents came from there, although they never spoke

Spanish at home so she didn't speak it that well...and I barely know a word of it. But Dad got it in his head that digging up the family roots was the way to form a more perfect union, if you know what I mean, and prevent future "misunderstandings" like the one I had with the car that didn't belong to me. Ever since I came back from my community service, Dad had promised to spend more time with me and Harry and Mom, and this was the way he did it—an all-expenses-paid summer vacation to sunny Costa Rica on his pride and joy, the *Second Chance*, a name Harry told me I should take as a personal insult (but he was always saying stuff like that). The *Second Chance* could sleep eight people comfortably if you liked each other, and four if you did not. Like most families, mine fell somewhere in between.

The reason Harry thought the name *Second Chance* was a reference to me is that Dad blamed himself for what happened. He seemed to think that I stole that car in Prado Verde because Dad had taught me to be prepared. That was pretty silly; for the record, I stole that car to impress Jenna Mason. And to see if I could. And to see if I could get away with it. (In case you're wondering...*it didn't*, *yes*, and *no*.) The *Second Chance* was forty feet long and when the wind was right she could make twenty-five knots, which is not fast enough to outrun a gang of pirates in speedboats...but if you shoot at them with a Dragon's Breath round, plenty of pirates will decide there's easier prey, which we'd had to do six times since leaving Costa Rica—three times before and three times after what happened to Mom and Dad.

The "Dragon's Breath" is an explosive incendiary shell made for the twelve-gauge shotgun, and in case you were wondering it's illegal in most states. It makes the shotgun belch out flame to something like fifty feet—creating the illusion that you're firing a cannon or something. To hear my Dad tell it, the round is utterly useless in a real fight—it's nothing but fireworks. But if you can fire it at a good enough distance, pirates—and everyone else—believe you're firing a rocket or a cannon at them, which leads them to believe you're far more heavily armed than you are.

It's a pain to fire because, one, make sure you put your ear-plugs in first, and two, you have to clean the gun every time you fire one because it leaves gunpowder residue everywhere. It also *stinks*, but on the Gulf of Mexico nowadays, "stink" is really a relative term.

My Dad had some pretty freaky toys, though he'd be pretty irritated to hear me calling them toys. I'd probably get a lecture. I wouldn't exactly say Dad was a survivalist, but he believed in always having your deck stacked against every nasty possibil-ity the universe could throw at you. Everywhere he went, he had everything ready for the very worst. You're going down to Wal-Mart for a new pair of swim trunks? Pick up another case of bottled water while you're at it, we've only got ten in the basement. Get some ammo while you're at it; you really can never have too much ammo, can you?

And as for the *Second Chance*?

She was "a hole in the water that you put money into," as Dad frequently put it, also alleging that the word "boat" was an acronym for "Blow Off Another Thousand." But the *Second Chance* was worth it, from the sound of what was happening on dry land. All across Latin America and the United States—and maybe the rest of the world, there's no way to know for sure—the dead laughers had taken over—the walking dead, their chests compressing in something like a weird, obscene semblance of a laugh. And without the *Second Chance*, we would have been be right in the middle of it. She was packed with all the good stuff. Satellite phone? Check. Shortwave? Check. Satellite Internet? Check. GPS? Of course. There was even a pistol-grip twelve-gauge shotgun from the Mossberg Just In Case series, packed in a waterproofed cylinder designed to keep it dry in case your boat went down.

And that's what saved Harry and me...when Dad went laugher about a week ago. Harry was the one who got it and fired it, while I was still standing there like an idiot. Dad went over the edge, and Mom sat there sobbing.

Harry said he didn't feel bad; after all, Dad had made us promise. "If I start to turn," he'd said, "Kill me. Don't even think about it. If that happens, I'm not your father anymore. I'm a *thing*. Put me down. It's for my sake as well as yours."

Harry did. Would I have done it? I'm two years older; I'm the criminal of the family. I spent a summer doing my community service under the authority of the Patterson Correctional Facility, in Morgan City, Louisiana sponging oil off sea birds with dish detergent. There, I made the acquaintance of guys with far bigger mental problems than I have. I won't try to tell you I didn't get in fights there; I did. You *have* to. I got in a lot of them, just like I got in a lot of fights back in Sunland Park. I was the family's resident tough guy.

But could I have shot Dad in the head with a shotgun, even with what he was trying to do to Mom?

I don't think so. He's always been the one I got along with. But when mom, pouring blood from her arm and starting to weep, put Uncle Frank's old service revolver to her head and tried to pull the trigger, she couldn't.

"You have to do it," she told me.

Why was *I* the one who argued with her? It wasn't till she came at me with her teeth bared and her eyes wild that I did it. Harry, on the other hand, hadn't even seemed to hesitate. He said the only reason he didn't shoot Mom, too, was because he didn't have a good line-of-sight; with a buckshot round, which the Mossberg was loaded with, he couldn't be sure he wouldn't kill me.

But just between you and me...she was always the one that *he* got along with.

Well, neither of them got along much now; they were floating somewhere, headless in the pea soup of crude-oil "mousse." Shortly after we lost Mom and Dad, we smelled the oil and hit the giant field of gooey off-brown sludge.

We knew it was the *Deepwater Miracle*, or another offshore drilling rig like it.

Somewhere at the center of this, a bunch of wildcatters were laughing.

※〜‹›

In some of the last AM reports from the States we picked up at sea after we left Costa Rica, the coverage was everywhere— threatening to squeeze out the stories of the contagion in Latin America. That ended when it became clear to the general public how major this all was...when the outbreaks started in California and elsewhere. Then it had all happened *fast*.

But for the first day the story of oil spill was everywhere. The

Deepwater Miracle was a deep-sea drilling platform about a hundred miles off the coast of New Orleans. The crew had gone dark. All contact with the rig was lost instantly. The wellhead had burst or uncoupled or something. It seemed obvious, now, what had happened—the crew had probably gone laugher.

The *Deepwater Miracle* started pouring crude into the Gulf of Mexico at an even greater rate than the huge 2010 spill.

I asked Dad if we shouldn't steer clear of the Gulf.

He said, "When this blows over, we're going to Corpus Christi. There's no way the spill will reach that far."

The substance covering the water was what they call "mousse," a frothy substance made up of mixed-together crude oil and sea water. It only gets whipped up when the water is warm and there's a certain amount of wind and wave action.

Why do I know? I told you, after I stole that car in Amarillo, I the whole summer fulfilling my community service by doing cleanup in the Gulf. Have you ever smelled frothy crude oil "mousse" on the water when it's ninety degrees?

"Will it burn?" Harry wanted to know.

I shrugged and said, "I don't think so. Not very well, at least. They talked a lot about the fire risk and said it was explosive. But they told us a lot of things that weren't true."

It wasn't easy to sleep, but it was harder to stay awake.

✖◞◇

Now there was no AM or FM, no GPS. There was nothing except the occasional scattered broadcast, fuzzy and indistinct, that told us how pirates were roaming the Caribbean preying on the thousands of small boats packed with refugees; armed boat-bound militias had formed and were covering the Texas coast. But it had been days since we had seen another boat.

We didn't know for sure what to expect on the Texas coast, other than that something *bad*. But could it be worse than what we'd done the first week at sea, before Mom and Dad went laugher—running from Cuban pirates taking pot-shots at us with rifles? Plus, Harry and I were running out of food, and fast. The beef jerky and the MREs were gone; so was the produce and the ramen and the cereal and of course the milk. We were subsisting on emergency rations, which are like the worst-tasting brownies you've ever had. They really didn't give us a lot of energy.

We'd decided we'd make for the coast: Corpus Christi, Dad's original plan. There, we'd try to hook up with Uncle Keith if he was still around, which we were beginning to think he wouldn't be. Maybe *no one* was left expect pirates and laughers.

But Corpus Christi had to be better than just floating out here, waiting for the pirates to find us.

So we cut a wake through the vast sea of mousse, choking hard on the petroleum stink. It sucked.

About three in the morning, I told Harry to go below and catch some shut-eye in the V-berth, which is the V-shaped sleeping compartment in the bow of most small boats. I told him I'd keep watch.

"You're exhausted," he told me, barely keeping his eyes open.

"So are you," I told him. "Don't worry."

I had the revolver in my belt, but Harry held up the Mossberg.

"You want the shotgun?"

"You'll need it."

"You're more likely to need it than I am."

"You might need it for *me*."

"Oh."

"We don't know for sure how it's spread."

"By bite," he told me, confused.

"I know," I said. "But we don't know *how else*. How did Dad get it?"

Harry had to concede that point. He shrugged. "All right," he said.

Harry is either a brother of amazing toughness, or a complete psychopath. Maybe both. I hadn't seen him cry once since we had to put Mom and Dad down. Then again...maybe he just hid it from me, the way I'd hid *my* crying from *him*.

I told Harry, "If I start laughing...you have to kill me."

He nodded, "You don't even need to say it, bro."

"Don't call me that." It freaks me out when Harry tries to use cool-kid slang. I said warily, "Same for you?"

He didn't even answer. He just looked at me and said, "You know you still look like a dork in that thing."

He was referring to my safety vest, which I'll admit was hot as heck even in the middle of the night. No sea breeze could get through it, and we were becalmed in the first place.

I had worn this dumb vest almost the whole trip, no matter how hot it was, *everywhere* except below deck. It was stupid, I know it.

The truth is, I'm terrified of the water; I hate to swim. I almost drowned at when I was about ten, and if there's one thing that scares me it's the idea of falling into the water, which was one of the reasons I wasn't hot on this whole stupid Costa Rica trip to begin with. Just thinking about falling into the water makes me break out in the sweats. It scares me more than dying. It scares me more than laughers. It scares me more than the idea of getting shot by pirates, but in this case, Dad's vests had that covered, too. Did I say he wasn't a survivalist? Okay, maybe he was. This one was ShurGuard Junior Masai combined ballistic fabric and flotation vest—in other words, a combination bullet proof vest and life jacket. Pretty bad-ass, even if it had me sweating up a storm. But like anyone would be able to smell me over that crude oil?

I tried to play it cool, because Harry likes to razz me about being scared of the water.

"What can I say? Dad knows how to pack. You should be wearing yours, you know."

He rolled his eyes.

My brother is one weird dude; he seems to think he lives a charmed life. Maybe he does. I know *I* don't.

He went below.

I took my post.

✗~⟨⟩

I don't know how far into the night I actually made it, pinching myself to stay awake.

I got some sleep, like it or not.

Then the world exploded.

I opened my eyes to the breaking dawn stillness.

I saw a vast bulk outlined against the rising sun.

I jumped up before I was awake and so I was more than a little punch-drunk, already sick from the crude oil fumes. I had the revolver out and leveled, instinctively.

Then I shoved the revolver in my belt and leapt for the wheel.

I screamed at the top of my lungs: "Harry! Get up here!"

What I'd seen towering above us, coming in at an angle and *fast*, was a vast grey Mexican warship towering over me stories-high, at like twenty knots. Written across its bow was the name, in block letters: *Veracruz*. Flying from its flagpole was the Mexican Naval Jack, the white-green-red, gold stars, white anchor—I knew it because Dad used to build plastic models of sea vessels, back before he got one of his own.

But this Naval Jack was sprayed with blood, and hanging in tatters. It had been partially burned away—and as for the *Veracruz*? There were holes in the deck—big ones, in a string, like from automatic cannon fire. It was coming at us at exactly the right angle to strike us amidships—and with its speed and its size and our side, and the *Second Chance* being made out of, you know, fiberglass instead of steel and all, it would have cut us in half as easily as a machete cutting a vine.

I realized there was no point turning the wheel without the motor going. I double-timed it astern and pulled the recoil start for the Yamaha two-stroke. It choked and sputtered. I pulled the recoil again and again and screamed and screamed and screamed myself hoarse for Harry.

"Harry! Get up here!"

He stumbled out in his board shorts and Dad's Johnny Cash T-shirt, aiming the shotgun at whatever he could see, which wasn't much; his eyes still weren't focused and his wire-framed glasses were on half-crooked. He howled, "What? What? What?"

I pulled the recoil start again and screamed, "Ship! Bearing down! Take the wheel! Turn it! Turn it! Turn it!"

Harry jumped to the wheel, staring up at the huge ship in horror. We were pointed straight at it, at an angle, and we weren't moving.

"Which direction?" screamed Harry, spinning around in the half-dark, his eyes still not clear.

I screamed, "Away!"

Under my breath, as I yanked at the recoil start, I muttered, "I'm sorry, I'm sorry, I'm sorry..."

The Yamaha outboard finally kicked in and went *vroom, vroom!*—the sweetest sound my ears had ever heard. At that point the *Veracruz* towered over us like a building. Harry started cranking the wheel, desperately trying to turn the *Second Chance* away from the onrushing *Veracruz* while I stood there trying to figure out what we did if it struck us.

Probably drown, I thought.

That's when I heard them: laughers.

There were laughers on the ship, hanging over the rails, reaching for us as they screamed out in hilarity. I could see them silhouetted against the pink light from the rising sun; as the sky paled, they howled, their ruined faces and broken fingers reaching for us as they neared. They were *hungry*—like all laughers, they wanted to eat us. That was the only way they could make the laughing stop. But the bite transmitted the virus and the second their victim got the joke and started laughing himself...he was no longer a nutritious breakfast.

Some of them tumbled over the railing of the *Veracruz*, trying to get to us. They must have been *starving*. How long had they steamed around in circles on that ship, getting hungrier and hungrier for human flesh?

Some laughers had already gone over the edge trying to get to us. They cackled out wet sounds in the water, uttering a gooey petroleum-slick cacophony that grotesquely imitated laughter. They were floating because they had safety vests, but not all of them looked like Mexican sailors. From what I could see there were fat guys in Hawaiian shirts and old ladies and little in pink swimsuits. Others were sailors, all right—twenty-ish, mocha-faced with their black hair cut military-short and their ears sticking out slimed with crude oil.

The ones who jumped kept splashing into the water all around us, if you can call that disgusting crude oil muck "water." They were evacuees and Mexican sailors both, and many of them—both groups—had weapons strapped on, rifles over their backs, pistols in shoulder holsters. I even saw one dangling from the railing with what had to be some kind of grenade launcher. But they weren't using their guns, of course—because laughers don't do that. (If they did, we would have already been dead.) When they struck the water, there were plenty who didn't have their vests on—it took only seconds for them to disappear into the gooey mousse and go down as I watched. Unable to keep their mouths closed because the Panama Laugh compelled them to keep them open—howling out laughter that turned to gurgles—they just vanished into the slime. They'd probably been evacuees on the Mexican destroyer. They'd been trying to abandon ship when they changed...and now they were trying to eat. We outpaced them as we turned away from the *Veracruz*. We left a long trail of orange-vested laughers in the water, paddling behind us and laughing in disappointment.

The orange-vested things in the water dog-paddled toward us, laughing wetly. The dry laughter on the rails of the *Veracruz* came from the sailors and evacuees reaching for us; in another few seconds they'd be close enough to jump for it and land right on our deck. By then we'd know if the *Second Chance* would clear the *Veracruz* or be struck by it.

"Turn! Turn! Turn!" I howled, not so much at Harry as to the universe, begging it for my thoughts or my prayers or whatever to lend the turning of the *Second Chance* some impetus.

"To everything there is a season," said Harry—ice-cool, as always.

But I could see his hands trembling on the wheel.

✳✳〈〉

The *Second Chance* cleared the side of the Mexican ship by about three feet. The *Veracruz* was listing badly, and seemed ready to topple on us. For maybe fifteen seconds, the railing was above us, even after it was clear that we were going to make it past the ship without hitting it.

But we were close enough for the laughers to jump.

Harry and I watched in horror as laughing sailors dangled over the edge—and got ready to leap on us.

I took the wheel away from Harry and said, "Get the shotgun ready." Harry picked it up and chambered a round. It made an ominous *rick-rack!* sort of sound, as a shotgun shell was forced into the chamber.

I took the revolver out of my belt and steered a path through the huge field of gloppy crude oil muck...as all around us, sailors hit the deck.

✳✳〈〉

The "freeboard" of a vessel is the distance from the water to the railing. That measurement is disrupted if the vessel is listing as badly as was the *Veracruz*, because the railing's a lot closer to the water than it ought to be. I had no idea what kind of ship the *Veracruz* was, but it was bigger than a destroyer; it had to be at least a frigate or maybe a missile cruiser or something. The freeboard was still at least thirty feet, even listing the way it was. The thing seemed ready to capsize any minute.

A thirty-foot drop onto the deck of a fiberglass-hulled sailboat is absolutely guaranteed to break a bone or two, unless you know how to land—maybe even then. Knowing how to land requires *knowing*, which requires higher brain functions. That is one thing laughers don't have.

They were dead; what was left of their brains knew how to do one thing and one thing only: seek out live humans to eat.

It was their *bodies* that knew how to do the other thing— laugh, or something like it.

Dad said the laughing was "real"; he said it was "neurological." He called it "cachinnation," and claimed it was the same kind of unexplained laughter one sees in extreme psychotics. How he knew that, I don't know, but I'm just going to be honest with you: I think he made it up. I think he'd read the term in some news story somewhere twenty years ago, and pulled it out of his brain to make me feel like he knew what he was talking about. I will say this. Dad was so used to being so smart about so many things that when he doesn't know anything about something, it seriously pisses him off.

I'd tell you Dad's pretending to understand the virus and the laughers was designed to make me and Harry feel better.

In one sense it was. But I've been watching my Dad do this on many topics since I was a little kid; Harry is the only one who'll call him on it, and he knew less about laughers than Dad did, so he let that one slide.

But whether they're laughing because their viral death throes make their chest muscles go *cachunk-cachunk*, or they're laughing because the only part of their brain that still works is the part that finds all this incredibly funny, I don't know. But I know one thing.

Those Mexican laughers couldn't jump worth a *darn*.

It's just that...well...

...there sure were a *lot* of them.

✖✖‹›

The jump did not dissuade them. They crawled like worms over the railing, heedless of how they landed—incapable of making that determination or that decision. They didn't tuck and roll; they didn't aim to land on their feet with their knees bent to absorb the impact. They just *went*.

They belly-flopped. Those who hit the deck hit it *hard*. Those who missed the deck and hit the water went plunging through the muck and sank—their rotting bodies would not float unless there was air in the lungs by pure chance—and in any event many of them had chest cavities that had rotted open, and clear damage to their lungs.

Then there were the ones who didn't hit either the water or the deck—but landed on the edge, over the railing of the *Second Chance* or on the various winches, ladders, handholds and the like that dotted the deck of the sailboat. Those sailors destroyed themselves—causing not just broken bones, but actually ripping their bodies apart from the impact. Some impaled themselves.

One landed squarely on Harry and knocked him off the flying bridge; the both of them went tumbling onto the main deck. The shotgun went rattling down and slid away. Harry screamed and struggled with the dead, laughing sailor. The guy was short for a sailor, but a lot bigger than Harry. His rotting flesh and septic muscles had no problem overpowering my little brother. Harry fought desperately, screaming. But I couldn't shoot without taking a chance on hitting Harry. The light was still not good and the *Second Chance* was careening wildly out of control, pivoting back toward the *Veracruz*—and all the remaining laughers who hadn't jumped yet. I didn't know what to do—if I let go of the wheel, we'd swing back toward the ship of laughers; if I stayed here that thing was *definitely* going to sink its teeth into Harry…and then it was all over.

"Luke!" he screamed. "Help! Get it! Get it! Get it!"

That's when he lost it; his cool was just an act. The terror took him over as he gripped the wheel, waiting on pins and needles

My brother *cried*.

I abandoned the wheel and it went spinning. As I dove for Harry and the laugher, The *Second Chance* heeled back toward the *Veracruz*.

✺~‹›

I made it to the main deck, kicked the zombie in the face and aimed Grandpa Frank's .38 revolver.

I blew its brains out.

It went limp instantly. I kicked the thing in the shoulder to tip it over the railing as Harry scrambled for the shotgun. It had slid practically over the edge of the deck as the *Second Chance* listed, but the pistol grip got hung up on the rigging. Harry grabbed it and took a quick circuit, evaluating the situation, which wasn't good. Freed from my guidance, the wheel of the *Second Chance* had spun like a roulette wheel. This turned out to have been good news and bad news; it was easier to kick the laugher over the side, and the sudden whipping of the bow back toward the Mexican ship meant that a couple rag-clad, rotting sailors that were almost over the rail went tipping over and fell into the thick slime of chocolate mousse.

But there were more coming down.

Some struck the railing, joining the remnants of the earlier ones, who had been practically ripped in half by the impact and hung there in parts, still laughing. There were damaged spines twisting through gooey sacks of limp flesh. They hung squirming over the railing , groping for us and gnashing their teeth as they laughed. Others had plunged into the water but been wearing flotation vests; they began crawling up the side of the boat and hoisted themselves up to come after us. By then another half-dozen had hit the deck in various places.

"What do we do, Luke?"

"Probably die," I said.

Harry and I started shooting.

※~❰❱

Only a head shot will down the laughers. Grandpa Frank's revolver held six rounds. I had more in my pocket. Harry had seven rounds in the Mossberg and another seven in a holder on the side for quick reloading. The laughers were everywhere. Some couldn't walk after they hit the deck, because their leg bones had been pulped. Others could walk, but did so in a broken shamble, on half-ruined feet with ankles sprouting jagged lengths of bone. They lurched at us violently, screaming out laughter. Harry and I pressed our backs together and fired and fired, both of us screaming and sobbing like idiots. The things were so close on Harry's side that shotgun could take out a couple, sometimes three at a time; their wet wreckage made it harder for the others to come for us, 'cause they made the decks slippery.

We cleared the *Veracruz* this time, just barely, but the wheel was still at the whim of the winds and the water. Then suddenly we heard a foul grinding noise—wet, and frothy. The Yamaha made a coughing sound, gave out one last scream, and began to pour out black smoke. It kinda went *thumpa-thumpa*, and then it was dead.

Harry and I both knew what had happened—a swimming crawler had gone to climb up onto stern of the *Second Chance*... and gotten caught on the propeller.

That was confirmed a minute later, as half-pulped crawlers writhed forward. They neared us, too destroyed to walk. They moved with excruciating slowness...as did the very last of them, who was nearly bisected, its abdomen ripped open. That was the one who had fouled the propeller, I was guessing.

There were maybe six of the ruined crawlers making very slow time toward us. I had maybe three shots left in the revolver.

Covered in stinking frothy crude-oil slime, the zombies began slipping and sliding across the wet residue of their fellows, laughing.

I aimed the revolver, but didn't pull the trigger.

Harry aimed the shotgun, but didn't pull the trigger.

"Why aren't you shooting?" I asked Harry, even though I already knew.

"I'm almost out," he said. "Why aren't you shooting?"

"I'm almost out," I said. I had reloaded twice; in my worst nightmares I had never thought I'd need more than eighteen shots, or Harry more than fourteen. I told Harry I had two rounds left. Harry said he had one. There were six laughers.

There was more ammo in the cabin, but the zombies were now between us and the hatch.

The zombies glopped toward us, leaking fluids and laughing out wet sounds.

"What should we do?" Harry asked me.

"Back up," I told him.

"What good will that do?"

"It'll give me time to think of something."

Harry, to his credit, is the one who thought to glance behind us to make sure there weren't more zombies coming from the bow. There weren't, but he saw something else that made his jaw drop.

He said, "Remember that part where you were gonna think of something?"

"Yeah," I said warily.

"Think fast, bro."

Behind us, there was a gunshot.

✖➝‹›

A big black powerboat towered over us. It was probably about the same length as the *Second Chance*, but sitting much higher in the water. Guys with guns sat or knelt on its foredeck—eight men, at least.

One guy had a cowboy hat; another had a "Git-R-Done!" baseball cap. I spotted one with a Jimmy Buffet shirt and another's said *Don't Mess With Texas*. They all had rifles.

For a second, I thought, *Whew, we're saved*. The feeling lasted right about until the time I saw the two flags flying from the back of the powerboat: the Confederate flag and the Jolly Roger. The pirate flag flew above the other.

On the bow of the boat was stenciled the name, in a hasty spray-paint job obviously done after whitewashing somebody else's name off the front; this was a stolen boat.

And now its name was *¡Adios, Vatos!* "Goodbye, dudes." This was one of the paranoid groups we'd heard about in those last AM broadcasts—pirating civilian ships in the supposed service of securing the border against invaders.

"Invaders," "refugees," "steaming cups of the American melting-pot," or just your average pair of Texan brothers trying to come home for the end of the world. Call us what you will, but I can tell you I'm pretty sure what the pirates would have called us would not have been polite.

That rifle shot wasn't aimed at the zombies on the *Second Chance*. They'd shot in the air just to get our attention. I guess, unlike Harry and me, these guys had plenty of ammo.

One of the guys shouted through a bullhorn.

"*¡Deja las armas, amigos!*"

Harry and I are half-Latino, and it shows. With a name like McAvoy, the topic of my ethnicity does tend to come up now and then, and I patiently tend to explain the simple facts: Irish-American father, Costa Rican-American mother, American-American kids...*whatever*. But I'll be honest, I was pretty sure what these guys had already decided Harry and I were, and it made me mad.

Sometimes when I'm mad, I do things that can be a bit reckless...like steal a car to impress a girl.

Or mouth off to pirates.

I did that second thing now. I said: "*Que? No hablo*, Bubba. I don't-a speak-a the-*Español*-a so-a-good-a."

"Put down the weapons, boys. We're taking your boat."

I was starting to panic, turning quickly from one threat to the other: the laughers as they crawled toward us on their broken bones...and the pirates pointing rifles at us.

"I said put down the weapons. We're taking your boat, boys."

"Don't you even want to know who we are, first?"

"We *know* who you are," said the guy, his voice dripping contempt even through the distorted electric crackle of the bullhorn. "Do not fire a shot, or you will be killed." The riflemen on the bow of the *¡Adios, Vatos!* had us in their sights, fingering their stocks. "Put down the weapons and put your hands up. You're within Texan territorial waters now, and you're under our authority. We're impounding your boat in the name of the..."

He kept talking like it meant something; these guys were a self-appointed government. The laughers were gaining; they weren't far away at this point.

I said, "We have to take care of these things...and then we'll talk, okay?"

"Do not fire a shot," the guy with the bullhorn crackled ultimately. "If you fire, we'll fire back."

"We're not shooting at you!" I pleaded. "Okay? Let us do this, then we'll talk."

"Don't shoot, don't move, put your weapons down."

"What about these laughers?" Harry howled.

There was a dry laugh through the bullhorn. "Sounds like you boys had better decide fast. We're taking your boat. If the laughers get you first? Well...just a little more mess to clean off of her."

I eyed the crawling laughers—*feet* away, now, gaining. They crawled on their ruined limbs, their bones broken in many places.

Harry shouted, "You'd do that?"

The answer came without hesitation: "This is getting old. At least it'll be fun to watch the laughers eat you."

✻〜‹›

While the writhing laughers came closer, I growled at Harry:

"Do you want to trust these guys?"

"No," he said. "Not at all. I think they'll kill us even if we let them take our boat."

I eyed the laughers. They were close. "You think they'll really shoot us if we take down the laughers."

"Yup," said Harry, flatly.

I shrugged. "You want to fight them?"

"I've got one shotgun shell left," he said. His voice wasn't shaking at all; he was back to the bad-ass Harry I knew. Cool as all get-out. "You've got two bullets. Would *you* like to fight them?"

There were at least eight men visible—all with rifles. "I guess we don't fight, then," I said. "What do we do?"

I said, "Uh-uh. The right question is, *where do we go?*"

Harry said, "Huh?"

I nodded off in the distance, where the *Veracruz* was still visible. She was steaming around in a circle, listing badly enough that she was now slowed down to just a few knots.

"I go left," I said. "You go right. Let's hope they're lousy shots."

The laughers were just a few feet away, then.

"I can't swim with the shotgun," he said.

"I can't swim at all."

Harry said, "I see your point. On the count of three?"

The nearest laugher reached out and grabbed at my foot.

I said, "No, bro. Let's just go *now*."

We jumped over the rail.

✖~‹›

Shots rang out behind us. But my prayers were answered; the pirates were lousy shots. *Mostly.*

I hit the foul-smelling, frothy-brown water and went under—and then I felt a punch in my back, *hard*. I felt the wind knocked out of me. I'd been hit. But I was wearing Dad's ballistic life vest. I was under the water for a sec, choked with the crude oil stink, and saw the bubbles of rifle bullets tearing through the mousse-fouled water. But I couldn't stay down with the vest on—not for very long; it drained my strength, and *fast*. So I came back up started swimming for all I was worth—which isn't much. Like I said, I'm not much of a swimmer. But I had a *lot* of incentive, with those pirates shooting at me.

Probably the only thing that saved me from getting hit a second time was that the vest I was wearing wasn't bright orange, like most safety vests—but camouflage. It looked pretty dorky; Harry was right about that. But it blended in perfectly with the gooey petroleum foam I was paddling through.

I'm sure as I swam, I left a wake that the pirates could have shot at.

But it didn't matter; there were so many laughers in the water that they couldn't have picked me out of the crowd.

%~<>

I dog-crawled slick and fast through the ripe winy stink of the chocolate mousse; it choked and burned me even under the water. My eyes hurting worse than they'd ever hurt before.

I was disoriented enough, sick from the petroleum fumes and lost in the mousse, that I barely found the *Veracruz*. But she was not far away—and she was coming closer, having taken her long slow circuit on her broken rudder.

Sputtering paddlers in Hawaiian shirts and naval uniforms chased me. I left a trail, thinking miserable thoughts about Harry—I must have lost him. No way he could swim through this whole crowd and make it safely to the *Veracruz*.

But Harry was a pretty strong swimmer.

When I made it to the Mexican ship and found the rope

ladder dangling and twisting and spinning at a crazy angle, my crazy brother was already crawling up it. I barely made it out of the stinky water before the zombies reached me.

Good thing the laughers couldn't climb.

✕~<>

Harry and I made it to the deck with great difficulty; I promised myself if I ever made it through this, I would learn to swim and climb. Harry, for all his being a bookish type and all, was actually pretty fit; he also weighed a lot less than me. He was panting on the slanted deck clinging to the rail and wiping crude-oil mousse out of his eyes by the time I got up there.

The passing of the *Second Chance* hadn't cleared the deck of the *Veracruz* —but it *almost* had. The *Veracruz* must have been at sea for a long time, from the condition of the laughers in the crew. The *Second Chance* represented their first chance at a meal...and the less living flesh the laughers eat, the more they rot, and the more they laugh. And the hungrier they get. These ones were *hungry*.

There were a few who had been too destroyed to move. Too rotted, too broken...shot to death, but not put down, because they hadn't taken shots in their *brain*.

Most of them were up against the railing, because the deck was titled at a terrifying angle.

"This ship is sinking," said Harry, panting and retching.

"I know," I said, panting and retching harder.

"We'll never make it to shore."

"I know," I said.

"Where are the lifeboats?"

I gestured at the big open bays where the boats had once been.

"Someone probably took them and ran. I don't blame them."

"Are there others?"

I said, "Maybe on the other side—but there's no way we'll get them down with the ship listing like this."

Harry took his wire-framed glasses out of his pocket. He put them back on and said, "Then what do we do?"

I spotted a laugher I recognized...the one hanging over the railing, dangling and laughing. The heavily-armed one.

The one with the rocket-propelled grenade.

✳⌄◇

The guy was wearing what I think was an officer's uniform, but it had been ripped apart and his chest was exposed. Across it was a big tattoo in deep black script: *¡Viva Mexico!*

I killed him with one of the last two shots left in my Grandpa's revolver. Or...he was already dead. I just finished the job. I took the RPG away from him—along with the binoculars he had dangling around his neck.

"Do you know how to work that thing?" asked Harry.

"Not a clue," I said. "Do you?"

"Not really, but I'm good with machines. I saw this History Channel documentary—"

"Stow it," I said. "Fine, you're elected expert." We were propped on the railing; the *Veracruz* was tipped at so steep an angle that we had to cling for our lives to keep from falling over. To get any further up on the deck, we'd have to crawl up the railing and find somewhere there were more handholds.

Then we could try to get below decks.

But then, I didn't like the idea of going below deck on the *Veracruz*—especially not with how bad she was listing.

I peered through the binoculars.

All eight of the gunmen had disembarked from the ¡*Adios, Vatos!* and were tearing through the *Second Chance*, tossing laughers over the side. They left a trail of them in the water, cutting a swath of writhing dots through the frothy brown mousse.

The *Veracruz* gave a horrible shudder and listed still more. I said something nasty. The ship felt unstable.

It was clear we were going into the water one way or the other.

Halfway hanging off the railing as the *Veracruz* tipped, Harry looked through the site of the rocket propelled grenade and fingered the trigger. It was basically like one of those bazooka things you see in World War II movies—except this one had a giant diamond-shaped tip on it that looked like a red and white bowling pin.

Harry said, "I've never killed anyone."

"Me, either," I said. "I can't imagine Mom would approve."

Harry gave me a frown.

"I think she'd be fine with it."

Then the whole world exploded.

✕⌣‹›

Everything seemed to happen at once—but at the same time, there was sort of a lot of time to think. The backblast of the rocket launcher practically blew my eardrums out; it was like being hit with a hot wave of exhaust from a jet plane, except the jet plane is your *brother*, who's squealing like a pig right next to you.

Whether it was the pressure of the rocket's backblast hitting the deck that made the *Veracruz* finally give up the ghost, I don't know. But I know seconds later, Harry and I were falling—and as we fell, I watched the guy whip off his glasses, right there in midair, and stuff them in the pocket of his board shorts.

Then everything was crazy. There was a huge blast—the *Second Chance* went up in flames. He'd scored a direct hit— right there amidships where Mom and Harry used to sit in the mornings and play magnetic chess.

The ball of flame went up, and I saw the bodies of the pirates tumbling end-over-end. Not all of them were whole.

Funny thing...I'd sort of figured he'd shoot the pirate boat, not *ours*. But when it comes right down to it, it made a lot of sense. The pirates were all busy looting the *Second Chance*—so that's what he hit.

That's why he's my brother...that, you see, is why Harry is the smart one.

Was, I thought. Because the *Veracruz* was going down, and sucking me and him and the laughers into the guts of the ocean.

As far as I knew, I was the only one who came up.

※～<>

It took me half an hour to swim through the crude oil muck after the *¡Adios, Vatos!*, which was drifting. There didn't seem to be a moving soul aboard. The *Second Chance* was nowhere to be seen—she must have gone down.

I thought of everything I owned, practically—on that sailboat, headed toward the bottom of the Gulf. I thought of my brother, probably dead in the undertow from the sinking *Veracruz*. I fought down a sob and buried my anger by swimming like a fiend.

The water still writhed with laughers, which was part of why it took me so long to catch up with the boat. Those things couldn't swim like I could—even being as bad a swimmer as I am—and I had to take big long wide circuits around them to avoid them again and again.

But I made it. I caught a rope that had dangled from the edge of the *¡Adios, Vatos!* and hauled myself up.

As I reached the railing, I hearing laughing on the deck.

I had shoved Grandpa's revolver into the thigh pocket of my cargo shorts; the three rounds left were thoroughly soaked. I had no idea if the revolver would fire. There had been pistols on the dead sailors of the *Veracruz*; I'd thought seriously about grabbing one, but the RPG had seemed more urgent...and then everything had gone *nuts*.

I pulled Grandpa Frank's revolver out and thumbed back the hammer so I could fire faster and with greater accuracy. I had one round left; I had to make it count.

I pulled myself over the railing and aimed the revolver at the laugher—guffawing, braying hysterically. *Harry*.

He put up his hands.

He stopped laughing *fast*.

"Whoa! Whoa! Whoa!" he said.

"What's so funny?"

"Didn't you see me waving at you?" he told me, his voice hoarse from the stink of the crude oil. "I thought you were dead."

"Why didn't you shout something?"

He rubbed his throat and said, "I guess I was laughing too hard." From somewhere he had grabbed a flotation vest—a bright orange one. I don't know who or what he took it off of, but he'd obviously put it on in the water. The thing was buckled in a haphazard fashion, and that's putting it nicely.

"I see you've finally realized the wisdom of wearing a vest."

"Whatever," said Harry.

Neither he nor I looked much improved for our adventure. We were both covered head to toe in petroleum slime. The stuff was revoltingly pungent; it burned your mucus membranes.

"I'm glad you made it," said Harry dryly. Then, with a smirk, he added, "I guess."

Then he and I heard it—up ahead, on the bow.

Laughing. Down here on the lower deck, we couldn't see who it was. But it was clearly a zombie—voice, an old one, ruined, wet. Cackling, ruined, revolting. It made me wonder how I could ever mistake the joyous, ironic laughter of my crazy brother for the Panama Laugh.

I gripped the revolver.

We found the last remaining pirate just about *halved*, hanging mostly off the bow, clutching his bullhorn. A piece of fiberglass shrapnel from the *Second Chance* had practically bisected him when the grenade hit. He lay prone, immobile, laughing, tangled in the thick ropes that had attached the *¡Adios, Vatos!* to the *Second Chance*. In one hand he still clutched the bullhorn; in the other, he had a boat knife. If, bisected or not, the pirate hadn't cut the ropes that attached the two vessels, the *¡Adios, Vatos!* might have been dragged down with the *Second Chance*. In a weird kind of way, that last pirate saved our lives.

I didn't feel much like saying "Thank you," though.

Harry and I looked at each other.

Harry sighed and shrugged.

The final pirate tried to rise. He couldn't. Tangled in the ropes and almost cut in half by the jagged sheet of fiberglass, he could barely move at all. He clawed after us, laughing uproariously.

I raised the revolver. Whuddaya know? The thing *did* fire wet, after all.

The last pirate stopped laughing.

"Get off our boat," I said, and kicked him over, bullhorn and all.

※~<>

The *¡Adios, Vatos!* was fully fueled; it was stocked with provisions and guns and extra ammunition. Nine men had planned to do a lot of pirating on this vessel—lots more than they got a chance to do. We were one of their early conquests, but not their first. We found wallets in the lounge—a bucketful. Dozens of them.

I don't know who they got them from...who they killed...but if I ever shed a tear, it's for them...not the pirates Harry killed.

There was no GPS, but at least they had a working compass. We got the motor going and aimed the boat north...toward Texas. But something weird hung in the air...and it wasn't just that me and my brother both stank like gasoline.

He and I exchanged a *look*.

"You thinking what I'm thinking?" I asked Harry.

He pursed his lips.

He said, "Don't mess with Texas?"

"I was thinking 'Texas sucks,'" I told him. "But it's basically the same sentiment."

I turned the boat around and pointed her south.

We left a trail of laughers dogpaddling after us through the muck. Man, they sure thought *something* was funny.

:/8}

COPYRIGHT ACKNOWLEDGMENTS

"Family Buisness" by Jonathan Maberry. © 2010 Jonathan Maberry. Originally published in *The New Dead: A Zombie Anthology*. Reprinted by permission of the author.

"The Wrong Grave" by Kelly Link. © 2007 Kelly Link. Originally published in *The Restless Dead*. Reprinted by permission of the author.

"The Days of Flaming Motorcycles" by Catherynne M. Valente. © 2010 Catherynne M. Valente. Originally published in *Dark Faith*. Reprinted by permission of the author.

"The Barrow Maid" by Christine Morgan. © 2007 Christine Morgan. Originally published in *History is Dead: A Zombie Anthology*. Reprinted by permission of the author.

"You'll Never Walk Alone" by Scott Nicholson. © 2003 Scott Nicholson. Originally published in *The Book of Final Flesh*. Reprinted by permission of the author.

HARRISON GEILLOR

"I am a big proponent of originality... of quality literature that doesn't pander to the masses... of books that speak to the deeper truths of the human condition. Harrison Geillor's *The Twilight of Lake Woebegotten* does **not** posses **any** of these qualities!"
— Epiphanie Neyer, best selling author of many books

the twilight of lake woebegotten

ISBN: 978-1-59780-284-0 • $14.99

A small town... a plucky heroine, a shiny vampire, and a hunkey Native American rival with a secret. But all is not as it seems in Lake Woebegotten. Let Harrison Geillor reveal what lies beneath the seemingly placid surface. You'll Laugh. We promise.

When Bonnie Grayduck relocates from sunny Santa Cruz, California to the small town of Lake Woebegotten, Minnesota, to live with her estranged father, chief of the local two-man police department, she thinks she's leaving her troubles behind. But she soon becomes fascinated by another student—the brooding, beautiful Edwin Scullen, whose reclusive family hides a terrible secret. (Psst: they're actually vampires. But they're the kind who don't eat people, so it's okay.) Once Bonnie realizes what her new lover really is, she isn't afraid. Instead, she sees potential. Because while Bonnie seems to her friends and family to be an ordinary, slightly clumsy, easily-distracted girl, she's really manipulative, calculating, power hungry, and not above committing murder to get her way—or even just to amuse herself. This is a love story about monsters... but the vampire isn't the monster.

NIGHT SHADE BOOKS IS AN INDEPENDENT PUBLISHER OF QUALITY SCIENCE-FICTION, FANTASY AND HORROR

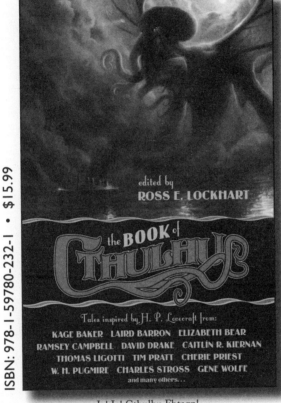

ISBN: 978-1-59780-232-1 • $15.99

edited by
ROSS E. LOCKHART

the BOOK of CTHULHU

Tales inspired by H. P. Lovecraft from:

KAGE BAKER   LAIRD BARRON   ELIZABETH BEAR
RAMSEY CAMPBELL   DAVID DRAKE   CAITLÍN R. KIERNAN
THOMAS LIGOTTI   TIM PRATT   CHERIE PRIEST
W. H. PUGMIRE   CHARLES STROSS   GENE WOLFE
and many others...

Ia! Ia! Cthulhu Fhtagn!

First described by visionary author H. P. Lovecraft, the Cthulhu mythos encompass a pantheon of truly existential cosmic horror: Eldritch, uncaring, alien god-things, beyond mankind's deepest imaginings, drawing ever nearer, insatiably hungry, until one day, when the stars are right....

As that dread day, hinted at within the moldering pages of the fabled Necronomicon, draws nigh, tales of the Great Old Ones: Cthulhu, Yog-Sothoth, Hastur, Azathoth, Nyarlathotep, and the weird cults that worship them have cross-pollinated, drawing authors and other dreamers to imagine the strange dark aeons ahead, when the dead-but-dreaming gods return.

Now, intrepid anthologist Ross E. Lockhart has delved deep into the Cthulhu canon, selecting from myriad mind-wracking tomes the best sanity-shattering stories of cosmic terror. Featuring fiction by many of today's masters of the menacing, macabre, and monstrous, *The Book of Cthulhu* goes where no collection of Cthulhu mythos tales has before: to the very edge of madness... and beyond!

Do you dare open *The Book of Cthulhu*? Do you dare heed the call?

NIGHT SHADE BOOKS IS AN INDEPENDENT PUBLISHER OF QUALITY SCIENCE-FICTION, FANTASY AND HORROR

"Terrifying, darkly hilarious, tougher and meaner and faster than a .45 hole-in-the-head—Roche delivers a fast-paced, gripping thriller where the showdowns make other zombie novelists look like they're playing with dollies."
—Violet Blue, author of *The Smart Girl's Guide to Porn* and many others

THE PANAMA LAUGH

THOMAS S. ROCHE

ISBN: 978-1-59780-290-1 • $14.99

Ex-mercenary, pirate, and gun-runner Dante Bogart knows he's screwed the pooch after he hands one of his shady employers a biological weapon that made the dead rise from their graves, laugh like hyenas, and feast upon the living. Dante tried to blow the whistle via a tell-all video that went viral -- but that was before the black ops boys deep-sixed him at a secret interrogation site on the Panama-Colombia border.

When Dante wakes up in the jungle with the five intervening years missing from his memory, he knows he's got to do something about the laughing sickness that has caused a world-wide slaughter. The resulting journey leads him across the nightmare that was the Panama Canal, around Cape Horn in a hijacked nuclear warship, to San Francisco's mission district, where a crew of survivalist hackers have holed up in the pseudo-Moorish-castle turned porn-studio known as The Armory.

This mixed band of anti-social rejects has taken Dante's whistle blowing video as an underground gospel, leading the fight against the laughing corpses and the corporate stooges who've tried to profit from the slaughter. Can Dante find redemption and save civilization?

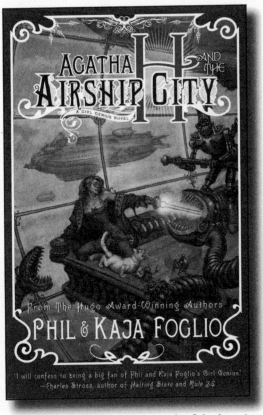

ISBN: 978-1-59780-212-3 • $14.99

The Industrial Revolution has escalated into all-out warfare. It has been sixteen years since the Heterodyne Boys, benevolent adventurers and inventors, disappeared under mysterious circumstances. Today, Europe is ruled by the Sparks, dynasties of mad scientists ruling over—and terrorizing—the hapless population with their bizarre inventions and unchecked power, while the downtrodden dream of the Hetrodynes' return.

At Transylvania Polygnostic University, a pretty, young student named Agatha Clay seems to have nothing but bad luck. Incapable of building anything that actually works, but dedicated to her studies, Agatha seems destined for a lackluster career as a minor lab assistant. But when the University is overthrown by the ruthless tyrant Baron Klaus Wulfenbach, Agatha finds herself a prisoner aboard his massive airship Castle Wulfenbach—and it begins to look like she might carry a spark of Mad Science after all.

From Phil and Kaja Foglio, creators of the Hugo, Eagle, and Eisner Award-nominated webcomic Girl Genius, comes *Agatha H and the Airship City*, a gaslamp fantasy filled to bursting with Adventure! Romance! and Mad Science!

NIGHT SHADE BOOKS IS AN INDEPENDENT PUBLISHER OF QUALITY SCIENCE-FICTION, FANTASY AND HORROR

{ *"The Loving Dead* is really kind of hot, in a very creepy way. Read it. You know you'd love you some sweet zombie sumpin' sumpin'. Buy it, bitches! Ride this zombie Zeppelin of love like there's no tomorrow." }
— **Christopher Moore**, author of *Lamb* and *A Dirty Job*

the loving deAd

ameliabeamer

ISBN: 978-1-59780-194-2 • $14.95

Girls! Zombies! Zeppelins!

If Chuck Palahniuk and Christopher Moore had a zombie love child, it would look like *THE LOVING DEAD*, a darkly comic debut novel by Amelia Beamer.

Kate an d Michael, twenty-something housemates working at the same Trader Joe's supermarket, are thoroughly screwed when people start turning into zombies at their house party in the Oakland hills. The zombie plague is a sexually transmitted disease, turning its victims into shambling, horny, voracious killers after an incubation period where they become increasingly promiscuous.

Thrust into extremes by the unfolding tragedy, Kate and Michael are forced to confront the decisions they've made, and their fears of commitment, while trying to stay alive. Kate tries to escape on a Zeppelin ride with her secret sugar daddy -- but people keep turning into zombies, forcing her to fight for her life, never mind the avalanche of trouble that develops from a few too many innocent lies. Michael convinces Kate to meet him in the one place in the Bay Area that's likely to be safe and secure from the zombie hordes: Alcatraz. But can they stay human long enough?

NIGHT SHADE BOOKS IS AN INDEPENDENT PUBLISHER OF QUALITY SCIENCE-FICTION, FANTASY AND HORROR

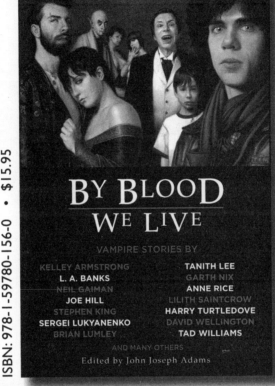

Vampires. They are the most elegant of monsters—ancient, seductive, doomed, deadly. They lurk in the shadows, at your window, in your dreams. They are beautiful as anything you've ever seen, but their flesh is cold as the grave, and their lips taste of blood. From Dracula to Twilight; from Buffy the Vampire Slayer to True Blood, many have fallen under their spell. Now acclaimed editor John Joseph Adams brings you 33 of the most haunting vampire stories of the past three decades, from some of today's most renowned authors of fantasy, science fiction, and horror.

Charming gentlemen with the manners of a prior age. Savage killing machines who surge screaming from hidden vaults. Cute little girls frozen forever in slender bodies. Long-buried loved ones who scratch at the door, begging to be let in. Nowhere is safe, not mist-shrouded Transylvania or the Italian Riviera or even a sleepy town in Maine. This is a hidden world, an eternal world, where nothing is forbidden... as long as you're willing to pay the price.

Edited by John Joseph Adams (*Wastelands, The Living Dead*), *By Blood We Live* features over 200,000 words of the very best in vampire fiction. Thirsty? *By Blood We Live* will satisfy your darkest cravings...